BABE

OTHER BOOKS BY ROGER A. MACDONALD

Memoirs
A Country Doctor's Casebook
A Country Doctor's Chronicle
A Country Doctor's Journal

Fiction
With Malice Toward All
A Question of Ethics
Fortune Cookie

BABE

The Remarkable Family of
Paul Bunyan's Blue Ox

ROGER A. MACDONALD

iUniverse®

BABE
THE REMARKABLE FAMILY OF PAUL BUNYAN'S BLUE OX

iUniverse books may be ordered through booksellers or by contacting:

iUniverse
1663 Liberty Drive
Bloomington, IN 47403
www.iuniverse.com
1-800-Authors (1-800-288-4677)

ISBN: 978-1-4917-9659-7 (sc)
ISBN: 978-1-4917-9658-0 (hc)
ISBN: 978-1-4917-9660-3 (e)

Library of Congress Control Number: 2016910067

Print information available on the last page.

iUniverse rev. date: 07/27/2016

*This account is dedicated to the memory
of those remarkable men of yesteryear who
proudly wore the title of lumberjack.
Their kind has vanished from the land.
Are we not the poorer for it?*

PROLOGUE

I became known as Babe the Blue Ox, and my association with Paul Bunyan is the stuff of legend, but the tag clipped to my ear at birth read simply S★2708.

My story began on a Northeast Texas cattle ranch. Awareness of beginnings after the fact depends on memory. I had to choose between those vague mental images that are little more than primal imprinting and those I acquired from life following the great transformation.

Transformation. An understanding of such a cataclysmic event will be best achieved by setting it in a proper time frame, later in this narrative.

This tale is mine. Still, not all of the events that shaped who I became were seen through my eyes. At times others must add to the story. Who better to begin this than Mrs. Sarah McAllfry, one of the humans who most impacted my life?

Mid-October 1880

The day was as bright and golden as October days are meant to be in the hill country of East Texas. Foliage was beginning to turn color. Brown oak leaves still clung to their branches, leaves of cottonwood trees fluttered to the ground like clouds of yellow butterflies, and sumac brush flaunted radiant crimson along a far ridge. Crisp nights gave way to days seductively warm, as though winter, with its dreary chill, did not lurk just to the north.

Sarah McAllfry drew air deep into her lungs for the pure joy of breathing. She walked along the road toward the Springdale Elementary School, grades one through eight. The school was one mile north of the farm where she lived. For fifteen years Sarah had been the teacher, the school marm. Her pace was brisk, and her cheeks were warm, despite the nip in the morning air.

A lad wearing neatly patched trousers, frayed but clean, a plaid shirt, and worn boots free of dust or grime stood up from a rock near the door. He appeared to be eight, probably nine. His features were solemn, his jaw set.

The boy was a darky.

He stepped in front of the door. "Is yo the teach lady?"

"Yes, I am. And you are?"

"I's called Henry. Ma'am. Henry Jackson. An' this here's a school?" He swung his arm toward the door.

"Yes it is, one for … children."

"I wants to learn me readin' an' how to do sums. I wants to come to yo' school."

Sarah's knees went wobbly. *Dear God in heaven!*

The sign nailed above the door of the building read Springdale Elementary School. Nowhere did it say White Children Only, three damning words that more honestly might have been written in fire by the finger of God.

"Henry. You, uh, can't come to this school. You have your own, down in Possum Holler. Don't you?"

"No, ma'am, not no mo'. Hasn't been no school fo' two years."

"But, you see, I'm not allowed to take students … please understand. You, uh, don't meet the requirements … oh dear."

"I's a child'en, ain't I?"

"Yes, but—"

"Then hows come I can't get me learnin'?"

Sarah held her hands together in a prayer-like attitude. "Because …"

The boy stood straighter, his shoulders back. "What's a matter, white lady? Can't say nigger?"

"I would never say … I …"

She studied the waif through the lens of awakening perception. *What do I really know about his kind? Despite walking through life side by side with coloreds, I have no more wondered about their concerns than I might have those of a stray dog lying beside the way.* Two clans sharing space so independent of each other that "those others" might as well have been invisible.

Inferior by God's decree—*I've heard that from the pulpit as well as from neighbors.* Incapable of graces flowering from intellect. Indifferent to dirt. Indolence anchors about their necks.

Why challenge convictions of a lifetime?

She looked down at the boy, engaging him at the level of his unblinking gaze.

Despised one?

Not on a level with …?

With me?

She believed that she must be Irish. And who were the Irish in nineteenth-century America? White trash. Micks. Sent out of Ireland by the shipload to skulk around the fringes of New World society. She cringed. *Is skin pigment such a difference between this lad and me?* Scorned is scorned.

So …

Say nigger? Say it with proper disdain?

A seismic shift rumbled in her soul. With understanding, she saw a boy-child human barely conquering fear, with courage born of some stirring from within, and he ceased to be a symbol of a smoldering past with its hatred and violence.

She straightened her shoulders. "No, Master Henry, I *won't* say that word. Does your mama know you're here?"

His eyes grew huge. "Uh, no, ma'am. I snuck off while she was a-workin' the garden."

"Do you have a papa?"

His head drooped. "He dead."

Decisions and their consequences.

She squared her shoulders and drew a deep breath.

She unlocked the door and ushered the boy inside.

"Henry, let's see what kind of storm you and I can stir up."

The boy's bravado appeared to flee, and he became merely a frightened, overwhelmed nine-year-old. "Eighth graders sit at the back here," Sarah said. She guided him toward the front of the building's one room, opposite the door. She seated him in an empty desk at the end of the first row, seven or eight feet from her own desk. "I'm going to introduce y'all to the other students. I'll ask that you stand and give your name. I'll decide what grade to assign you to after I test what you already know." He swayed, and she steadied his shoulder. "Sit before you fall."

She sat at her own desk, her gaze on its scarred surface. She felt oddly detached, given the maelstrom she was initiating. *Now the cow has kicked over the lantern, and who will feel its fire?*

She glanced at the lad. Like her, he sat quietly, wrapped in his personal cocoon of apprehension.

Fifteen years before, when she had first moved to East Texas, the cacophony of battle had barely stilled. A rage of defeat, of a society torn to shreds, had made it easy to turn anger onto the same people who had so recently been its slaves. But now, in 1880, Sarah realized that coals of despair and vengeance had grown cold in her own psyche.

She had come to Springdale in 1865, fresh out of normal

school, her one-year teaching certificate in the drawer of her desk. Sarah was "city," from a place called Dallas. A precious job was the reason she had come to the East Texas hill country, a stepping stone on a path surely leading back to the city.

Except …

A single teacher, a city lady new to a rural community, needed a place to stay during the academic year. School officials referred Sarah to the home of Betsy ("Ma") McAllfry. For the best part of two decades, that gracious lady had provided quarters for the contemporary schoolmarm—room and board and use of a washtub once a week. Sarah learned early on that Ma's husband, Hale, had not returned from the Battle of Vicksburg. Not even his body, lost somewhere in the anonymous horrors of bloody mud and fragmented flesh that the Great Conflict had spawned. Their son, Jonas, had survived the war. A shattered leg and a year in bed back at the homestead, and he had assumed responsibility for running the farm.

Matches are made in heaven, or so Sarah had heard it said. Proximity has a better record in that department—her wry judgment. She and Jonas "courted" over suppers in the McAllfry dining room. Having seen her son united in the state of matrimony, Ma slept peacefully away one night.

Then a fever took Jonas, and Sarah was alone, no children from their union. Jonas was surely settled by now into that dust the Good Book describes as destiny. His modest headstone was fourth in a row of McAllfrys in the tiny family plot out beyond the pasture.

The farm had come down to her from Jonas, along with its mortgage and the yoke of labor required to make it fruitful.

Memories were ghosties more painful than soothing.

Seven thirty arrived. Voices filtering in from the school yard announced her pupils. She stood and pulled the rope that rang the bell in the squat belfry above her.

The door burst open, and children cascaded into the room.

"No running!" Sarah called. The sounds of voices and tramping feet slowed, stopped. Like a wave cresting, one by one the students seemed to spy Henry.

"Take your seats," Sarah snapped. To her own ear, her voice sounded strained. Murmurs, hesitancy, but the students sat in their usual desks, all except third-grader Ellie Farnham.

"Do you have a problem?" Sarah asked.

"I can't sit next to one of them!"

"It's temporary, until we assign permanent seating for our new student."

Ellie dragged her desk away from Henry, as close to Jimmy Marquette's as the laws of physics allowed, and eased into it.

Sarah nodded at Henry. He stood, the effort obviously a painful one. The boy was tall for a nine-year-old, slender to the point of being skinny. His hands, with their darky-pink palms, were large, fingers clenching and relaxing. Sweat beaded his forehead. If he paled, his complexion hid it. One knee peeked through a tear in cotton britches. He glanced around wildly and straightened his shoulders to look squarely at Sarah.

"I's Henry Jackson," he said softly.

"T'ain't a proper name for a niggah," called an adolescent voice from the back of the classroom.

Sarah snapped, "There will be no talk like that!"

Zeke Beaugarde, Sarah noted. Seventh grade, for the second time. Class bully. *Why is he still in school?*

Ingrid Hanson waved her hand. She stood and made a

green-persimmon face. "My daddy is chairman of the school board, and he tol' me we don' allow his kind in a school." She tossed a head of golden curls and sat daintily.

Murmurs of support rumbled from the back two rows, the seventh- and eighth graders.

Seth Pringle stood. "I ain't breathin' the same air as that one. 'Sides, my pa prob'ly needs help puttin' up hay. I'm leavin'." He stomped to the door, then turned back and shook a fist at Henry. "Y'all show your ugly face here again I'll personal make sure you gotta grow new teeth. Go back where you belong, black boy." He turned to the others in his row. "Anyone else comin'?" He swung the door back against its stop with a bang and stomped out into October exuberance.

Henry collapsed onto his desk seat.

A calm of cold resolve claimed Sarah. She had mounted an untamed horse and its gyrations held her captive. She knew where she was headed, yet despite awareness, she knew that she would stay to the end of the ride.

So. Be. It.

The students left, one by one. Some stomped out. Phillip, son of Pastor Yates, detoured to hawk and spit at Henry. Some sidled out or crept out with downcast eyes. None of the white students remained behind.

The stillness settling over Springdale Elementary School smothered any sounds of breathing. Henry sat like a mahogany figurine. What his staring eyes saw was not apparent, nor did he show any emotion.

Sarah drew a chair opposite Henry's desk and sat quietly before him. She waited, as solemn as he.

A boy wanted to read and write. By definition, the business

of a school was teaching such a fundamental need. Was it a monstrous expectation?

If! Oh, those ifs. They are monstrous. *Why have I never questioned such an obvious thing before?* Education is deemed to be a right for every citizen in this nation, one trying to heal fresh scars from a bloody war with itself. When the stroke of a pen creates thousands of new citizens, there must be a first, and firsts are terrifying. Why did fate choose *this* frightened child to trigger an explosion?

She sighed and cupped Henry's hand with hers. "Best you and I find your mama. She needs to know what happened." She leaned toward him. "She needs to know what a brave son she has."

Like a bit of ice melting in a warming sun, Henry slumped. Tears filled his eyes, brimming for release. His lips trembled.

Sarah slid her chair alongside his and pulled his head onto her shoulder.

"Let them come. Tears wash away a pile of hurts."

Henry cried. And cried. Sarah wiped her own eyes.

Sarah trudged after her would-be student. Henry and his mother lived in an old shack so decrepit that it had to have once housed slaves. She realized suddenly that she had never before given thought to living conditions for the Henry Jacksons of life. A roof minus a few shingles and four walls of vertical planking with many a gap between them gave access to the elements. Three similar shacks lined up alongside it. Half a dozen black youngsters spilled out of these, marveling aloud at sight of "Henry and a white woman" trudging toward them along a narrow, dusty trail.

Henry stopped short of the brief, low porch to his home. "I'd better let Mama know y'all ... she didn' know I's went to school." Head down, he walked slowly into the hovel.

A shrill feminine voice sounded through its open door. "Henry Jackson! Where yo bin? I oughta tan yo' hide."

"Mama, I gots somepin' to say."

"I tol' an' tol' y'all—lemme know where yo is."

"That's it, Mama. I went to school an' teach lady brought me home."

"What?"

A statuesque black woman, who appeared to be in her late twenties, stormed from the cabin. Henry edged onto the porch to stand just outside the door, solemn, his face taut.

The woman was tall and muscular, her features regular, her skin ebony. A bandana covered her head. Black curls peeked out here and there from under the faded cloth. She wore a skirt banded horizontally with exuberant colors and a cotton blouse that acknowledged a firm figure. On her feet she wore sandals made from the bark of a tree.

She moved with the lithe coordination of a feral creature. Her face was rigid with mistrust.

Sarah came to stand before her, looking up into eyes guarded by squinting lids. The oddity of the situation stole away Sarah's breath. *Am I safe, after all? Will this panther-like woman from God-knows-what-kind of world see me as some threat? How might she react? And ultimately, what* am *I doing here?*

Still, for those moments at the school Sarah *had* felt a connection with the boy. She recaptured her convictions and drew a deep breath.

"My name is Sarah McAllfry. I'm the teacher at the Springdale schoolhouse. I'm here to talk to you about your son."

"Why?" The flat sound was like a slap across Sarah's face.

"Henry is a remarkable boy. He wants to read and write. I want to teach him how to do that."

"Dat ain't no school fer us Nigras."

"Then we need to work around the problem, don't we, Mrs. Jackson?"

No response.

"Please, I want to help. Look … may I come indoors with y'all? To talk?"

"No. Cain't jes' walk inna my house."

Sarah sighed. "I understand." She stepped up the few inches onto a sloping porch. Mrs. Jackson jumped back a step and fisted her hands on her hips belligerently. Sarah raised hers in peace. "I was getting a crick in my neck, standing down there looking up at you. I want to tell you about how brave your son was today. You should realize."

Standing three feet apart, Mrs. Jackson's gaze locked on Sarah's face.

Sarah related in her firm teacher's voice what had happened. "Seems to me that if a body wants to better himself, he should have the opportunity," she concluded softly.

The silence between them lasted for part of a minute, for a century was Sarah's wild fantasy during the living of it. A trickle of sweat ran down her cheek. Buzzing insects whirred and sang somewhere. Disputing chickens clucked. The flock of children watched silently from a discreet distance.

Henry's mama dropped her hands to her sides and looked away. She sighed. "Dey called me Florenda while I was still a … before." She raised her chin, her voice a challenge. "Thinkin' I might brew up some sass'fras tea. Could make 'nough fer three."

Sarah bowed very slightly. "I would love a cup of tea." She followed Florenda into the cabin. As she passed Henry, she winked at him. He grinned, a flicker.

Sarah expected dust and grime. Instead, she found a single

room adorned with splashes of vivid color, whitewashed walls scrubbed down to the wood, a swept hard-packed earthen floor, a neat corner devoted to a kitchen/dining area, and beds screened by calico curtains.

Florenda pointed at a caned chair beside a simple wooden table. She busied herself with tea and cut three squares of johnnycake.

"Pone?" Her voice was brittle.

"Please."

She poured tea into three unmatched cups and sat on a chair that was obviously homemade, crude but sturdy. Henry brought a three-legged stool to the table.

"Is yo some kinda missionary?" Florenda asked. "Iffen yo is, we don' need none yo' kinda that. Nobody ever 'gain tellin' us what's we does."

Sarah smiled. "No, no. My only mission is ..." *Is what? Encourage freedom to think? Teach skills to keep one free?* "I've never considered what I do to be missionary work, but I believe that every person should have a chance to better himself. In that, I can help."

Florenda smirked, a cynical grimace. "S'matter, white school-teach lady? Y'all tryin' tell us yo *unnerstan'* where we'uns been?"

Sarah set down her teacup and leaned across the table toward Florenda. "Of course I don't *understand*, not the way you mean it. I'll be honest, more honest than I've ever been. I never thought before what it has been like for you and Henry, for all your people. Never even felt guilty because I *hadn't* thought about it. But this morning, when I saw your son subjected to the cruelest mental torture I could imagine, it was as if a great door opened onto my very soul."

She clenched her hands and felt her freckled face redden. "Those self-righteous, vicious children spouted what they had been taught." Sarah's voice broke. She shook her head impatiently. "Mrs. Jackson, I felt their hatred. Like an outside force, I felt it. For that instant, I was Nigra!" She dug in a pocket for a handkerchief.

Florenda stared at her hands clutched on the table. "Grand words," she said softly. "Now yo kin go home feelin' like a saint a some kind. Pat nice black folks on de head. Then y'all kin forget 'bout dat whole t'ing—no guilt 'cause yo jes' done did dat."

Sarah straightened and felt her cheeks flush again. "Not so. I broke the *rules* of my employer. I most certainly will not have my contract renewed. The rest of this school term, my students will shut me out, and I will be teaching no one. Some of the older boys made threatening gestures toward me, as well as toward Henry. Will they act on those feelings?"

Florenda's lip curled. "Yo's still white. Y'all talkin' 'bout a 'maybe' kinda thing. Try bein' like me. No man. No protection from the law. Huh! I walk into yo' house like y'all done mine, would yo' neighbors keep from doin' somethin' 'bout it?" She glanced at Henry. "Go outside," she said curtly. "Shoo."

Looking alarmed, the boy dragged out the door.

Florenda leaned toward Sarah. "Yo gotta man?"

"No, my husband died of a fever. After the war. We never had any children."

Florenda snorted. "The war. Him a hero, fightin' to keep us in our place. My man ..." Her voice shut off and tears brimmed.

"He … my man was lynched when Henry t'ree years old. For why? We was in town. Rained heavy. He accidental tripped and mud splashed on a white woman's skirt. Her husban' was a *gentleman,* a officer in dat war. Six years ago … nine years after it ended, he still struttin' 'round wearin' a great sword."

Her voice quavered to a stop. Her hand shook when she picked up her cup and gulped from it.

Sarah waited, silent.

Her eyes downcast, Florenda said, "He … he yank out dat terrible sword an' jes' ran it t'rough my Ben liken he stickin' a pig." Her voice became a wail. "Left him bleedin' in de mud, not a soul botherin' to he'p me lift his dyin' head outta the slime. An' not a po-lice man in sight."

Florenda rose abruptly and put the teacups beside a washing basin. Without looking at Sarah, she said, "Bes' y'all go now. Don' wan' yo messin' up my son's head, dis readin' an' writin'. Won't he'p him pick cotton one bit better."

That evening, Sarah sat in the kitchen of her house. A pot of vegetable boiled dinner simmered on a wood-fired iron cookstove. She considered dishing up a bowlful for her supper, but didn't when the effort seemed exorbitant. It was not hunger that occupied her thoughts.

October dusk stole the sun's bright cheer, mocking Sarah's mood so bitterly. *My morning started out full of contentment. An explosion of black powder could not have shocked me, terrified me, any more than did the explosion of raw hatred at the school. Then to be rejected by these Negroes whom I tried to help? Have I risked my career for nothing?*

Recalling the woman's curt dismissal goaded Sarah's pulse into a bounding response.

A pounding on her front door broke through the melancholy of Sarah's thoughts. She groped in the dim light for the lamp at her elbow, found a match, and lit the wick. She rose wearily and went to the door that was still resounding to thunderous knocks.

When she opened it, a man, whose frame filled the opening, pushed past her and stomped out of darkness into the front room.

"Explain yourself!" he roared.

Irritation quelled Sarah's initial jolt of fear. She followed him and held the lamp to illuminate the face of Thorwald Hanson, chairman of the Springdale School District. *How like a wild Viking*, she thought. Hair and beard bright red and shaggy. A broad face, creased now with a frown. Chest like a barrel; a belly even broader. At inches above six feet, he towered over her.

"Well?" he demanded.

Sarah set the lamp on a table. "Have a seat, Chairman Hanson. We'll talk."

"This won't take that long. My little Ingrid says you kicked everyone out of class this morning so's y'all could teach a *nigger*? True or not?"

"A nine-year-old Negro boy presented himself at the school, requesting that he be allowed to attend. I kicked no one out of the school. The students took it upon themselves to depart. I believe we need to face a new challenge, since the alternative school intended for his people has closed. I'm glad you came tonight so that we can plan—"

"No plan. No niggers. Given your attitude, *no teacher.* Y'all are fired."

Sarah drew a breath deep. "I have a contract, Mr. Hanson. The law says that you cannot abrogate—"

"Hogwash." He pulled out a legal paper, thrust it into Sarah's face, and tore it in two, in four, into confetti. "I don't see no contract. Do you? Don't you come near my school again." He tossed the contract into a shower of paper scraps.

"You can't—"

"I just did." He started toward the door.

"I'll contact authorities."

He thrust his face inches from hers. "You pathetic prune, I *am* the authority."

He shoved against her shoulder and lumbered past her.

Sarah called, "The students need a teacher!"

At the door, he turned back. "They got one. Me. The Bible's our text from now on. Them kids gonna be taught God's truth. No nonsense. And no black apes in *my* classroom."

Sarah collapsed into a chair and closed her eyes.

Two evenings later, a commotion arose outside of Sarah's house. She went into her parlor and peered through the window.

Four white-clad men, wearing pointed covers over their heads and faces, lit a fiery cross in her front yard. Astride nervous, prancing horses, they rode in a circle around it. Rebel war cries shattered the still air.

Sarah plopped onto the settee, fighting a lightheadedness determined to put her down. Like a blow from a fist, she missed solid, unflappable Jonas with a fierceness she had not felt since the day she had watched him lowered into the ground. A swoon—surely the right of a Southern lady in peril.

But no, damn it, no!

She stood and squared her shoulders. Jonas had shown her a way …

She loaded his deer rifle and brought a chair to her porch. She fired one shot between the feet of the horse ridden by the apparent leader of the four and plunked down on her chair.

"Wanted y'all to know," she called, "I always hit what I aim at."

She sat with the gun pointed toward the yard.

The intruders trotted back onto the road, milling about, arguing and cursing. One of the men fired a shot that pierced her front window before they broke into a gallop, heading toward town.

Sarah watched until the fire burned out.

4

The next morning, Sarah raked ashes of the cross into a pile. Movement behind her …

She whirled, the rake held aloft like a weapon.

Florenda Jackson stood straight, arms folded across her chest.

Sarah lowered the rake from an attack position but held her grip on its handle. She stared at the other woman between taut lids. "You have something to say?"

Florenda shook her head side to side and grimaced, her face a mask of despair. "Y'all got no idea what yo' meddlin' do to others. Crawl inna our lives like a water moccasin snake, den come home to yo' pretty house, full uh pride fer what yo' done. Leave de troubles to us!" She clenched her fists and stamped a foot.

Sarah tightened her grip on the rake. *Am I in danger?* The

venom she sensed in her visitor made her wish she had Jonas's rifle at hand.

The woman sighed, and the tightness in her frame sagged. "Now I see a bullet hole in yo' window, a burnt cross in yo' yard. Dey come here too."

"Too?" Sarah's voice sounded thin to her own ear.

"Dey do dere shit in the dark. I din't know dey tooken after yo. 'Least, y'all still got a house."

"You'll have to explain," Sarah said.

"Dem burnt down my house an' all my t'ings. Chased Henry an' me into the woods, whippin' our shoulders all the way."

Sarah lowered the rake and glanced around. "Dear God. Where's Henry?"

"Dey a holler'n 'bout hangin' him by his thumbs and hackin' off his man parts. He's hidin'. Dat's what yo' messin' in our lives done to us."

Sarah chewed her lower lip. She walked in a tight little circle. *How could this Florenda person so misunderstand my intentions? Differences in life or not, aren't some experiences, some feelings universal? Should I accept a degree of responsibility for the woman's plight? Am I to blame?*

Then there was Henry to consider. For the boy, innocence wouldn't spare him.

Decisions upon decisions in unending hordes …

She mentally slapped her own cheek. *Oh stuff it, Sarah,* she thought. *In for a penny?*

Sarah squared her shoulders and tossed the pound after the penny.

She dropped the rake on the ground. "I was thinking I

might brew some tea. Could make enough for three …" She raised her voice. "If Henry happened to be nearby."

Florenda's face twisted. "Y'all think I'd set foot inside yo' house?"

Sarah said, "I set foot inside yours. I'm asking you to return the courtesy." She stood like the hostess of a grand restaurant, one hand pointing toward her door.

"Ain't gonna!" Florenda screamed. She screwed up her face, shook her fists, and stamped her feet. "Settin' me up fer dem bastards to come a huntin' me again?"

Sarah held her pose. "I'm sure you and Henry must be hungry. I have a venison roast simmering in the pot. I'd welcome your company, you and Henry."

She waited.

Tears trickled down Florenda's cheeks. She stamped her foot and clenched her fists again.

Sarah heard a quivery voice coming from within a brush-choked swale bordering her yard.

"Mama, I's hungry an' ain't nothin' to drink. Teach lady—I think her all right. Please?"

Florenda swung around. "Henry, stay put! Don' let dem catch yo. Oh Lord Jesus, he'p us. He'p us." Her voice trailed off, and she fell to her knees. She buried her face in her hands.

Sarah lifted Florenda to her feet. "Henry, give me a hand with your mama."

Running feet came behind them. Henry took Florenda's other arm, and they hobbled into the house.

Sarah led them to the front room and found chairs. She pulled hers to face Florenda. Henry sat as close to Florenda as the chairs allowed.

Sarah said, "I am greatly sorry for what happened to your home. The question is, what are you going to do now?"

"Do now? Like I's some choice?"

"Snap out of it," Sarah said. "You're alive, even unhurt, and Henry is too. We just need to find a way for you both to survive."

Florenda's eyes sharpened. "Don' talk to me 'bout survivin'. What yo know?"

"I know what it has meant for me."

"The law on yo' side—white people wit' the power—"

Sarah clapped her hands together sharply. "Enough!" She grabbed Florenda's arm and rubbed vigorously; then rubbed her own. "Black stays black—doesn't come off any more than my freckles do. So what? Cry and moan about what we can't change? I accept that you have had hideous experiences because you were a slave. Things I can't ever rightly know about. But others of us have had to fight to survive too. Do you know who your parents are?"

"If I do, so what?" Florenda brushed her skin where Sarah had rubbed it.

Sarah said, "As a newborn baby, I was abandoned on the steps of a foundling home in New Orleans. So I am told. I'm probably Irish—hair's too red to be French. One of the nuns told me once, all the while smirking piously, that my father was a priest and my mother a … I won't defame her name. After that, I refused to call the orphanage priest 'Father.' I fought my way out of there, ran away, made my way to Texas, and earned an education."

Sarah leaned toward Mrs. Jackson. "On my own. Why do you think I connected so strongly with your son? His gumption reminds me of myself when I was his age. I too realized that 'readin' and writin'' were the means of my salvation. Henry has a God-given *right* to discover how far he can go, and education is his best chance to succeed."

Sarah leaned back in her chair. "I could use a hand setting the table, brewing tea, and making some gravy. Henry, there's a kitchen garden out behind the barn. I need a few carrots and an onion or two." She stood up. "Let's go."

5

Two weeks later Sarah, Florenda, and Henry sat around the dining room table. They were sated from a roasted chicken meal and tired after a day spent digging the last of the vegetables, now stored in the root cellar.

Sarah said, "Henry, please clear the dishes and start washing up. Your mama and I have business to discuss."

Henry glanced apprehensively at his mother before pushing back his chair. Florenda tensed. She stared at something—or nothing—over Sarah's shoulder.

Sarah said, "More tea before we begin?"

"No."

Sarah filled her own cup. She waited until Henry dragged into the kitchen.

"I've been thinking on our dilemma, yours and mine. I accept what you said, that my trying to help you and Henry cost

24

you all that you had. I don't have the resources to find another home for you. I do have an idea, though."

She took a sip of tea. "Given how those cowards in dirty bedsheets regard y'all and me right now, when word gets around that you're my guests, we're likely to have another visit, another cross, and a danger that things could get out of control."

She leaned forward. "This past while, I pushed you and Henry. Cutting the last of the hay with the scythe, hoisting it into the barn, digging potatoes, cleaning this house indoors, down to the corners and sidewalls. You and Henry are good workers—don't grudge any. This is a desperately rundown farm. Since my Jonas was taken, I've managed to grow my food and earned cash from teaching. The fields, though, have gone fallow. No cotton, no barley. The land is there, waiting, but I can't manage by myself."

Without asking, she poured tea for Florenda and refreshed her own cup. "A hundred years ago, there was a custom in Europe where people owing someone could work it off by becoming what was called an indentured servant. For the various reasons I've touched on, I'm offering you and Henry home and board here with me, ostensibly as my personal indentured workers."

Florenda jumped to her feet. "Servants? *Slaves?* Ain't *never* goin' do dat again. An' what dat *ostent* mean?"

Sarah leaned toward her. "Ostensibly. It means giving the appearance of something not true in fact. The idea is that we publicly declare you and Henry to be 'indentured' but with no obligation between us. No paper. No contract. If we make a profit off the land, you would earn equal parts of it."

Florenda's face was like a gathering thunderhead. "If y'all ain't lyin', why yo do all dat?"

"Please, be seated again. I'll be blunt. I feel no personal guilt over what happened to you. Evil people harmed you. History is a continuous record of the damage evil people do. I am not evil. You said that you are a survivor. So, survive. I'm a teacher. I intend to teach your son as much as he wants to learn so he can have a life that is more than just surviving. There it is. The decision is yours."

Florenda said, "If I say I will, yo don' own Henry or me?"

Sarah smiled and shook her head. "Absolutely not. I would never do that, even if I could. A bargain?"

After a pause that stretched a minute into two, Florenda nodded.

Sarah said, "I'd like to hear you say so."

Florenda ducked her head for a moment before staring Sarah straight in the eye. "I says I do dat, Miss McAllfry."

Sarah beamed and turned toward the kitchen door. "Henry, you can quit eavesdropping and join us for a cup of tea. Bring those cookies with you."

When Henry was seated and munching an oatmeal cookie, Sarah said, "One more thing. Names. We are going to be living together from now on. My name is Sarah, and I want you both to call me that. In return, I would like the privilege of calling you Florenda. With your permission, Mrs. Jackson."

Florenda shrugged. "Massa can call … de boss say what *she* wants to call me."

Sarah shook her head sharply. "No. A name is special, unique."

"Lemme t'ink 'bout dat."

Sarah nodded and turned to the boy. "Henry, call me Sarah."

He swallowed a bite of cookie. "Yassum, teach lady."

Sarah shook her head, a twitch. "Sarah."

His eyes widened. "Yassum, teach Sarah lady?"

"That'll do for now. Florenda?"

"Oh lawsy, lawsy, Miss McAllfry. I was to call Massa by his name I'd be—"

"Sarah, Florenda."

Florenda covered her eyes with one hand and squeaked, "S-S-S-ar." She peeked between her fingers. "Can't say it."

Sarah nodded. "All right, Fl-Fl-Fl-or."

Florenda dropped her hands to the table, stared at Sarah, and threw back her head in a laugh so hearty it seemed to rattle the windows. "Sarah!"

"Now I can say Florenda with comfort. And Henry. For this to work, we must become friends."

Laugh lines in Florenda's face smoothed out, and she said softly, "We see 'bout dat, Miss Sarah. We see."

6

Sarah had kept a journal since her arrival in East Texas. She jotted her thoughts and yearnings onto tablets of the same paper her students used to record their lessons.

One spring day in 1887, she sat at the small writing desk in her front room, pencil in hand. She laid it aside to muse—to remember that day seven years before, when three unlikely people had signed on together. Friends, Sarah remembered saying. To succeed, it would require that they become friends. "And by God," she declared aloud, "we have succeeded."

Months had piled up, along with that distant October's castoff leaves. Seasons paraded by. Sarah, Florenda, and Henry worked the land and made it fertile. And Henry. He grew tall, prodded by genes from far Africa, his strength annealed by work, until, at sixteen, he had become the *de facto* man of the place.

Henry learned to read; oh yes, he did! He discovered equal facility at doing sums. Sarah's eyes misted at the memories that fact provided. Pride too? *Yes, I enjoy it for what it means to me.*

Sarah had passed on one skill learned at the shoulder of her Jonas; she taught Henry how to use a rifle and shotgun—to hunt deer, turkeys, the endless abundance of passenger pigeons darkening the sky overhead, and even the lean, feral swine roaming the back country. The boy's eye proved to be sharp, his aim true.

The porcupine quills of Florenda's suspicions gradually blunted. Sarah and Florenda explored their differences and discovered that they mattered not a jot. Sarah's thought was smug, yet sincere in gratitude. Insulated by remoteness, the unusual little island of harmony escaped the notice of those devoted to hatred and turmoil.

Sarah filed her addition to the journal and sat back. Life was good, so unexpectedly good after the losses and pains that had brought three friends together.

He did not know that he was Babe the Blue Ox until after he had become both "Babe" and "Blue." He found advantages in being bovine, for he had not met a creature stronger than he. Still, having front legs ending in hooves instead of nimble fingers made any attempt to record his adventures a frustration.

His earliest life experiences clung precariously to the loose pages of memory. When he settled down at night for quiet time, early impressions oozed up from murky hiding places. He called these his primitive memories. He clung to them, for they provided proof of roots and roots validate existence. As in ...

There was a sense of bodies lying close around him, close to each other. The complex aromas of being alive. Soft rumbles from bulging bellies. Rhythmic crunches from the processing of a thousand cuds. Whining creatures, nearly too small to see; the sting when whining gave way to a bite of ear or eyelid. The sudden gush when a nearby companion released body water. The odor of the odd material coming from someplace just beneath one's tail. The lingering taste of Mother's milk, warm and comforting, from teats reserved for him. Such was the earthy nature of primitive memories.

During those placid days, he was vaguely aware of occasional visitors. They called themselves humans, he later discovered. He learned that these intruders insisted on classifying all creatures, great and small. They tagged him and his kin with a Latin word, *Bos*. They were scrawny, these Two-Legs, standing upright on spindly hind legs. They gave every appearance that a good Texas breeze would blow them along like tumbleweeds.

He soon noticed that the adults of his herd paid little attention to them unless they approached directly. Many rode animals as large as Mother, even taller, if slimmer of build. Creatures they called horses.

He recalled endless sweeps of lush grassland. Grass as a carpet and as fodder. Pine-covered hills bordered the grazing area in the direction where Sun awoke each day. A shallow stream meandered through the meadow. He neither questioned nor anticipated the seasons. He was incapable of wonderment.

Life for a Texas longhorn calf was simple and uncomplicated.

Until one day of stark horror. A warm, bright, innocent-appearing day dawned. He had been butting heads playfully with another calf, proud of his budding horns, testing their strength. He ran and chased the other for the pure pleasure of doing so.

Then, a small herd of Two-Legs arrived. Humans, riding atop horses.

Along with a gaggle of his comrades, he was forced into a confining chute and dipped in foul-smelling tarry material. He was thrown on his side to endure the sting of hot iron against one flank and ghastly pain when a human clamped another piece of iron onto an odd sac dangling from his belly, near the source of body water. When a human approached with another iron implement, intent on cutting off his developing horns, he bolted. He butted one human into coals of the same fire where he had heated branding irons and swept the feet out from under another with the very horns the human was trying to mutilate.

He ran until he plunged into a pool of water contained behind a dam of sticks and mud. He waded and swam to the far bank and hid in a tangle of willows and cottonwood trees from one of the humans who came searching for him. Two-Legs gave up when mosquitoes swarmed around him. Babe waited until darkness before slinking back to the anonymity of the herd.

Fear and distrust of these puny-looking two-legged sticks, these humans, seared determination deep within him, as unrelenting as were the irons they used against his flesh. Two-Legs could not be trusted!

Pain of what had been done receded. Events seen through the lens of such limited understanding didn't allow introspection. Forgetfulness carried its blessing. He roamed with his herd in search of fresher grass and drank from the stream with simple-minded lack of concern. Days followed nights in vaguely noted succession.

Babe was officially a yearling longhorn steer—an ox, by other definition. He grazed amid his herd.

The spring day was hot. Along about the time when Sun rode straight overhead in Sky, a haze began to dim its light, just enough to notice. Clouds rumbled up from the horizon, from that direction where Sun disappeared each night. Black, tall as a *Bos* can see, they devoured the blue that Sky has always worn. Restlessness pricked at his being, deep in parts he had been unaware of. Call it fear, an apprehension similar to that which he felt whenever one of the Two-Legs seemed to notice him. Even the adults of the herd, so stolid most of the time, twitched and turned aimlessly. They raised snouts to sniff at eddies of air moving in haphazard swirls. Mother and her sisters lowed plaintively.

Sky darkened. No blue remained in sight. A petulant wind rustled the leaves of trees lining the nearby small river.

A cloud black as night extended a horn downward from Sky and probed Grass. A roar like a full stampede swelled, even as members of the herd circled aimlessly—anxiously. Jagged streaks of light, blinding in intensity, flashed from edges of the cloud or lit it from hidden depths. Thunder swelled from angry rumbles to crashing explosions of sound. A black frenzy swallowed the herd.

Mother! His playmates!

He panicked in primal terror and ran without thought or concern for direction. Chance directed him toward the river. He stumbled and slid down its bank into water up to his knees. He lost footing and collapsed.

Leaves lying on the ground trembled. A robust branch, fallen in the past, moved and turned over, and he was minded of a snake. It lifted off the ground. A rumbling shook water around his knees into oddly peaked directionless ripples. Kinfolk on the plain next to the stream raised their snouts as though each was bellowing in full voice, yet the uproar of the storm overwhelmed sounds from the entire herd in chorus.

A cottonwood tree on the bank of the stream whipped wildly about before it tore free of the ground with groans of deep agony. It whisked into the air and disappeared upward! Water in which he stood followed the tree. Up, up, beyond up, swallowed by black, swirling terror …

From the clutter of impressions that were his primitive memory, one stood starkly. *He* was swept up along with water from the stream, among trees dangling torn roots, high into a dark swell of dust and clods of sod and shredded leaves. Circling rain turned dust into mud. He pawed frantically at nothing but air gone rabid. He could no longer see the ground.

These images branded so strongly on his mind ended in a flash of light. That he recalled, remembering how every hair of his body stood straight, pricking darkness, each with its own tiny spark. Flickers of blinding light flashed past his eyes from the tip of one long horn to the other.

His nightmare, the very act of *transformation*, ended in darkness even deeper than the black air of the whirlwind.

8

Sarah peered at the window across the width of the barn. Its glass was translucent from decades of grime. There, the sunlight and blue skies of a warm spring day lost out to time and hay dust. It was humid—yes, even for East Texas. Caused a body to drip sweat down her chin and arms. From the very tip of her nose. Dust motes stirred to life by tiny breezes glittered in sunshine leaching into the place. Thinking about all those specks made her itch. She grinned suddenly and scratched in places a lady never would if she weren't unobserved.

The old barn creaked in the way of such a poorly built structure. Sunlight slanting through the doorway dimmed while she watched. A restless breeze thrummed through a thousand cracks in old wooden walls.

Sunlight diminished. Curiosity prodded her. Mucking out the milk cow's stall could wait. At the doorway, she looked up.

A cloud stretched a surprisingly sharp line across the sky directly overhead. The sun had slipped out of sight behind it. Sarah stepped out into the barnyard and squinted past the corner of the building. In the southwest, a cloud mass reared massive shoulders, threatening heaven itself, black as the ebony keys on a piano, shaped like a gigantic anvil. Muttering breezes subsided. It was as though nature and God himself waited breathlessly for … for what?

Sarah shivered, chilled despite the heat.

A pointed streamer appeared, whirling between the bottom of the cloud and earth herself. It grew wider, devouring the horizon in its path. Wider still. Continuous threads of lightning stitched the cloud overhead as well as in the broad funnel. Thunder grumbled, growling constantly in rising chorus. A gout of violent rain slammed her hard enough to make her stagger. The writhing funnel scoured the earth a quarter of a mile away from her, drawing into itself dust and tree limbs and what had to be the roof from the neighbor's shanty of a house. A madness of tortured air roared toward Sarah, momentarily paralyzed by the sight.

She knew what was about to engulf her!

A tornado as relentless as a promise of God's vengeance.

She ran toward her house, some hundred feet away, toward the storm shelter Jonas had dug into a bank of soil just north of the building. No time! She wasn't going to get to it, let alone warn the others. Florenda? She had been sewing in the dining room. And Henry? The last she had seen of him, he had been headed out to the fields.

God help them!

Wind screeched. It slammed her to the ground. She turned

her head to the sight of her milk cow, airborne into a devil's cauldron, soaring higher than the tallest tree. The oak in her yard thrashed in a frenzy of pounding air until its two-foot trunk twisted off as she might twist a stalk of celery. The top disappeared into the funnel.

Wind tumbled Sarah along the grass of her yard, her lovingly tended patch of green. She fetched up against the stub of the oak tree with a thud that drove breath from her. She grabbed the stump and held on grimly, even as wind tried to lever her free to join the tumult overhead.

Her breath came back. She closed her eyes and prayed in a shout lost in the snarl of wind.

"Oh God of my fathers, spare Henry, somewhere in this hell. And dear Florenda. Take me if you must. But damn it all, if you do, make it quick!"

She glared up into the belly of that wind monster and a flash of lightning so bright it near seared her eyes. "And addled my senses," she afterward told any who would listen. "That bolt of lightning sizzled straight from the tail of a longhorn calf flailing along in the middle of the storm, high overhead. His whole outline was pricked out in beads of light, and lightning arced between his horns. The poor critter went limp as wash left on the line during a rainstorm. It fell smack onto the old haystack out by the barn."

Oblivion shielded Sarah from further chaos of the storm.

9

What caught Sarah's attention when she opened her eyes onto what was left of her life was the utter silence. The quiet after such a cacophony created by the tornado was almost painful. She fancied that nature listened, stunned by what she had wrought. All of death and wreckage so dreadfully still; all of timid life so hesitant to announce itself.

Sarah heard no raging wind. Not a breath of air moved. No insects chittered; no birds called to each other. Sunlight once again filtered through last wisps of cloud.

Sarah still clung convulsively to shattered splinters of the oak tree. She willed cramped hands to relax, and she flexed her fingers. She sat up and looked around.

A foundation of field stones marked the spot where her house had been. She looked over her shoulder. Defying reason, the miserable wreck of an old barn, minus some shingles, still stood.

Florenda! And Henry!

She tried to stand, wobbled back to her knees, and crawled toward the open basement of her house. Collapsed flooring, pieces of furniture, and her cookstove had dropped straight down as her house splintered. She peered into the hole.

"Florenda?"

Florenda's voice came from beneath a pile of linoleum-covered boards.

"Sweet Jesus, is you callin' me home? I's here."

"It's me. Sarah. I'm coming."

From the basement came a resolute, "Oh when de saints, go marchin' in ..."

Sarah stood, steadying herself by holding on to the foundation. The stairs leading into the basement were intact in one corner. She edged toward them.

Now the basement rang to another tune. "Come to de church in de wildwood, oh, come to de church in de dale ..."

Sarah clambered over debris to a thumping rhythm. "Oh, oh, come, come, come, come ..." She tossed broken boards aside, levered up a section of flooring, and leaned it against the basement wall.

Florenda lay flat on her back, her hands folded prayerfully across her chest. "Come to de church in de ..." She opened her eyes and stared straight up at Sarah. "Land o' Goshen. Is you ... is we ..." She sat up abruptly. "I believe we's still here."

Sarah dropped to her knees beside Florenda. She cried, great tears overflowing, sobs wracking her chest. She threw her arms around Florenda and clung to her. Florenda returned the hug.

They stood, facing each other.

Sarah touched a livid bruise on Florenda's forehead. "That is going to be all black and blue. Oh no, I'm sorry—didn't think."

Florenda threw back her head and laughed, a robust guffaw. "Better on me den y'all. Sarah, I forgives you fer bein' white, now and fer all time."

They leaned back against the wall of the ravaged basement, laughing, crying, until Sarah said, "Henry! He was out in the cotton field." They scrambled up the stairs to ground level.

They met Henry trotting across the barnyard, his face taut with anxiety.

He touched Florenda's face and her shoulders, testing.

"Mama! Are you hurt?" He put his hands on Sarah's shoulders and then enclosed Florenda and Sarah in a tight embrace. He drew a breath deep into his lungs. Sarah realized his voice was bubbly with suppressed tears. "And you both seem to be all right."

The three survivors hugged fiercely.

Henry walked toward the stone foundation and peered into the basement. "It's gone. How could a house just vanish?"

Sarah pointed toward a debris field across the road. "More like, it came undone. How did you survive?"

"I saw it coming, the dark cloud, a funnel. I remembered hearing tell of tornadoes and knew I had to find a low place to ride it out. I ran to the drainage ditch at the end of the field and hunkered down as tight as I could. There was unbelievable stuff up in the cloud. That old wagon of Morris's sailed past, fifty feet in the air. Someone's leghorn chickens, the top of a tree."

Sarah said, "Yet there stands that near worthless barn. My

poor milk cow gone in the wind." Her eyes widened. "The longhorn calf."

"What calf?" Florenda and Henry said in unison.

"It was up in the cloud too. Lightning shot out from its tail."

Florenda and Henry exchanged glances.

Sarah strode toward the barnyard and looked up at the haystack. Nothing was visible from her ground-level vantage.

"Henry, fetch the ladder from the barn and crawl up to the top of the haystack. See whether I was dreaming, or if there really is a cow on top."

Henry returned with a homemade wooden ladder about twelve feet in length. He leaned it against the stack and climbed quickly.

"There's a cow up here," he said solemnly. He climbed out of sight. Sarah hitched up her skirt enough to climb after him. They knelt beside the animal. It lay on its right side. The beast's long, straight, right-side horn had been driven deep into the haystack. The animal lay motionless.

"Steer," Henry said.

"Yearling calf, I'd say. I wonder if lightning barbecued it." Sarah poked at the animal. "What? Three hundred pounds? Three fifty? Imagine a wind strong enough to carry that weight."

"Don't have to imagine it, Sarah. It'd be nice if we could save the meat."

Sarah lifted the creature's eyelid. No flicker of life. She pressed her ear against its chest wall. No breath, no sound other than a dull thump. Thump.

Thump?

What did the heart of a longhorn steer sound like?

Is the creature alive?

She pounded its side. Again, two-handed. No response.

She crawled around the top of the haystack, found a two-by-four that had anchored a canvas cover in place. She raised it high and whacked the animal's side with all the strength of her tough, skinny arms.

The steer grunted, pulled in its tongue, and drew a breath deep.

Sarah decided that the critter was about to regain an interest in living. He tried to raise his head. *Must be weak as a newborn kitten.* The horn buried into the hay held his head captive.

Sarah and Henry straightened onto their knees and stared at each other across the animal. "Rope," Sarah said. "Saw a hank last week … where? And a block and tackle. Ah. We used them to fill the hay loft last fall." She descended the ladder, with Henry right behind her.

They fastened the block of pulleys to a post supporting the hayloft inside the barn, ran rope through it, and dragged the long rope end out the door. A few pitchforks of hay were used for a landing place beside the stack. They clambered back atop the pile of hay to kneel at the animal's head.

The steer was awake. His eyes rolled wildly, and he thrashed his legs feebly. Baby steps for such a hefty animal. His chest heaved as though he tried to bellow. To Sarah's ear, the sounds resembled the bleating of a lamb taking its first breath.

Sarah wound rope around the base of each horn and tied it firmly into a loop. She made a fist and thumped his broad forehead between the eyes.

"Y'all listen up," she snapped. "We're going to help you, but you have to cooperate. Hear? We'll drag you off this stack onto some hay on the ground. Slow and easy does it, but there's going to be a bump at the end."

The creature groaned. His legs twitched, like a sleeping dog running in a dream.

Sarah and her two helpers went into the open doorway of the barn and began to pull on the business end of the rope. A snort came from atop the stack. She saw his tail flick into the air for a moment. The pulley block exerted its power and the creature slid to the edge of the stack. The imbedded horn dragged a bale-sized wad of hay with it.

Sarah called, "Can't help a jolt now, so don't give us any guff."

They pulled. The animal's head hung down limply. It bleated. Another pull. *Easy …*

The critter slid over the edge of the stack. Pulleys or not and despite their dug-in heels, his weight dragged them across the barnyard. He landed with a solid thud and a puff of hay dust. With legs now folded under him, the animal looked like any cow chewing a cud.

Except that he seemed unable to hold up his head. Sarah used the pitchfork to pry hay off his right horn. He shook his head weakly before letting it droop again.

Sarah studied him. "Looks as though you may be here for a spell. We need to give you a name. Like a baby, you are. So Baby, what'll it be? Y'all way too big for that to stick. Maybe just Babe, till I figure what works better. Time to bed you down."

Sarah and Henry readjusted the block and pulleys to drag the animal across the central aisle and into a twelve-foot-square calf pen opposite the door into the barn. Sliding on hay, the task was readily accomplished. She set three saplings into slots confining the space.

Sarah said to Henry, "I heard somewhere that if a cow can't stand when ill or injured, it might develop breathing problems. Don't know if that's true or not, but since we've come this far, let's not take chances. I believe a sling should do the trick." She and Henry fastened the tackle to an overhead beam, with a piece of canvas under Babe's belly.

"So, up you go, Babe."

A three-person hoist, and the animal stood on four feet. Part of that effort went to the sling; part seemed provided by Babe's gathering strength.

Sarah, Florenda, and Henry lined up in a row, chins on folded arms resting on the top pole of the calf arena.

Florenda asked, "What y'all goin' to do wit' him? Can't give no milk. He already near dead an' half cooked when he came. So why wake him up?"

Sarah found a stem of hay to chew on. "I'm that curious to learn where he came from, dropping out of the storm, and what he's about to do next."

Babe looked at her and waggled his horns. The effort seemed to do him out of energy. His head drooped until his muzzle rested on straw covering the floor.

10

Babe learned details of how Sarah got him down off the haystack and into the barn months later. From that beginning time, primitive memories still dominated. A mélange of brief flashes—fear when he slid off the stack—a determination to gore the Two-Legs-in-a-Skirt if she came close enough. Would have if he hadn't been so exhausted.

She got a canvas sling under his belly, used the ropes again, and hoisted him high enough for his legs to take over. They quivered, and a sneeze would have sent him tumbling, but he remained upright.

He experienced an unlikely moment of tenderness when Two-Legs fed him a paste of oats, fresh eggs, and molasses. She held a pan of water under his nose for him to drink. She—he did recall this—she patted his neck, lowing with odd sounds, a steady stream of them. Somehow, the effect was soothing.

Much of what he recalled so dimly was of sleeping. That is, waking to find Sarah Two-Legs standing in front of him, coaxing him to eat or drink.

One overall primitive memory persisted: a sensation of being comforted that awoke memories of Mother.

11

Sarah forced herself to take stock of her shattered resources. For a brief while, like blinders on a horse's harness, attending to the sky-riding steer shielded Sarah from full appreciation of the devastation the tornado had wreaked upon her life. Once she and Henry got Babe upright in his sling, Sarah headed across the yard toward her house.

Her house! Gone. A year's supply of kindling wood, a jumble of bricks that had been a chimney, a battered iron cooking stove ... these lay in the dug basement where the house had stood. Pieces of shattered wood, roofing material, shards of furniture, clothing, and her lace curtains were spread across her front yard, across County Road 17, across Crosby's hay field and wood lot beyond. The footprint of the whirlwind traced the fruits of her life.

Her legs folded under her. She sat on sodden earth, her

certainty of faith in any God as shattered as her home. *So this is what hard work and frugal living and honesty came to—a piece of hardscrabble, hilly land; an old barn capriciously spared; a henhouse barely stout enough to keep out foxes; my milk cow certainly dead; chickens and geese scattered like so much cottonwood fluff; my gentle old plow horse, Ned, unaccounted for.*

And a mortgage hanging overhead like an anvil suspended by so hopeless a thread.

The warmth of two bodies settling one to each side roused her from her reverie. She stretched out her arms and hugged Florenda and Henry close. They sat without speaking, slumped. Day crept off to the west, rosy with the cynical promise of a bright tomorrow. Darkness came, a moonless veil to fit Sarah's mood.

In the morning, seated on piles of hay in the barn doorway, Sarah held council with Florenda and Henry, they big-eyed and solemn.

"That's it," Sarah said. "I'm wiped out. No house, no prospects for rebuilding. A quarterly mortgage payment is due in another month. And unless the bank would accept this old barn as collateral ..." She snorted. "I'd apologize, except none of this is my fault." She smiled wryly. "Florenda, that 'Sweet Jesus' of yours has a deaf ear."

She bowed her head for a moment and then looked each of the others in the eye. "You two are free to go wherever you want. There must be some place with better prospects than here. I have a little money to share with you, as I promised.

I'll divide what cash we have accumulated into thirds. It'll tide you over."

Henry and his mama looked at each other. Florenda shrugged and glanced over her shoulder at the barn's dusty interior. "This don't look no worse than mos' places I lived. We'd best round up them chickens before foxes git 'em."

Henry said, "I found the rifle. I cleaned it up, fired it once. I can get us a deer this evening."

Florenda grinned, her teeth bright against her complexion. "Y'all ain't the only one what got curiosity about that ol' steer." She sobered and leaned forward to put a hand on Sarah's knee. "T'ain't often 'at I gits to know a white lady who is a *real person*. I want to stay."

"And my learning lessons aren't finished," Henry said.

"Well." Sarah found a handkerchief. "It's time this *family* gets to work. The cotton field needs attention, and peas in the kitchen garden were ready to pick, if they didn't follow our house into the storm. We need to check whether the canning jars survived in the basement."

12

During the days that followed, Sarah scavenged what she could of her belongings. A tintype wedding picture, wrinkled and water-damaged. Odds and ends of clothing. A blanket and Grandmother McAllfry's old quilt, torn but mendable. A surviving high-flying chair from her dining set, come to earth a mile away. Half a dozen dishes not reduced to shards.

Caring for Babe became the focus of her efforts, a hold on her sanity. Of necessity, Florenda, Henry, and she moved under the only roof still standing—into the barn. They banged together beds from boards dragged over from the demolished house, a stall apiece at the opposite end of the barn from Babe's calf pen. Henry gathered stones and made a fire pit just inside the barn door.

Sarah had never previously considered the idea that an animal might have … what? Call it personality. Barn cats existed to catch mice intent on stealing grain from the bins. She paid them little heed. The milk cow produced butter and cream. "Best not to personalize her since she'll be meat for the winter," she had chided Henry. Chickens were useful producers of eggs, meat, and feathers for a down jacket. While Babe …

Sarah considered the dilemma. By any rule of reason, the steer was a year away from being a winter's worth of meat for the larder. As such, it made sense to keep him alive long enough for the investment to pay its dividends. When keeping him alive required more than feeding, providing water, and mucking out his stall, the rule of reason shifted in an odd and disorienting way.

The morning following the tornado, Sarah removed the sling she had used to get him onto his feet. He promptly collapsed onto his belly, his legs askew in an unnatural tangle. The beast's eyes rolled wildly, and he coughed and bellowed. She and Henry hooked up the sling again and ratcheted him once more to his feet. On day three, she loosened tension on the hoist rope but left the sling in place. She chuckled; the poor fellow's legs quivered.

On the fifth day after the whirlwind, she decided—the steer was either going to make it, or he was not. She loosened the sling and snaked it from around his torso. Babe turned his head to watch her over his shoulder.

He stood quietly, shifted his weight without apparent difficulty or trembling.

"Let's do it," Sarah said. "Might as well find out where we

stand, you and I." She removed the railings of the calf pen, slid the barn door open, and stood aside from the opening.

The animal bolted out of the pen to the barn door opening and stopped for the briefest of moments. He looked back at Sarah.

"Well," she snapped. "Git, if you've a mind to go."

The animal snorted, shook his head, waggling those horns of his, and took off at a brisk trot. He headed for the spread of pine trees covering a knoll next to the pasture. Headed for the place where split-rail fencing had blown off during the whirlwind. She watched him disappear amid the trees.

"Like the kid I never had," Sarah muttered. "Save him. Feed him. Clean up after him. Right when a body could maybe find a use for him, off he goes. Good thing I don't care."

She took her reading chair into her stall, a dark place with no window. She tossed the book aside and curled up on her bed. Coma too deep to be called sleep claimed her. It dragged her into a nightmare full of ice and cold and loneliness too black to reveal any figures.

Something warm and moist touched Sarah's cheek. She awoke with a jerk and swatted the jaw of a yearling steer. From her elbows, she looked up at a broad snout, at an eye rolling wildly, and saw with discernment the size of this creature of brute instinct and strength.

She reared up and screamed.

Babe jumped, a full-body four-legged twitch. He backed away from her bed so abruptly that his off-horn hooked the shard of salvaged mirror glass she had hung on the rough boards of her stall. It fell with a clatter and disintegrated into slivers of silvery glass.

Babe spun like a spring uncoiling and bolted to the barn door.

"Babe?" she called. "Babe! Wait …"

He stood in the door opening, quivering.

"You came back. You didn't run away. You … Babe! Go to your pen this instant." She pointed, her arm extended.

The animal lowered his head and waggled his horns.

Last light gleamed off the wicked point of the horn nearest her. A stab of fear sent blood pounding through her ears. She groped behind her and found the handle of a hay fork.

Babe raised his head. He looked over his shoulder at the open barn door and then back at Sarah. He turned, as though studying the calf pen.

He walked into it and swung around to face her. Her hands and arms trembling, she located the poles that closed the pen's opening and dropped them into place.

He came toward her and rested his chin on the top pole.

Sarah looked into his broad face and at the hay fork she had clutched so convulsively. She tossed the fork aside, climbed onto the bottom pole, and leaned to hug Babe's head and neck.

"What manner of creature *are* you?"

He snorted softly in her ear.

Sarah decided that she was honor-bound to try to locate Babe's owner. A branding scar on the steer's flank appeared to be a T within a circle.

She and Henry set out on foot one day to investigate. They followed a path of destruction created by the tornado. En route, they passed the rotting bodies of three steers, one of which looked to be more than five hundred pounds.

Grassy plains began some three miles west of the McAllfry farm. A herd of cows and steers was attended by a quartet of cowboys astride horses. The cattle each bore the brand of a Circle T.

As Sarah and Henry approached, one of the men fired a rifle at a cow lying on the ground. The animal jerked, trying to stand. A second shot, and it collapsed.

Sarah heard a grizzled, gray-haired cowboy say, "All them with broken legs, shoot them. Any that look hurt or ailing, don't fart around. Shoot them too. Those killed by the tornado are damned ripe, and I wanta get outta here."

The man turned his horse toward another cow lying on its side. When he spied Sarah and Henry, he reined in to face them. "Hey," he said. "Get away from here."

Sarah stood looking up at him. "Are you in charge?"

"Zeke Franson, foreman," he said. "If it's any of your business."

"Do you own these cows?"

"Work for the owners. I told you to skedaddle. Don't want nobody gettin' hurt on my time."

"Were these cows injured by the tornado?" Sarah asked.

The man spat a wad of tobacco. "Lost a quarter of the herd. Losing that many pretty well wipes us out."

Sarah said, "If a person were to find one of your steers—say, three or four miles from here—would you be likely to come and claim him?"

"You expect some kinda reward?"

"More asking. Theoretical."

He snorted. "Keepin' another man's steer's considered rustlin' in Texas."

"That's why I'm asking, being a good citizen."

Franson asked, "How big's this theoretical steer?"

"Probably a yearling."

"Walked into your place, did he?"

Sarah squinted in thought. "Actually, thanks to the tornado, might say he flew in. When the lightning shot out of his tail, he was still fifty feet up in the air. That's when he fell down into our barnyard."

"He *what?* Christ, lady, is he alive?"

"Yes, as a matter of fact, although he might require some nursing for a while. Unforeseen late complications. Theoretically."

"Lady, a steer is either marketable meat on the hoof, or he's food for coyotes and vultures. A banged-up yearling ain't worth the effort to come for him. Now get the hell off our land."

Sarah smiled, her sweetest variety. "Thank you, Mr. Franson. No need to escort us as we leave."

13

Over the next weeks, Sarah fancied that Babe was adapting to her. Skittishness gave way to cautious trust. He no longer swung his swordlike horns at her if she approached him. He moved aside when she mucked out his stall and spread fresh barley straw.

She allowed Babe to leave his pen for extended periods. He grazed on summer's lush grasses. He was growing, she was certain—growing quite remarkably. His hair had all fallen out, effects of the lightning, she supposed. More unexpectedly, he seemed to be shedding skin. Not in swatches but more subtly, as though cell by cell it replenished itself.

His dun-colored hide was becoming brighter. She realized one day in midsummer, when sunlight caught him just right, that he was becoming blue. Real blue. As true as a bright June sky. Almost iridescent, like an indigo bunting when sun's rays came at the best angle. She tried to convince herself it was a figment of imagination or sign of eyestrain.

Blue? A steer?

Herm Corcoran decided to stop by Sarah's place one day, attracted by the sight of a new animal in the barnyard.

"Dangdest color I ever seen," he told Sarah. "Liken y'all dipped him in dye or somethin'. Where'd ya get the thing?"

Sarah winked. "New breed, so they tell me." She headed back toward the barn before Herm could ask more questions.

Herm's mission in life was to spread the news. Of course, he was also known to embellish a story if it needed spicing up, so not many folks in the hill country actually believed there was a true-blue longhorn steer at the Widow McAllfry's farm.

"Come on, Herm!" old man Polk said to him.

"Get glasses, Herm." Bertha Smith waved a hand of disbelief at Herm.

"Into the hooch kinda early, ain't ya, Herm?" Howie Longstreet asked.

Howie Longstreet was a twice-removed cousin of the illustrious Confederate general, or so Howie loudly maintained. A blue steer? He decided that rumors of its existence provided excuse enough to call on the critter's owner, the widow Sarah McAllfry. Prudently, he first searched courthouse records for a description of her land holdings.

Assessment time. Sarah wandered around the periphery of her farm. Possum Creek, the crick, meandered through the south pasture. It was handy to the stock and seldom inclined to flood. Besides the pasture, thirty acres were once again planted to cotton and twenty acres in barley. She smiled. At least nature, in all her resilience, was already healing the scars from the storm. Here, an acre grew field corn for the milk cow, now deceased, and another sizable patch was the kitchen garden, food on which the family subsisted.

She turned her face toward the south. The rest of her land—120 acres, more or less—was a sweet-smelling piney grove. Breezes talked to the trees, music that, to her ears, soothed beyond any hymn sounding from a church meetinghouse.

She grinned at the thought. Nature's voice was never out of tune.

Howie sat in front of his favorite saloon, his heels cocked up on the hitching rail. Think time. Decision time ...

Widow McAllfry pure puzzles me. When, by chance, we meet in town, she ducks around me without a by-your-leave. Even if I spit-slick my hair and call the biddy ma'am, she acts liken she don't notice the effort. No man puts up with a woman bein' uppity. No suh. A bachelor can pick and choose, and there ain't no harness on my shoulders.

Thing that gets me to ponderin', though, is the twinges of middle age, hinting at what being truly old might hold in store. Makes a man consider the advantages of having a long-term female around the house. Take care of a fella. Might be handy to have someone with a name a man can remember for more than a couple of hours after he leaves her. Someone to look after him when his chilblains bark.

All right, women bein' so danged high-toned 'bout life means a dad-blamed wife.

The widow Sarah? I probably could do worse.

Given a proper bit of remorse on her part, I might forgive her for the way she always ignores me.

Howie owned a thirty-year-old roan horse named Robert E. Howie realized from things he'd heard that even in horse years, that made the beast barely older than its rider. An age with implications. Robert E's concept of speed these days seemed to Howie no better than that of a basking turtle on a summer beach. Slow and easy does it.

Howie knew well where Widow Sarah's place was located. His official visit as a Klansman enforcing the will of God those years before had left a sour taste that still nagged when he thought about it. There's that business of uppity again—the widow. Too handy with a rifle. Still, time does wonders to smooth memory's sharp edges. Yep. Under his firm hand, she could be taught her proper place.

He unhooked his heels from the hitching rail and used it to pull himself erect. He climbed aboard Robert E and set out for Widow McAllfry's farm, filled with benevolence … and a generous draught of Southern comfort.

The warmth and humidity of mid-July promptly raised a sweat. Insects of some kind twittered and chirped at each other. Noisy little bastards. Mirage waves of heat shimmered at the horizon. Robert E clip-clopped at the slowest speed consistent with forward motion. Howie's morning hair-of-the-dog pick-me-ups had their way, and he swayed in the saddle, more asleep than not.

Sarah stood in the barn doorway, massaging sore back muscles. Babe had grazed all morning and lay just outside the opening, contentedly chewing his cud. His hide glowed, softly blue in the radiance of the sun. A hint of fuzz had begun to grow, replacing the hair he had lost to the whirlwind's electrical storm. The bristles appeared to be dun colored, but the blue of his skin still blazed through.

She trundled soiled barley straw from the calf pen into the barnyard and dumped it onto a compost pile. On impulse, she stopped before Babe.

"Those who make messes should have to clean them up. If you weren't above such things, I'd train you to do your business outdoors like the rest of us have to." She shoved the empty manure cart close under Babe's nose. He snorted and drew back his head. She blew a lock of hair away from her forehead and wiped sweat onto her sleeve. She steered the reeking cart back toward the barn, muttering to herself. She glanced back from the barn door.

Babe stopped chewing, levered himself to his feet, and walked to the compost pile. He sniffed at what Sarah had deposited before returning to his spot in the sun. *Now what was that about?* she wondered.

Sarah sat in the opening of the barn doorway with her belated lunch—a slice of cheese, a slab of bread sweetened with elderberry jelly, and a bowl of strawberries, picked that morning while still covered with dew. Half of a passenger pigeon, cold, left over from last night's repast, gleaned from the swarms passing within range of Henry's shotgun, filled the menu. She did miss her moo-cow's milk. It was time to think of a way to replace her.

The sun's rays warmed shoulder aches that her morning chores had provoked. She tuned in melodies of nature—the hum of a foraging bee, a robin's chirping, the liquid warble of a cardinal bird. Peace spread broad wings. Face to the sun, her eyelids drifted shut.

A shadow blocked the sun's benevolence. She jerked to attention. A man stood before her, close, in her space. Howie Longstreet. He of the lascivious smirks. He of skill at contriving an "accidental" full body collision in the aisles of Burton's Department Store. The master of double entendre slyly delivered.

Rules of Southern hospitality decreed that a mealtime guest be invited to the table. Sarah suspended such an arcane rule.

She looked past Howie.

He shifted his feet and spat a wad of tobacco juice. "Y'all doin'?"

She nibbled a strawberry.

"Heard y'all got yourself a blue steer." He sniggered and pointed at Babe. "Didn't believe it till now, seein' the critter for myself."

She ate another strawberry.

"Talk is, y'all claim he"—he sniggered—"dropped outta the sky. Sorta like a miracle."

Sarah stood and brushed crumbs from her skirt.

Her voice was as cool as a stormy day in December. "You've seen him. Now you'll be wanting to head back to town, it being so hot and all."

"Dad burn it," he muttered. "Did she done it again? Uppity?" He edged closer to her. His face reddened. "Heard y'all claims that critter is a act o' God. Talk around town, though, the real act o' God might be your house layin' in a thousand pieces in yonder field. Some folks wonderin' what a woman done to earn that kinda die-vine punishment."

She turned away and stepped toward the doorway into the barn. Howie jumped in front of her again.

"I come by today, full of concern. Poor widow an' all. Property wiped out. Livin' in a ratty old barn. Thought maybe I could help, maybe rebuildin' your house." He stroked a chin days past a shave and lowered his head, as though offering a confidence. "Cost y'all cheap, 'specially iffen y'all was real nice to me, gettin' my meanin'." He edged closer to her.

The stale-sweat stench of the man felt like something crawling on Sarah's skin. Florenda and Henry were out in the barley field, dispatching weeds—she was alone. Her pulse bounded, and her hands trembled when she clenched them.

She closed her eyes for a brief moment. *Courage!*

She swung past Howie, entered the barn, and left dishes in the tack room/kitchen/all-purpose space to the right of the door. Howie grabbed her arm and spun her around.

"I talkin' to y'all. I know your type. All prissy fussy. I've a mind to take that outta you—"

She bit his wrist and shook her head like a terrier with a rat.

He roared and jerked his arm away, staring in shock at blood dripping from a gaping crescent-shaped wound. He raised his arm in a towering threat. "I gave you a chance. Now I'm gonna take what I want—"

Abruptly, he bellowed.

Howie dangled from Babe's left horn. The animal's horn had slid under Howie's pants from behind, down the leg, to emerge at the ankle. Babe snorted and shook his head, backing out the barn door, the man dangling helplessly. Howie's arms and the unfettered leg thrashed about like windblown long johns on a clothesline.

Babe trotted around the barnyard, shaking his head, tossing it—and Howie—wildly. With a last heave of his shoulders and neck, Babe flung Howie head first ... into the compost pile.

Babe galloped across the yard, spun in a tight circle, and came to a stop just outside the barn door. His eyes bulged, and his sides heaved from panting breaths. Head high, he stood directly in front of Sarah.

She touched his nose—a small gash oozed blood—stroked his broad forehead. She threw her arms around his neck.

"You dear lad!" she shouted. "Let's clean out the barnyard."

Side by side, the two walked toward Howie, who was just emerging from the detritus of a ripe composting pile. He brushed at clinging straw and manure.

"I gave y'all a chance," Howie squealed. "You're a witch, Sarah McAllfry. And that critter of yours is the devil himself. God-fearin' folks gonna stay clear." He shook a fist at her.

When Babe snorted and lowered his head, Howie ran to his horse, slumped in sway-backed lethargy. From atop Robert E, his feet searching for elusive stirrups, his arms waving, Howie screamed, "Y'all ain't heard the last a this!"

Legs flailing far out from the flanks of his steed, Howie lost control of Robert E's reins. He clung to the horse's mane. Robert E broke into a tooth-jarring trot and headed north toward Possum Creek, the town, four smelly miles away.

Sarah's shoulders slumped. "Dear God, what if he had ... I've never felt vulnerable here on the farm before."

She stood directly in front of Babe and looked him straight in the eye.

She spoke her thoughts. "Babe, something remarkable occurred here. I never heard of a steer—any cow, for that matter—actin' like y'all did just now. I have goose bumps thinkin' about what coulda happened. More bumps from seeing you take care of that gooby. Wondering what was going through your mind."

Mind? Does a dumb steer actually have what a body could call a mind?

The warm summer day had been full of sunlight and soft breezes to chase away flies and a sweet cud to chew. A Two-Legs stranger had appeared at the gate into the barnyard. Babe stopped chewing, tightening muscles. The human had gotten off his horse and walked up to Sarah.

His own Two-Legs-in-a-Skirt had occasional visitors—Two-Legs who arrived in a carriage pulled by a horse, or riding on top of a horse, or even on foot. He had learned that such visits didn't need to cause anxious feelings deep inside him.

But this Two-Legs roused tension from the moment he appeared. Babe watched him, lying still as a shadow. When the stranger confronted Sarah, Babe received a stronger jolt of tension. He stood up and faced the newcomer, head lowered, gaze intent.

Sounds passed between them. Babe sensed fear in Sarah's tones. Herd instinct, he readied himself to gallop.

The newcomer seized Sarah's front leg and jerked her into the barn. Babe felt danger from him, terror from Sarah.

Flee! Run! Blind escape.

Sounds erupted from the barn. The strange Two-Legs roared; Sarah screamed, a frantic wail.

Babe bolted toward the pasture.

And stopped after only a step.

Sarah-Mother sounds. Hurt sounds.

He trotted to the barn door.

Two-Legs-the-Stranger raised one of his front legs.

Babe sensed a threat. He lowered his head and swiped a horn along the intruder's back. It pierced the human's odd removable skin and emerged by his back foot. Babe jerked his head, shaking it side to side. He bellowed and charged around the barnyard, twisting in tight, stiff-legged, jolting circles, before arriving at the pile of used straw. He flung his head in a wide arc, and intruding Two-Legs landed in a heap on the pile of compost.

Babe turned toward the pasture when …

A feeling he had never experienced came over him. *I must not run away again. A member of my personal herd needs me.* He turned and trotted back to Sarah Two-Legs.

She wrapped her front legs around Babe's neck and nuzzled a sore place on his muzzle. The warm feeling that swept through him in a great wave told him things were good.

14

The iron cookstove survived its fall into the basement. Using salvaged boards as skids, once more supplementing muscle power with block and tackle, Sarah and her willing helpers skidded it into the barn. They set it up in the tack room, just to the left of the door. Cooking once more became an indoor activity.

Sarah wryly acknowledged awareness of her own nature. She was a talker. She had dealt with the aloneness of widowhood by conversing with her world. Birds on the wing. A goldfinch in subdued winter plumage while perched on her finger to accept a seed. Flowers in her garden joined forces with a breeze to nod, as though responding to her words. Photographs lined up on the cherry-wood bookcase became her confidants. She scolded the God with whom she had previously had a trusting relationship, now sorely tested by events. She whispered to trees and to bees in their hives. Winter's grumpy winds; she talked to them all.

Now, she talked to Babe.

Chance had dropped the bookcase into the basement when the rest of her house had taken wing. She removed a cache of books to the barn, carefully drying pages that had been soaked. Mark Twain's collected writings. A set of *Collier's Encyclopedia*, A to Z. *Ben Hur*, and the Bible, of course. She set out to read her way through her small library, and the books served as focal points in the course of Henry's ongoing instruction.

September arrived; October's crispness loomed. Patterns evolved. It was dark in her stall, so she moved her chair to the barn door opening. She read aloud, sharing Dickens and Mr. Poe's eerie vision of reality with Florenda—she, busy with her sewing needle—and with Henry—he, absorbed.

She augmented her supply of resource books with a leather-bound copy of *Gray's Anatomy*, bought for pennies at an estate sale in town after the death of old Doc Smithers. In order to guide Henry through the mysteries it revealed, Sarah had to study the text right along with him.

More and more, she had him read aloud. His growing facility—in comprehension, in natural science and mathematics, in logic—brought shivers to Sarah. *What if his potential had never been allowed to flourish?*

One afternoon, cold rain splattered the barnyard. She drew a sweater tight and closed the door. Dark. She and Henry moved to the calf pen, where Babe lay chewing a cud. The window in his pen gave best light. This day, Sarah chose the poetry of Lord Byron.

She closed the book. A pensive quiet settled over Sarah and

her companions. A low-pitched moan told of cracks between wall boards.

"Winter is harsh," Sarah said. "We'll need to plug as many of those openings as we can."

"How?" Florenda asked.

"I've been thinking on that," Henry said. "We have straw. Stuff canvas and rags we collected from the house blowing down into openings. Maybe use mud, like chinking a log cabin."

Sarah smiled. "We just decided tasks for tomorrow."

"An' I's gonna chop firewood," Florenda said. "I love swingin' that mighty ax."

Sarah swiveled to face Babe, lying placidly in his pen. "I haven't mucked out his stall for more than a week."

Henry said, "Ain't you noticed? Babe does his duty outdoors now."

"But the door has been shut because of the weather."

Henry beamed. "I showed him how to open and close the door." He whistled softly. "Come on, Babe. Open the door."

Babe abruptly stopped chewing his cud. He tossed his head side to side.

Henry stood and snapped his fingers. "I want you to show Sarah."

Babe snorted and rose to his feet. Grudgingly? Sarah mentally chided herself. *He's just an animal, one bred for brawn, not brains or emotions.*

Babe hooked the tip of one of his horns under the top pole closing off his pen and lowered one end onto the ground. He repeated the process with the middle pole and stepped daintily over the bottom pole. He went to the barn door, hooked its handhold with the tip of a horn, and slid the door open along its track. He walked through the opening, turned around, and, again using his horn, drew the door shut from the outside.

"Y'all come back in now," Henry called.

The door rattled open. Babe walked inside, turned, and closed the door. He retreated to his pen and carefully hooked his horn under the end of the middle pole, settling it into its slot. He then repeated the process with the top pole.

"Sweet Jesus," whispered Florenda.

Sarah felt as stricken as Florenda sounded. "I see that we can dispense with bars to Babe's pen." She took them down and went to stand beside him. She rubbed his neck and looked him in the eye. "What kind of miracle was in that tornado of yours?"

"Sweet Jesus!" Florenda repeated with conviction.

December brought a pervasive chill that made Sarah huddle in her worn cardigan sweater. Winds whistled across the plains of Texas to moan through a thousand openings in the old barn. The family spent waking times in the area just inside the barn door. The iron cookstove provided warmth, fueled by wood from trees surrounding the farm. Gallows humor … splinters of the demolished house served as kindling. Occasionally, they awoke to the sight of an inch or so of snow. It melted by noon.

One day, after such a baptism, Sarah watched Henry from the barn doorway. He scooped up a handful of snow, touched it to his tongue, and shrugged. He compacted it and threw at the bole of a tree. Missed it. He leaned against the side of the barn.

A red fox appeared at the edge of the forest, surveying the expanse of white between them. A female. She walked cautiously toward the henhouse. Quick flicks of her head as she glanced about. She sniffed at the door to the henhouse and walked around behind it.

Henry darted into the barn and grabbed the shotgun. He sidled back outdoors, the gun halfway to his shoulder.

The vixen reappeared and barked, a boy-soprano yip. Two nearly grown foxes trotted out of the forest. Mama Fox wandered about the barnyard, her nose to the ground, trailed by her kits. She paused over an area of undisturbed snow and then jumped straight into the air from all four feet. She repeated the maneuver, flipping a mouse or vole into the air with her jaws. When it tried to tunnel back into the snow, one of her offspring jumped à la Mater and flipped the mouse in an arc. The second kit finished the lesson with a quick snap of dainty jaws. He (or she) picked up the prize, and the fox family headed back into the forests.

Henry lowered the shotgun with a sigh.

"You didn't fire," Sarah said at his shoulder.

"No. I … couldn't."

"Next time, she'll be after our chickens."

"Then I'd better make sure there are no chinks in the henhouse."

Sarah hugged Henry tightly. "I love you."

He hugged her. Fiercely.

Sarah was pleasantly surprised that so many of the chickens that had survived the whirlwind had been rounded up; many returned on their own. Eggs and the occasional roasted bird supplemented a diet of venison—and pork, when Henry one day shot a wild tusker. She and the boy rigged a harness, allowing Babe to drag the prize to the barnyard for processing. Turkeys, coaxed within range of his shotgun by an offering of dried field corn, donated meat and feathers to stuff the quilts that kept them warm in bed.

One day, Sarah slipped on loose hay in the barn, landing on a scythe blade. The result was a four-inch cut, deep enough to expose calf muscles in graphic display. Florenda clucked at her. "I wash dat out an' den stitch it for yo."

So, she did.

"I's sorry to hurt yo, Sarah. Dat'll heal nice now."

"Where did you learn to do that?" Sarah asked.

Florenda's smile vanished, and her face became a stolid mask. "In de bad ol' days, Massa din't spend no money treatin' sick or injured slaves. No suh! My granny learned me about herbs what he'p a fever or sores, willow bark tea for pain, and Mrs. Munson teached me how to sew. De first time I had to sew up a cut in a field hand's arm, I near fainted, but I got it done. After dat, Massa expected me to put splints on broken bones and take care of cuts." A grin broke through her somber expression. "Some de peoples started callin' me Doc."

Henry's determination to learn had not withered. Sarah spent every morning with him, reading, quizzing him, challenging him to solve problems in logic. She added to her personal journal, writing in tablets she had purchased for the use of her students.

Henry took over caring for Babe. He spent hours in the calf pen, sitting beside Babe, his voice a soft murmur. Reading to the animal? Sarah smiled. A way to learn.

Sarah was fascinated by Florenda's skill with needles and thread—stitching, decorating, mending. She created scenes of birds, animals, and imaginative patterns in glowing color to be sold as art pieces at market.

Then there was Florenda's gift of music. Her singing voice was a throaty contralto. Sarah was reminded of a brook in the hills, water stirred to melody by its passage over rocks and ripples.

Afterward, Sarah marveled that such a simple event had brought the issue into focus …

Florenda asked Sarah if she could buy some colored thread to use in a tapestry she had outlined.

Sarah was deep into her own head while she prioritized expenses for the coming spring planting. She jotted figures in the asset column and toted up expenses. A tight squeeze if—

Petulance in her voice, Florenda demanded, "Is yo sayin' yes, or is yo sayin' no?"

Sarah blinked and looked at Florenda. "What, yes or no?"

"What I done asked yo."

"What did you ask me?"

Florenda shook her head and snapped, "Yo done that again."

"Did what?"

Florenda spoke with exaggerated precision. "Yo din't listen an' I still got no answer. Dis happen all de time."

Sarah felt her face flush. She leaned back against a bale of hay. *Relax. Nothing personal. Stay rational—even if others sometimes are not.* "Start over. What didn't I hear?"

"I need a spool of crimson thread for my sewing project."

Sarah squinted. "So?"

"Can I buy one?"

A jolt of irritation straightened Sarah up. "Why are you asking me?"

"*Yo'* de boss."

Sarah studied Florenda's troubled face. *Has some serpent of discontent crawled into our midst?* "I think something important just happened. This reminds me of another discussion. Henry, the last time we were in town, you asked me if you could buy shells for the rifle."

Henry returned her gaze unblinkingly. "And you got irritated with me over it."

Sarah nodded. "I did. I believe I know the reason. Florenda, why do you ask me for permission to buy what only you know is needed? The same to you, Henry."

Florenda and Henry exchanged glances. Her voice was sullen. "I always ask."

"That's what annoys me. Why do you put the burden of all decisions onto me?"

Florenda's eyes were round, her voice soft. "Before, Massa *tol'* me everything I do. Slave peoples in big trouble if dey decided *anythin'* they se'f. It's terrifying to think 'bout decidin'."

Sarah said, "But we—you, Henry, I—all decide things every day."

Florenda shook her head. "Not big things, we don'."

Sarah smiled. "Like buying a spool of thread?"

"Don' fun me!"

"I'm not. You seem to feel free to contradict me when you disagree; do it all the time. I actually need that to happen. What's different about this?"

Florenda twisted her fingers in a tortured snarl. "It already a thing that is when yo decide something. I can like or not. It *not* a thing when it undecided. I never allowed to *decide* somethin' before. What if I decide wrong?"

Sarah held out her hands to Florenda. "We're a family. Remember? Right, wrong—makes no difference between us. Each of us has an equal voice in deciding things." Sarah beckoned to Henry, and the three joined hands. "The responsibility to decide is the price of freedom and the blessing of freedom. Are you ready to shop for a spool of crimson thread without involving me?"

Florenda said, "It still feel like I standin' on the edge of a cliff."

"Let's jump off your cliff together." Sarah hugged the other two tightly.

Babe snorted in her ear and pushed his muzzle into the middle of the group hug.

16

Florenda told Sarah that she wanted to honor the birthday of her "sweet Jesus." She covered her mouth and stepped back.

Sarah nodded gravely. "We can work out details. I'm a little surprised that you gain something from a Christian celebration."

Florenda's face relaxed into lines of peace. "His message done reached me t'rough my heart. Person's gotta believe in somethin'. Ain't no life otherwise."

"Even so, where did you learn about Christianity?"

"Granny had a brother who was owned by a godly man. He let Uncle Seth learn to read, 'long's it was outta de Bible or de hymn book. Seth taught Granny 'bout sweet Jesus. She could sing. Lordy, Lordy, Granny could sing. Massa done let her teach us slaves songs in de Baptist hymn book. *Him* was no Jesus Christian, way he treated peoples, but he t'ink we all content when he hear us singin'. Mostly, life was easier iffen we let him t'ink dat was so."

She started to sing a hymn softly, one vaguely familiar to Sarah. Florenda's voice sounded to Sarah's ear like a soothing clarinet.

The day of celebration arrived. Warmth and contentment misted Sarah's eyes when she glanced at her comrades—at Florenda, across the dining table of rough planks; at Henry, beside her; at Babe, lying close by. Henry had shot a wild turkey for the Christmas Day meal. Between courses, Florenda insisted that Sarah and Henry take turns reading the traditional accounts of the Nativity from Sarah's tattered Bible.

Sarah passed the Bible to Florenda. "Your turn to read."

Florenda winced. "I too slow. Words don' jump offen de page for me like dey do for yo an' my boy." She tipped her head at Henry. Sarah heard pride in her voice.

Henry said softly, "Maybe if you considered print the same as instructions for your sewing needle—"

"Instructions? Those I hear. From Missus Munson, her tellin' me. I learn best from my ears."

Sarah retrieved the Bible. "Have you heard the Nativity story before?"

"Yes."

"Do you remember what Saint Luke said about it?"

A sudden smile lit Florenda's face, and she closed her eyes. "I do. 'An' there were shepherds living out in the fields nearby, keepin' watch' ..."

Sarah reached out and stroked the steer's broad forehead. "Look at Babe there on his bed of fresh straw. Put a manger beside him, and we have a picture of what we just read."

After dessert, pie created from a pumpkin out of their own patch—a raw pumpkin was Babe's special treat—Henry stood and said, "I have a surprise for you. Actually, Babe and I do."

Drowsy and sated from the meal, Sarah said, "Has he learned a new trick? Maybe mucking out his stall?"

Henry said with quiet dignity, "Don't make fun of Babe. He has feelings too."

She tipped her head toward Babe. *Feelings?* "Sorry. I bow to no one when it comes to respecting our Babe."

Henry frowned. "That sounds flippant."

Sarah raised her eyebrows. "What should I say?"

"Best y'all wait till we do our little demonstration before you decide."

Babe lay in his pen, staring at them quietly. Henry turned his head away and said softly, "Stand up, Babe."

The steer promptly stood up.

"Are you cold?" Henry asked.

Babe shook his head side to side.

"Do you know who I am?"

Babe nodded twice.

"Tell me."

Odd sounds emerged from deep in the animal's throat.

Henry turned toward him. "That's right. I'm Henry." He handed Sarah a piece of paper on which the alphabet had been written, each letter followed by dots and/or dashes. "As smart as Babe has become, his throat anatomy and lack of something called Broca's speech area in his brain don't give him the ability to *speak* words, to talk about all the things he knows. I looked that up in your encyclopedia and Mr. Gray's anatomy book. He has a vocabulary of several thousand words, and he's learning more every day. We decided, he and I, to communicate using the telegrapher's Morse code. He picked it up in a week; I'm getting better as we practice. He just now gave my name in code. Now, Sarah, ask him a question. He will answer in code. Use that table to check him out."

Sarah twitched as though she had just awakened. "A question? Of *Babe*?"

"Anything."

"Well … what day is today?"

The throaty sounds began.

"Slower," Henry said. "Start again."

The glottal sounds resumed in short groupings. Sarah searched the listing.

"Dec 2 5, sweet Jesus day," she said.

An odd ringing filled Sarah's ears, along with shivers and goose bumps. *Some things simply could not be.* She glared at Henry. "An elaborate trick? You signaled him some … let me ask him a question while you are out of sight or sound. Scoot!"

Henry grinned, winked at Babe, and sauntered to the far end of the barn.

Sarah stood next to Babe's ear and said in a soft voice, "How did you get here?"

Babe snorted gently and began the sounds.

"Wait. Slow down." She grabbed up the listing. "In … a … great … wind. Much … lightning …"

"Sweet Jesus," whispered Florenda.

"I can't believe that I'm talking to a dumb animal as though it could really understand."

A stream of clicks. "I … can't … speak … but I … have … a … mind."

"Sweet Jesus," Sarah said as she collapsed onto a bale of hay.

17

To Sarah's perception, the winter months slogged past in frozen sluggishness. Babe taught her the Morse code and readily agreed to practice with her until communication between them became as facile as any depending on words. Their bizarre teacher/student relationship still left her breathless.

A howling blizzard in February piled enough snow onto the old barn's roof that Sarah rigged up a harness and crawled atop it to dislodge as much as she could safely reach.

Tempers among family members rose, even as chronic chilling persisted. Runny noses, coughs. Confinement and monotony. Even Henry rebelled at further lessons. He spent hours with Babe, the two of them wandering around the countryside; or he stretched out on his cot, sleeping for hours or merely staring at the blank wall of the stall.

Sarah asked Florenda, "I'm worried. Is something really wrong with Henry?"

Florenda sighed. "He's in his teens. Dey's only half human fer a while. He all right."

"How can you be sure? What if he's ill or … something?"

Florenda snapped, "I sure 'cause I's his mama. I tooken care my younger sisters when dey growin' up. Yo ain't the onlyist one knows t'ings. Hush up now."

No one spoke to anyone else the rest of the day.

One evening, Henry and Sarah discussed the upcoming season of planting. Absence of Ned, the plow horse, lost to the whirlwind, was looming over them.

As they brooded, chewing the topic once again, Babe erupted into a frenzy of coded sounds.

Sarah interpreted and turned toward the calf pen.

"You want to pull the plow?"

"I … can … do … it."

"We could adapt the harness," Henry said. "He's strong enough. Look at him."

Sarah studied Babe. He stood with his head raised. He nodded briskly.

My word, she thought. *Babe is nearly three years old. Shoulders massive, haunches hard muscle, another hand or two taller. The tips of his horns must be more than five feet apart. The animal is huge, growth unnoted in the day-to-day closeness of our existence.*

She stood and hugged Babe around his stocky neck. Her arms barely contained it. He rumbled deep in his chest.

Florenda burst out laughing. "Sweet Jesus," she said, "dat fella purrin' like a kitty."

18

Once a week Sarah and Henry hitched Babe to a two-wheeled cart, loaded it with garden produce available at the time, and headed for Possum Creek, the town. Market day brought a chance to earn a few pennies. It took three hours to walk each way, the axles of the solid-oak cart wheels squealing like a pig at sight of the knife on every down slope.

It was a steamy day in late August. The cart held bags of the last string beans, new carrots, tomatoes, early squashes, half a dozen watermelons, two chickens tethered to the cart by their legs, and a four-pound catfish, caught that morning from Possum Creek, the crick. Henry walked on one side of Babe, Sarah on the other. Henry carried a long, flexible willow switch. It was for appearances only, as Babe understood his role.

"Henry," Sarah called across Babe's broad back. "A word of caution. Last week you were quick to answer back to casual insults. You can't win arguments with white-trash ruffians, and if they take after you, no one in town is going to stand up for you. Please, for my sake, be docile."

"Playin' dumb never gained us a thing."

"I know! Just pick your fights thoughtfully."

His face screwed into stubborn lines. His head bent forward, he stalked along and finally muttered, "For you."

"Thank you, Henry."

Sarah understood her community well—its breath, its pulse, its quarrels with itself. She relished a role as a dispassionate observer.

Possum Creek, the town, was home to 624 citizens, or so said the census takers. Well, probably more than 800, if one counted Nigras, but who, she wondered, actually did that? Pine Avenue divided the town—white to the north, the North Side; and black to the south, the South Side. All commerce was conducted to the north of Pine Avenue. Black folks were tolerated on the wrong side of the avenue if employed as a maid. Mammy crossed over, cash in hand, to buy groceries or dry goods. For a man, spading up a garden, clearing away trash, or other menial services granted amnesty. Curfew began when stores closed. Respect for laws of probity in both the South Side and the North Side led to peace.

A sure threat to peace was for a South Sider to become uppity.

Sarah led the way off Main Street. The market place sat like a half-acre knob on the eastern end of Pine Avenue. The result was one spot where North Siders mingled with South Siders in that eternal search for the best produce at the lowest price. Haggling, Sarah decided, was the chess match of commerce.

Arrived at the market place, Babe drew the cart into a spot shaded by a huge pecan tree. Sarah said to Henry, "I've got to get change from the bank. Set up the display." She strode away toward Main Street.

Henry unhitched Babe and walked with him to a wooden watering trough fifty feet away. "Sarah says we'd better tie you to that tree, Babe. Have to keep up appearances." He chuckled at Babe's coded response. "Wasn't that long ago I would have been tied up too," he said.

Henry arranged their offerings on the lowered tailgate of the cart.

Next to his slot, a wagon full of sweet corn was attended by a middle-aged Nigra named Joseph.

He glanced at Henry. "Y'all by yo'self today?"

"Sarah had to get change money from the bank. How's business?"

Joseph chuckled. "Iffen I was sellin' fer m'self, I'd declare it po' to bad. Since I's mindin' fer white boy, ain't no concern o' mine. Oh-oh, here come trouble. To de left."

Henry turned and stared.

Perched atop saggy Robert E, Howie Longstreet rode their way. Six more years had deepened Robert E's swayback to historic proportions. Six more years of moonshine whiskey had left their mark on Howie. Red, scaly cheeks complemented a bulbous nose laced with veins. His belly battled the belt attempting to contain it. For reasons divined only by himself, Howie was dressed this day in the style of a French cavalier. The effect of pantaloons and fitted stockings, a frilly shirt, a buccaneer's coat, and a broad-brimmed hat sporting a long feather were blunted by their air of grime. A flintlock pistol had been replaced by a long-barreled Colt revolver.

Joseph whispered, "Look, son, mebby y'all gets away with bein' bold but in the name of Jesus, don' stir nothin' up wit' this un."

Joseph doffed his dilapidated hat when Robert E stopped before them.

"Mornin', Massa, suh." Joseph never raised his gaze above the rider's silken shoes.

Longstreet flicked Henry's shoulder with a riding crop. "What's this, *boy?* The witch trusts you to bargain for her?"

Henry appeared to writhe with uncertainty. He stared at the ground. "Yassuh, but nosuh, but yassuh. Sorta."

Longstreet levered Henry's chin up with his crop. "Look at me when I give you permission to talk, *boy.* Is you pretendin' y'all know how to count?"

"Oh nosuh, but yassuh, I knows countin' real good." He held up the fingers of his left hand and touched them one by one. "They's one—that un, he come firstus—an' two an' four and seben an' num'er eleben, only he like one two, or else two ones. I t'ink. I ain't sure. Suh."

Longstreet leaned down from the saddle and smirked, his face contorted into a leer. "Do the witch snuggle up to you?" He mimed lasciviousness grotesquely. In a falsetto, he said, "Warm me up, nigger."

Henry straightened and threw back his shoulders. "She is a lady. If you don't see that—"

"Henry!" Sarah's voice echoed sharply. "Be still."

"But—"

"Now!" She turned on Longstreet. "Did you have in mind to purchase produce? If not, move on. You are blocking traffic."

"You's a witch," Howie snarled. "People's gonna find out." Longstreet stood straight in the stirrups to tower over her. One foot slipped out of its stirrup, and he lurched halfway out of the saddle. He grabbed Robert E's mane, yanking it in preventing a fall. The startled horse broke into a jarring trot, further loosening Howie's precarious seat in the saddle. Clinging desperately, his body projecting at near right angles to the back of his steed, the laws of physics and torque did the inevitable. The cinch to Robert E's saddle slid north, vertically speaking, allowing the saddle to slide south, depositing Howie on the ground.

The dashing cavalier landed directly onto a collection of fresh horse apples.

The saddle dangling under his belly, Bob E broke into a lurching gallop. He disappeared around the corner of Main Street.

Sarah turned toward the egalitarian mixture of North Siders and South Siders sanctioned by rules of market. Citizens of substance and mere folks of color exchanged glances. There was a silence of pending Vesuvian intensity, merely awaiting a proper trigger.

Howie did the honors.

He lumbered to his feet and pointed dramatically at Sarah. "She done that. She a witch, she un is." He picked up his hat with a dramatic sweep and replaced it on his head.

The hat. Adorned with a crumpled feather that had impaled one of the horse apples.

Vesuvius erupted those years ago with historic effect. So

now did pent-up laughter explode from all those at market. Even as Sarah struggled to contain her own mirth, clamoring so for release, she marveled at the sight of North Siders leaning on the shoulders of South Siders in laughter's warming embrace, while South Siders borrowed handkerchiefs from North Siders to mop up tears of pure pleasure.

She wiped her own eyes on the back of her hand. *Could such a thing provide an iota of healing?* she wondered. *Perhaps one can't revile another quite so convincingly when tears of any sort have been shared.*

Still ...

She shivered despite the charm of the day.

"Henry," she said, "fetch Babe. We're leaving."

1 9

Directly upon their return home from market, Sarah gathered the family to a council in the barn.

She said to Babe, "For Florenda's benefit, tell again what you overheard."

Babe signaled to her, "You say it quicker."

Florenda's eyes were wide in apprehension. "Sweet Jesus, what? Did somethin' happen at market?"

Sarah stared into the fire around which they sat. "I guess it was inevitable." She chuckled wryly and told Florenda about the day's events. "On the way home, Babe told us what he overheard those Klansmen deciding. All of Possum Creek laughed at Howie Longstreet, and that determined our fate. The Klan is going to burn a cross here on Friday night. Given Howie's embarrassment, he'll burn more than a cross, and I'm sure he's itching for a hanging."

"*No!* Oh, oh, oh!" Florenda wailed.

"They bragged of barbequing Babe. We can leave with fewer regrets after what happened. This is Wednesday, so we probably have a day to prepare for our departure."

"Departure?" This from Henry.

"We's leavin?" asked Florenda.

Sarah said, "What choice do we have? Say that we stay and defend ourselves. If we shoot one or two of those ruffians, after all is said and done, who do you think will end up on the end of a rope?"

Florenda sobbed, her face in her hands.

Sarah hugged her briefly. "We can't abide despair. It's survivor time again, and each of us *must* do his or her part. Babe, I'm counting on you to carry most of the belongings we decide to take with us, but each of us must carry what we can. Florenda, think what you value enough to carry on your back for perhaps hundreds of miles. There is no place for sentiment.

"Henry, this day, this hour, you have become a man, and you *must* carry a man's responsibilities. I too am faced with difficult choices, but I promise to be as ruthless on myself as I am asking each of you to be.

"While Babe heard Longstreet and his cronies plan for Friday, we must assume that they might come before that. In case that means tonight, we need to sleep somewhere other than here. I hope that we can be well on our way by tomorrow night."

"On our way to where?" asked Henry.

Sarah sighed, the deep kind. "West? There are hundreds of miles of land out there. Or north? I've heard that attitudes toward families like ours are more lenient than here. It is closer, as I read maps, and there is no shortage of water or grass for Babe. East? I have a prejudice against that direction. Any comments?"

"It sounds as though north might be best for us," Henry said quietly.

Sarah stared across the fire at the boy. *Is his voice deeper, more confident? Is my wish what I hear?* She sighed again. "I favor going north," she said.

"Yes," Henry said.

"Sweet Jesus, I'm with y'all."

Babe nodded briskly.

And so were four lives decided.

Wednesday night the family camped without a fire in a dense grove of pines at the farthest reaches of Sarah's property. "We might as well get used to this," Sarah declared briskly. "Up north might prove to be a long ways off and a roof overhead a rare comfort."

No one grumbled, but the only one who slept comfortably on the ground was Babe. He stationed himself below the crest of a modest knoll, from which the barn was visible between trunks of trees. About midnight, Sarah crept alongside him. She spread out blankets and crawled into them.

"I'm counting on your sense of hearing, Babe. Any disturbance at all, wake me."

Babe rumbled briefly. She grinned at his purr. She closed her eyes.

Dawn arrived as silently as a stalking cat. Sarah roused Florenda and Henry.

"Voices carry," she said softly. "From now on, never forget that. Henry, you will be our scout. Keep under cover, but see whether Longstreet or any of his friends are over there at the barn. Take the rifle, but *don't* use it against them unless you have no choice."

Henry nodded, his face solemn.

"We must become like panthers if we are to survive. Sharp claws, but we need to rely on stealth in the night. If this sounds melodramatic, it is not. I have seen what Klansmen are willing to do."

"As though we'uns haven't?" Florenda said sharply.

Sarah turned on her. Her voice was soft, yet as pointed as a stiletto. "And that volume of voice, Florenda, would lead them straight to us. Until we are miles away, we speak softly and as little as possible."

"Yassum, missus," she muttered sullenly.

Sarah leaned toward her and seized her shoulders. "Don't pull 'po' abused darky' on me. Y'all hear?"

A pout dissolved into a giggle, and Florenda's face turned dark with laughter controlled.

Sarah kissed her forehead. "To return what you once did for me, I forgive you for all time for being black. Henry, off you go. If it seems safe, wave from the corner of the barn. We have a lot to do today."

Alerted by what Babe had overheard at market the day before, Sarah had, while still in town, bought a sheet of canvas six feet wide and twenty feet long. Florenda cut it into two ten-foot pieces and set to work, stitching them into a twelve-foot-wide canopy that would serve as protection against weather. A saturating coat of melted canning paraffin made it as water repellant as rubber and half as heavy.

Henry and Sarah collected the items each thought most vital to their survival.

Sarah's list:

A waterproof can of matches

Metal dishes, utensils, one boiling pot

Homemade lye soap, half a dozen bars.

Towels and rags

Two Bowie knives, a butcher knife, and a whet stone

A hoe blade and round-point shovel

Hatchet, axes ... one single-bitted, one double-bitted

Set of common carpenter tools

Crosscut saw, three spare blades for cutting firewood

All the barley set aside for seeding

Two blankets and a down quilt, stuffed into a canvas bag

One pair of binoculars

Clothing: two pairs of heavy woolen trousers, Jonas's, refitted by Florenda

Three pairs of wool socks

Three flannel men's shirts, mementoes of Jonas

Cotton underwear, four sets

One woolen jacket

One cotton sweater

One woolen skirt

Condiments: salt, pepper, cinnamon, unrefined sugar

Bacon slabs, seven sides

Potatoes, twenty-five pounds

A mesh bag of carrots and onions

Flour, seventeen pounds

Lard, three pounds in solid blocks

Corn meal, three pounds

Money, $1,744.53 in federal money, gleaned from six years of markets

Candles, tapers and three-inch-base tallow candles

Rope, 100 feet, from the barn

Her wedding picture

Journal and eight blank writing tablets and a dozen pencils

Henry's list:

The rifle

A shotgun, its stock checked, its metal dull but functional

Ammunition: four boxes of rifle cartridges; four boxes of shotgun shells

Gun-cleaning supplies

One heavy blanket, one down quilt

An assortment of fishhooks, stout line, sharp filet knife

Books: Calculus theory, a dictionary, *Gray's Anatomy*

Six pads of blank paper and a dozen pencils

Florenda's list:

All the sewing needles; thread, fine and heavy-duty

Scissors, embroidery hoops, yarn, darning needles

Lengths of ribbon: red, yellow, green, lavender, crimson

An illustrated Bible

An etching of sweet Jesus looking soulfully aside,
framed, with a chain to hang it on the wall
An ivory hairbrush, a rare gift from her owner
Medical tools and herbs, salves

Clothing:
Necessities: warm, woolen pants; shirts; a jacket
Non-necessity-necessities: ("Ain't leavin' wit'out 'em")
Her gorgeous multicolored skirt
A silk blouse, aqua-colored
Underthings "what don't look like flour sacks"

Sarah and Henry spent the afternoon fashioning a well-padded harness to fit Babe's broad back. Babe insisted that he could easily carry about four hundred pounds of weight; Sarah set the limit at three hundred pounds. Apprehension chewed at her belly. In her mind, there was no doubt that Longstreet had been humiliated beyond restraint. Get him adequately stoked with moonshine …

She paused regularly during their work to walk to the middle of the road and listen toward the north. It was the first day of September, warm still with the lazy seductiveness of summer. Yet time was mercury, escaping through her fingers.

At five o'clock, her nerves, her breathlessness, demanded a halt in preparations and the beginning of action.

"Family Council," she snapped. "It's time. We have to leave. Now! We eat, then light the candle in the hayloft, and leave."

"Like that," Henry said softly.

"Better than ropes around our necks. Go!"

They loaded Babe's packs, strapped on their own, and

choked down a last meal. *Dear God,* Sarah thought, *let that not be as grim as it sounded.*

She lit a half-inch stub of candle and set it on the floor of the hayloft, surrounded by loose hay. She strode resolutely out the barn door. *I will not look back …*

Possum Creek averaged twenty-five to thirty-five feet in width. Its flow varied between gurgling rapids and lazy currents through ponds where movement of water became almost too slow to detect. They would start their escape by wading in the stream for the first mile or so. Their point of entry was into a brisk ripple over gravel near the back of the pasture. She and Henry laid down old planks at the place they would enter the water. No tracks; no hoof marks from Babe, so heavily laden. Once in the water, they retrieved the boards to be discarded as they traveled.

Dusk covered them with blessed darkness as they plodded through water ankle deep for stretches to mid-thigh in shallow pools. Catfish havens, beyond a doubt. It was low-water time of year, a gift.

For a distance of a quarter mile or so, the crick roughly paralleled the road but hidden from view by dense willow brush and cottonwood trees. Babe halted suddenly. He grunted in code. "Riders, coming south. At least half a dozen."

Whoops and savage cries erupted from the farm left behind, a barrage of gunshots, then silence.

They splashed onward.

No light remained from the day's passage. The family slogged through murmuring currents, urgency riding their backs. Sarah thought surely they must give themselves away, so noisy.

The crick bent away from the road in a broad, sweeping curve. Henry glanced off to his left and stopped. "Look," he whispered.

Orange light, a writhing ball of smoke lit from below, scalded the sky visible through branches of trees surrounding them.

Sarah whispered, "Our fire? Or theirs? At least they won't prosper from our work. Move on."

Sarah had remembered correctly. Long abandoned, nearly forgotten even by old-timers, a foot trail crossed Possum Creek at a shallow ford. A surfacing of bedrock and a wealth of gravel made it a place for fugitives to exit the stream. They slogged through darkness, lit only by a fingernail of new moon and stars as bright as God surely intended them to be. For more than a mile, to a dense grove of pine trees, the family groped their way. Babe led.

"We'll stop here for the rest of the night," Sarah said. "We're a good three miles from the farm and the road. I've hunted back here many times. It's desolate, no settlers. We need to dry our feet and shoes, so we'll stay put during this day. Organize; get ready for night travel until we are well clear of Longstreet and his ilk."

"I'm a-scared," Florenda said softly.

Sarah hugged her. "So am I, but we are *survivors*. Remember?"

21

Sarah paced restlessly through the fringes of light supplied by the dying campfire. It was time to begin the night's journey, which only accentuated her dilemma.

I understand what I have done.

The family had *chosen* north as a destination? North, with all its vast imprecision, chosen because, emotionally, it was the antithesis of south? Sarah faced a realization so crushing it haltered her breath. Henry, in his youth, and Florenda, for all her spunk, so unworldly and unaware of life beyond a few acres of backwater farm land, had been blindfolded pawns in *this* game of life.

She—Sarah—had chosen!

"God," she whispered into night's cooling air, "if you monitor these beings you are said to have devised, give me the gifts to decide wisely and the strength to cope with results."

She resumed pacing. With an acknowledgment of how things were, Sarah faced the reality that north, as a designation, was impossibly vague. *Veer west through Oklahoma?* she wondered. *Or east through Arkansas? Perhaps straddle the boundary. How can I burden Florenda and her son with a request for advice when their knowledge of what a choice means is, at best, based on some flat-dimensional paper map?*

She had once chided Florenda and Henry about making decisions. *Quite the stern teacher then, Sarah,* she scolded herself. *Yet now, I find myself standing on the same cliff of indecision that terrified the others.*

Yes, I understand!

So? Decide.

Now!

Sarah allowed herself a deep breath, consulted the compass, and strode resolutely into gathering dusk.

This night, the moon showed a slightly larger rim of light. Piney forests crowned small knolls, backed by the brooding hills Sarah knew vaguely of as Ozark Mountains. Each valley contained a stream rushing to find the next valley. They walked all night and camped in another valley to the north.

Patterns evolved. Nights of stumbling through brush and feeling a way between towering trees alternated with days of restless sleep. Days as numbers on a calendar lost pertinence and were replaced by events—the day it rained, the days when leaves first showed a change in color, the day Florenda fell and scratched her arm. On day six, Sarah decided that travel could be safely conducted during daylight. At their present speed, probably no more than four or five miles a night, they would be caught in winter weather too close to those who might have heard about them.

Henry shot a small deer. They spent a day and a half smoking and drying meat before pressing onward. Sore muscles eased while they rested.

Daytime travel allowed them to cover ten to eleven miles a day. When they neared a hamlet or small village, Sarah huddled the family a short distance from outpost homes to study it and watch interaction of its people. Florenda was assigned the task of sensing attitudes toward black folks. In the absence of obvious trouble, Sarah set out for its main street, her demeanor reserved, her stride confident. Henry and Babe followed her. Henry slouched in what they came to call his "yassum" mode, a servile three steps behind Sarah. He, in turn, led Babe, a rope around the bases of his horns, a long willow "whip" much in display, used briskly to steer the huge animal.

The rope ended up around the hitching post of the nearest saloon.

The family had long been accustomed to Babe's hue and sheer bulk. By whatever combination of genes and lightning's prod to his growth factors, he weighed at least a ton. Two thousand pounds bound within an extravagantly blue hide, he was like an aquamarine rhinoceros bearing Texas longhorns.

When a crowd inevitably gathered around Babe, he and Henry went into their act.

"Big fella." Farmer Jake prodded Babe's flank.

Henry jumped between Farmer Jake and Babe. "Oh my, suh. Don' rile 'im up none. I jes' dun got 'im unriled down. He don' like strangers touchin' 'im. Suh."

Rancher Ferguson said, "Y'all sayin', boy, you uns can control this beast?"

Babe raised his head and roared. And then again, for effect. A full-throated bellow rattled window glass in the saloon.

The crowd jumped back a step. Or three.

Henry touched Babe's flank with the willow "whip." Babe rolled his eyes and ducked his head like a scolded dog.

"Lil' Baby! B'have, now." Henry nodded to Rancher Ferguson. "Yessuh, I's sayin' jes' azackly dat. Gotta be careful whats yo calls 'im, 'im bein' sensitive ta dat kinda talk. Suh."

Jack Schmitze drawled, "Cow pokey."

Babe turned his head and waggled his horns in a wide arc that missed Jack's midsection by inches. Jack mentioned an errand and strode away. Briskly.

Bob Boyson wore a cap advertising a feed store. "Boy, what's his asking price? Although I s'pose you ain't the one selling him."

"No suh, no suh. I's onliest pusson inna whole world can manage Lil' Baby—"

Lil' Baby's head came up and he snorted like a fabled dragon.

Henry punched Babe between the eyes. "Hush yo mouf! Hear?"

Babe nodded his head, with one eye squinted at Henry.

"Y'all gotta ask my lady what hired me fer my special talent wit' Lil' Baby 'bout sellin.'"

Mrs. Preacher's Wife Annie asked, "How come Lil' Baby is blue?"

"Is *dat* what color he is? Be damned."

Mrs. Preacher's Wife Annie sniffed and headed away. Her

voice carried clearly as she scolded, "That kind of *language*, not to mention that awful *saloon*."

Henry stretched, yawned, and sat down on the boardwalk in front of the "awful saloon." He leaned back, a picture of indolence. In seconds he seemed to fall asleep.

For a few minutes, talk buzzed among gathered townspeople. News of the day passed, as well as the news that could only be whispered. In the mysterious nature of such things, a tacit decision emerged.

"A beer?"

"'Bout time."

"Who's payin'?"

Meanwhile, Sarah filled out her shopping list. She haggled over prices long enough so that the owner couldn't regard her as just another silly female. She quietly collected Babe and Henry.

No one in the village seemed upset by their presence. Neither she nor Henry nor Babe, with his acute hearing, had picked up any talk of a heretical un–Godlike family on the run, let alone a freak longhorn steer.

The terrain leveled out after they left the Ozarks. Farms and small villages were the order of things. Always quiet when they moved, with Sarah and Babe in the lead and Florenda and Henry a docile step or two behind, they hardened to travel, some days covering as many as twelve or thirteen miles. They went always toward the north. By the end of the first week in October, they were deep into Missouri. A right city called Kansas City was said to lie in their path.

The place was located where the Kansas River met the Missouri River. As though awaiting this union, the combined flow of western waters turned abruptly and headed eastward toward Saint Louis. Sarah was leery of how the family might be perceived in an urban setting. She steered a course, taking them to the east of the city.

They paid for a ferry ride across the Missouri River. Babe attracted his usual crowd of admirers.

"That un likens to sink my barge," said the ferryman. "Charge is a extra dollar, in case."

He provided them with the date—October 23—without further expense.

Once camped on the north bank of the Missouri River, Sarah called a council meeting.

"We need to find a place to winter over," she said.

Huddled in a blanket, Florenda spread her hands to the fire. "It already winter. How people live here when it so cold?"

"It hasn't frozen yet. No ice or snow. Still, that can't be far off. What we need to decide is, do we want to settle in this area? Do we want to continue farther north? Follow a river out west? If we spend a winter here, we can consider options."

Florenda rocked back and forth. "Lawsy, lawsy, Sarah, I cain't do dis. My bones ache—"

Sarah gripped her arm fiercely. "Survivors do what they must. Do you want to live under the threat of Howie and his friends? We will adapt!"

Henry shifted uneasily. "Sarah ..."

She turned to him. "Do you want to cut cotton for the rest of what might be a very short life? Or, if you are servile enough, to answer to *boy* when you are white-haired? Have your education go for nothing? You heard the grisly plans Howie and his mob had for Babe.

"I am as much a Southerner as y'all, and I will survive—in an Eskimo igloo if I have to, as long as I am free. You three are my family. If you want to return to the South, I can only wish you good fortune, and may God watch over you. I am not going to let hoodlums in bed sheets ruin my life."

The only sounds were flame-flutters from the fire. A log settled, shooting a cloud of firefly sparks aloft.

Florenda straightened. She wiped tears from her cheeks with the heels of her thumbs. "Well. I's glad dat's outta my system. What's next?"

Sarah's shoulders relaxed. She giggled. "How about you, *boy*?"

Henry grinned. "I's mos' certainly not nobody's boy. Except Mama's." He ducked his head. "And yours."

Babe snorted softly. His chest throbbed with "purring."

The family drew its bonds tighter.

23

The travelers interrupted their trek every ten or twelve days to rest and catch up on domestic chores. As Florenda put it one day, "Clothes don' mend dey selves, and dey need help gettin' clean." The day after they had crossed the Missouri River, they decided to use its copious water to advantage.

The campsite they chose lay two or three rods off a trail ground into the north bank of the river by wagon wheels and the hooves of countless horses. That evening, Florenda and Henry hunkered on logs beside the fire, while Sarah bustled about with cooking chores. Babe lay a few feet back from the fire, working on a cud.

Clothing laundered earlier was draped over bushes to dry. Stew simmered in their iron pot, suspended from a tripod over the fire. Vegetables bought at a farmer's market in a village a ways west of their location were augmented with the flesh of two rabbits, courtesy of Henry and the shotgun.

The aroma of stew shamed any perfume sold by a fancy department store.

Sarah smiled, at peace. October's early night settled about them. Bright Venus was an evening star this fall, she noted, and all was right with the world.

Babe abruptly raised his head, sniffing. He lumbered to his feet and turned toward the narrow path leading to the riverbank.

Sarah's pulse bounded. "What, Babe?" She spun to face the opening into the clearing where they camped. Nothing visible.

Babe sniffed again, sampling the air. "Heard … something …"

A cone of light created by the fire rendered darkness beyond it impenetrable.

Nothing …

Henry stood and went to stand beside Babe. Nothing, nothing …

Sarah returned her attention to the stew simmering in the pot.

A rank stench of old sweat and fresh whiskey engulfed Sarah. She whirled away from the fire. Two men astride horses regarded her from the edge of the firelight's reach. White men, scruffy of dress, with untended beards—the reek from their presence drowned the scent of stew. One man urged his horse into the cleared space of their camp.

He tipped a grimy wide-brimmed hat onto the back of his head. His hair was tangled and gray, shaggy around his neck and ears. "Eldred," he rasped, "smells like we just in time for our supper."

Sarah took a step toward him, and Henry joined her. Florenda gasped and stood. Babe held his head high, muscles taut.

The second man—had he been called Eldred?—a decade or more younger than the speaker but every bit as grimy, spurred his horse into the space lighted by the fire. He stopped at a point opposite the other man. He got off his horse and pulled a long-barreled revolver from its holster. He held it at his side, glowering from beneath the brim of a stained Stetson hat.

He gestured at Florenda. "You. Nigger. Dish up supper fer my brother Courtney and me." He raised the gun to point at the sky, lowering it slowly until it pointed at Henry. "Wouldn't want nothing to happen to the boy, now, would we?"

The man named Courtney remained on his horse. He said, "Eldred, we won't need to use no force, 'counta these folks is so generous. Was goin' to say, they glad to give us that pot of stew." He studied Babe. "But I look around, an' what do we have us here? Somethin' hell of a lot more interestin' than chowder." He scratched his chin through its tangled beard. "Iffen them folks don't cause us no trouble, they likely won't come to no harm."

He spat a wad of tobacco juice at Sarah's feet. "Might help y'all to cooperate iffen you know that I once rode with Will Quantrill. Remember him, don't ya? Quantrill's Raiders. We uns kept the good fight goin' against damn Yankees an' other nigger lovers fer ten more years, we did. After that, joined up with old Jesse James, till he got his self killed."

He launched another wad of tobacco juice at Sarah's feet. Henry made a move toward the man; Sarah grabbed his arm.

Courtney snorted. "Enough talk. Time fer business."

In a move too quick to anticipate, he drew a pistol from a

holster on his hip and whipped it against Henry's head. The boy collapsed at Sarah's feet.

Florenda shrieked and ran to where Henry lay crumpled and silent. Sarah seized a burning stick from the fire and threw it at the rider. His horse snorted and reared. For several seconds the man was held to controlling his horse, but Eldred slugged Sarah alongside her head with his pistol, and she fell across Henry.

Babe roared, his eyes bright with a wild bloodlust. The man called Eldred danced around the fire, keeping it between him and Babe. He raised his pistol in a two-handed stance and aimed at Babe.

"No!" roared the older man. He swung his arm, and a whip flicked out to wrap itself around Eldred's wrist. "Use your head! That freak steer is a gold mine on four feet. My God, the size a him and that color. Ain't never seen his like, so don't even think about hurtin' him. Rope him and tie on to your saddle."

Florenda scrabbled on hands and knees toward the shotgun Henry used for hunting. She swung around to aim at Eldred. Courtney's whip lashed out again. Red welts appeared on Florenda's arms, and she dropped the gun.

Babe had stopped in his tracks. Code crackled from his throat. "Florenda! No! I go. Not stop us. Care of Henry, Sarah. I manage these two."

Eldred worked the loop of a lariat around Babe's neck and cinched the other end to the horn of his saddle. Babe stood without twitching until Eldred swung up onto his horse and drew the rope straight. Then Babe strode toward the trail beside the river, the rope linking him to Eldred's saddle as tight as a banjo string.

Courtney chuckled. "Look at that old steer. He's as happy

to be shet of this crazy bunch as any good white men is. Kinda like him already."

Eldred grunted. "Yeah, maybe, but he's near pulling my saddle off. How we gonna control him?"

Babe let Eldred's horse catch up with him and then held to a steady surge away from camp, following the riverbank trail east, downstream.

Eldred grumbled, "Court, we never did get any that stew. I'm hungry."

"You wanta go back? They was to put a bullet in you, might not be worth it."

Eldred muttered, "Still, sounds right good about now."

"Don't forget; might have been fixed by that nigger woman."

"Even so, smelled good."

Courtney threw his hands in the air. "Ahhh. You're hopeless."

Florenda built up the fire. She checked her two patients, straightening them out alongside the blaze. She placed the rifle beside the shotgun, within quick reach.

She dampened cloths with cool water and gently cleaned Henry's and Sarah's wounds.

Henry winced and mumbled.

"Hush," Florenda said. "Yo be all right, no thanks to that bastard."

Sarah tried to sit up. Florenda scolded her like a banty hen did her chick. "Hush up, yo hear? Y'all gave dat Courtney somethin' to t'ink about when yo threw de fire brand at him. I thank yo fer defendin' Henry, but now jest lie back down, an' let me take care uh yo."

Henry mumbled, "What about Babe? I should follow them, help him escape."

"Land sakes, son. Yo dizzy from what happen. Dey's two of dem; dey on horses. Besides, dey got Babe to contend with. He tol' me to leave dem to him. My money's on Mistah Babe any day of de week, including Sundays." She settled her charges beside the fire before stationing herself at the mouth of the path they themselves had trodden down. She laid the shotgun in weeds beside her log. The night was dark and moonless. Quiet—the only sound was a ripple murmur from the mighty river flowing inexorably toward some place beyond her imagination.

Morning stillness. A slight hint of frost provided a nip to the air. No clouds promised a sunny day. A few travelers headed east on the riverbank trail; a couple headed west. Nobody hassled Florenda. There was no sign of Babe.

Florenda shivered. *I know dat Babe can handle t'ings. I know dat in my bones. I don' need to worry, no ma'am, no need. Only t'ing ... I worried.*

She returned to the campsite, adding fuel to the low flames she had kept burning all night.

Henry raised his head and sat up in his blankets. "Babe?" he asked.

"Not yet. He be all right. He Babe."

Sarah pushed blankets aside and crawled to her feet. She moaned softly. Florenda hurried to her and steadied her. "Sit on de log. Do it, Sarah. Lemme see dat bruise yo' head."

Sarah sat quietly on her log after her wound had been attended to.

Florenda sputtered, "Big fierce bushwhackers, cowards, hit

a lady an' a boy when dey not even expectin'.'" She fussed over Sarah, over Henry seated on his own log. "Huh. You two's a matched set, dem bruises. Reckon all you got to worry 'bout, though, is a whoppin' headache. I brewed up some willow-bark tea fer y'all. Help de pain."

The sky was exuberantly blue when the sun reached its October-day zenith. For lunch, Florenda warmed the stew intended for supper the evening before. She handed a bowlful to Henry, when he exclaimed and set it on the ground. He stood and pointed.

"Babe!"

The blue ox walked slowly toward the campfire. A noose of rope with a ragged end hung loosely around his neck.

Florenda hugged him fiercely. "Thank God yo' back. And dose two mens?"

Babe coded, "No worry. I'm all right. Need to chew a cud; you'd best eat that stew."

Florenda consulted her appetite and realized she was hungry.

When spoons had scraped the last morsel from each bowl, and Babe declared himself ready to explain, he lay at the center of attention.

"I tol' dem what y'all tol' me," Florenda said to him. "Dey was on de ground when yo left. So what happened?"

Babe sorted out his thoughts. *Yes*, he acknowledged to himself, *and my feelings*. Clicks rumbled from his throat. "I wanted to get those monsters away from the rest of you as quickly as possible. Their greed was like blinders, and I knew I was safe. I pulled that Eldred's horse along as fast as I could walk until we were a good ways downstream. Then I played dumb ox and didn't cause trouble for them. They were in a hurry to get away from here, so it was easy.

"I watched for the right place to carry out my plan. Strange country; no light. Made it hard. Had to pass up a couple of possibilities when the louse called Courtney drifted too far behind me." Babe sneezed and shook his head.

"That Eldred thought he was leading me, so he was always under my control. It was the other one …"

About four miles from the family's camp, they came to a suitable location. Courtney had closed on Babe's right side to talk to his brother about camping for the night. A murmur of water close at hand …

Babe turned abruptly to his right, lowered his head against the flank of Courtney's horse, pinning its rider's leg between his head and the horse's flank. Babe charged relentlessly toward the river. Before the rider could respond, he and his horse fell off the bank into the water, causing a stupendous splash.

Like so many rivers flowing through relatively flat land, the Missouri meandered in broad curves. That bend where Babe sprang his trap had a six- to eight-foot drop into water that was both deep and flowing briskly.

Babe tugged the lariat that Eldred had looped around his neck taut and stepped off the bank into air. He hit the water with a splash seconds after Courtney and his horse did. The end of the lariat was still cinched around the horn of the saddle on Eldred's horse. Just before leaping into space, Babe gripped the rope in his mouth, even as the rope pulled the saddle—and Eldred's horse after it—into the river. A third mighty splash. Babe and the two horses swam with the current, heads easily above water.

Babe was never certain how far they drifted, what with darkness and the unknowable speed of the current. Eventually, his hooves hit a sand bar. He was able to turn toward the north bank of the river again. Mighty splashes, the sounds of legs thrashing in shallow water beside him … the two horses kept pace with Babe when he reached dry land. He finished chewing the lariat in two, but he could do nothing about that portion around his neck.

"I'm glad you can swim," Henry said.

Babe said, "Water has never been a problem for me." He sneezed again.

Babe's Two-Legs, his family, sat in silence for a spell. Finally, Sarah said, "You haven't mentioned the bushwhackers. Are we still at risk from them?"

Babe coded slowly. "The horses seemed able to swim very well." He sat motionless for another silent interval before he said, "Judging by what I heard, neither Eldred nor Courtney could swim a stroke."

24

The family left at first light the next morning.

Three days later, they found what Sarah had been hoping for—a vacant house, an abandoned homestead gone back for taxes. Sarah visited the county courthouse and arranged to "rent" the place for the winter, the cost to be considered a down payment on a contract for deed, should they decide to buy it.

The winter allowed time for rest and thought. In the spring, defined as the final week in March, the family had reached several conclusions:

No one favored returning south.

One actually could adapt to cold—Florenda and Sarah bought woolen outer garments; Henry bought a tanned leather-fringed frontiersman's jacket.

Missouri was still part of the South for Florenda and Henry.

The land was settled. No Hunting signs abounded.

Babe continued to grow. Sarah estimated his bulk at more than 2,500 pounds of impressive bone and muscle.

Babe attracted attention—no surprise.

Henry and Babe worked out a moneymaking game of mind reading. Sarah put an end to it when she learned what they were doing during shopping days in town.

Henry was ready for college. He had decided that he would become a doctor. He had memorized *Gray's Anatomy*.

Early spring 1889

One day near the end of the following March, the family walked into Farmdale, the town serving the area, to do their weekly shopping. Henry tied the ceremonial rope around Babe's horns and then looped its other end around a hitching post in front of the grocery shop. Sarah went inside to haggle with the proprietor.

A rugged, middle-aged man wearing a plaid shirt, woolen trousers held in place by broad red suspenders, a woolen cap with a bill and earflaps, and heavy, much-used boots rode a large roan gelding along the rutted road of town. When he spotted Babe and Henry, the rider detoured abruptly and dismounted alongside them. He looped the horse's reins around the hitching post and walked next to Babe.

He sized up the steer from several angles and bent to inspect his fetlocks and hooves.

He whistled.

The man asked, "Is this animal for sale?"

Henry said, "Oh no, suh, not him. Massah, suh, be careful 'cause him don' like strangers too close a-him. Suh."

The man said absentmindedly, "I'll be gentle."

He rubbed Babe's foreleg softly and squinted at his flank. "I've never seen skin that shade before."

"No, suh, but yessuh. Ain't good to poke little ol' fella. He be upset."

On cue, Babe provided a full-chested bellow.

"Good lungs," the man said. Unperturbed.

"Yessuh, but you got 'im upset-like, an' I can't be 'sponsible fer what he do to someone dat upsets 'im—"

"Young man, I'm all right, and so is he. Relax. Do you own this animal?"

"Oh no, suh, da mistress, she do dat. She don' like 'im get his se'f riled up, so best y'all—"

"Laddie, it looks to me as though you're the one upsetting him." The man pulled a small card out of a wallet and gave it to Henry. "I'd much appreciate it if you would give this to your mistress. I must speak to her. When do you expect her back?"

"Well, uh, sir ... suh ... she be ... here she comes."

The usual crowd of admirers surrounded Babe when Sarah returned from the grocer's shop.

A man intercepted her by stepping directly into her path. She frowned at him.

His features were weathered, his face clean shaven. Streaks of iron gray gave his auburn hair a brindled look.

He doffed the cap. "Pardon me, ma'am. My name is Jock

MacPherson. I couldn't help noticing your animal. The lad controlling him tells me that he's not for sale, or I would make an offer on the spot. Heck, I might anyhow. Thing is—he would fit in our operation like a hand in a mitt." He gave her a business card. "I'm Paul Bunyan's marketing agent. Usually, I've only got an eye out for new customers, but this magnificent animal … I know Paul would take to him quicker'n a bolt of lightning."

Sarah cocked an eyebrow at him suspiciously. "How did you know about that?"

He looked puzzled. "Ma'am?"

She shook her head. "Y'all couldn't have known. What matters, Babe is not for sale." She nodded politely.

"His name is *Babe*? God al-blooming-mighty! But you haven't heard what we are willing to offer."

"I don't need to hear. Good day, sir."

"Now, now, little lady. Everyone, everything, has a price. I'll go double what a young steer usually brings. Say—"

Sarah felt her pulse bound. "Did you just call me 'little lady'? As in, 'Hush yo pretty lil' mouf, you lightheaded fluff'?" She walked past him coldly.

His face turned scarlet. He trotted alongside her. "Please. I was … good Lord, I was an oaf. Look. If Paul knew about … *Babe!* … if he didn't see me busting my briskets to have him join us up north, he'd skin me for a throw rug. I'd be most honored if you would allow me to buy you a cup of coffee while we discuss it further."

Sarah studied the man. Six feet tall, maybe an inch more; humor lines around his eyes; a lopsided grin. His complexion was a curious mix of freckles on deeply bronzed skin. "Does your offer include my sister and my son?" she asked.

"Bring a party, if you wish. Where are they?"

Sarah smiled wickedly. "Find a table. We'll join you."

He said anxiously, "This isn't a way to duck out on me?"

"Not on those briskets of yours."

MacPherson went to a café across the street. She saw him sit inside at a table in front by the window. He peered out at her.

Sarah joined Florenda and Henry, standing beside Babe.

"Let's go."

Henry unwound the tether and tossed the end across Babe's broad shoulders.

Florenda said, "That man's ... he gave yo trouble?"

"He's an ass."

Henry looked back over a shoulder. "He's a fast-running ass. Here he comes."

The man lumbered to a walk beside Sarah. "You said you wouldn't run out on me."

Sarah continued a brisk pace. "I lied."

"Why?" He matched her stride.

"Why should I please you?"

"And where is your son? Your sister? Lies too?"

"Not so. You're walking right here with them."

"But ... these ... they're ... you're ..."

Sarah said, "Henry, what do you think about the ass's dialectic style?"

Henry rubbed his chin thoughtfully. "He seems a tad disjointed. Whether he favors Euclidean logic will require further elucidation."

MacPherson jumped in front of Babe and shouted, "Stop! Whoa!"

Babe hoisted the man up between his horns and plodded steadily along the road. Coded dits and dots rumbled deep in Babe's throat.

Florenda said, "Mr. Ass, Babe, he askin' whether he should jes' toss y'all inna ditch or mebby trample yo down. Wonders him which way yo be less of a pest. Dat's what he say."

Sarah sighed. "Set him down, Babe."

Babe stopped and lowered his head until MacPherson's boots hit the ground.

Sarah stood close to the man and thumped his chest with her firm index finger. "Sir, we are a family. Our bonds were forged on the devil's anvil. That café back in town would not have served my *son*, Henry. My *sister*, Florenda, would have been thrown out the door. And Babe? They would have called the sheriff to shoot him, had he joined us. Where one of us goes, we all go."

She pushed past him and resumed her resolute strides. The man trotted to catch up. "We can't negotiate, walking at this pace. Why don't we—"

"No."

"But—"

"Be quiet."

He kept up with her. He seemed to be rehearsing speeches, hands waving, fingers pointing, but silently. Eventually, he seemed resigned to merely keeping up. So it went for a mile and a half.

She pointed at the house where they were staying. "It was kind of you to escort us home. You may leave now, Mr. Ass."

MacPherson massaged his face with both hands. He looked beseechingly at Sarah. "I don't even know your name."

"No, you don't. It is enough that I know yours."

"I don't want to call you 'Hey, you.' And please, even if I earned it, don't call me Mr. Ass."

Sarah studied him and turned to Florenda. "Tea would be nice. Would we have enough for this one too?"

Florenda's eyes widened. "Is yo invitin' him into our home?"

"Yeah, Sarah. Why?" Henry said.

"Just a hunch," Sarah said.

Babe rumbled and hiccupped.

"I'll bring you up to date later," Sarah said. She turned her back on MacPherson and headed up a long driveway. "If you want a cup of tea, we will allow you to join us."

MacPherson trotted to keep up with her. "Did I hear … it sounded like the beast was somehow signaling. Morse code? It … someone asked what … what something was all about?"

"Imagine that," she said.

"It's just that … I mean … I can't believe … steers don't … do they?"

She said, "I would have guessed that a man of the world might be more articulate."

A kitchen table had been crafted from one-by-six boards resting on sawhorses. MacPherson sat across from Sarah. Henry and Florenda faced each other from the other positions, while Babe lay in the corner of the room on a pad of hay.

MacPherson said, "I don't mean to be indelicate, but—" He tipped his head toward Babe.

"Delicate is nice," Sarah said.

Babe rumbled.

Henry grinned. "He asked whether you are housebroken."

MacPherson's face was crimson. "I heard! My God, this is *Alice in Wonderland*. Who *are* you people? All right, you too, Babe. God. I'm talking to a steer with a blue hide and the heft of an elephant, two sisters who really can't be, with a son ... I give up. Help me."

Florenda said softly, "Henry's my son. Sarah and I jes' share 'im."

"And they're my mother. Both of them," Henry said.

"And, uh, Babe?" MacPherson stammered.

"He a miracle," said Florenda.

"Dropped out of a storm cloud one day," Henry said.

Babe rumbled.

"'And a bolt of lightning,'" MacPherson translated. "'Don't forget that.'"

Sarah said, "Babe taught me Morse code so we could converse."

"*Babe* taught *you* Morse ... no. No!"

"It seemed best. Communication is important in a civil society, don't you think? More tea?" Sarah poured. "You said something about 'up north' earlier in the day. Someone named Paul."

MacPherson blinked. "I thought Paul Bunyan was surreal. Claims to be the strongest man on earth, and he probably is. One of the largest as well. 'A man who can fell trees with an ax in each hand while running through a grove of pines'—a quote from his own publicity. A legend in his own time, which he is happy to acknowledge. More important, head man of the logging company for which I work." He looked quizzically from one to the next. "This family you talk of. How did it, uh, evolve?"

It was the family members' turn to inspect one another.

Sarah shrugged and said, "I was a foundling, until I escaped. I received enough education to become a teacher. I lost my husband to a fever and lost my school when I chose to teach Henry. Klansmen drove me from my farm. I am a survivor."

Henry said, "My daddy was killed for no reason by a *gentleman* with a sword. Sarah saved me. She taught me." He glanced at Sarah. "I'd die for her."

Babe rumbled, in code. "A Texas rancher owned me. A tornado rescued me and sent me to the family."

Florenda said, "Massa owned me too, until a man I never knew heard my cry. He fought a war to set me free. He was a good man."

Sarah looked at MacPherson. "Your turn."

He made a wry face. "Holy cow, I'm just a working stiff."

Sarah nodded abruptly. "You'll be wanting to leave. Don't return."

"Look. I didn't mean … man, I said cow … I meant no disrespect. This whole thing has been very unsettling. I want to help you. Especially Babe. Henry and … what's your name again, missus?"

Florenda turned her head aside.

Sarah did not blink.

He snapped his fingers. "Oh Jesus."

Florenda said, "He sweet Jesus."

MacPherson stood. "I left my horse tied up on the hitching post in town."

Babe rumbled.

MacPherson translated. "The name of my *horse*? I don't …
he's just a livery stable … I rented him in Saint Joseph. I had to
see a client here, then one in Saint Louis, and … I came down
the Missouri River on a boat as far as Saint Joe. Paddlewheel.
Stern paddle … so I …"

Babe went to work on a cud. Henry stepped outdoors to
chop kindling. Florenda found a sewing project and sat beside
a window to catch last light.

Sarah went to the sink and began scrubbing potatoes. "Hard
to say how long an unattended, *unnamed* horse might still be
around after dark."

MacPherson seized his hat, crammed it down around his
ears, and stomped to the door. "I'll be leaving." He turned back
from the door, suspending time a long second at a clip.

Babe chewed; Sarah scrubbed. Florenda bit off the end of
a piece of thread. The sound of a hatchet cleaving wood came
from the yard.

MacPherson slammed the door behind him.

A man or a legend named Paul Bunyan, sure to have an interest in Babe. *Is that a threat or an inducement?* Northern Minnesota or a state called Wisconsin? This MacPherson—a man of honor or a bag of evil wind?

Sarah debated with herself. She called a family council that decided nothing. They still had a no more definitive goal than "north," and how would they know where the North began? At any rate, the North still sounded safer than the South.

A week passed, with tension such as that while waiting for the explosion of a lit firecracker, the flash and noise seconds away … away?

The family held a council again on Friday. No one offered an alternative. No one objected.

So for want of a more definitive destination, the North it remained. *This mysterious Paul*, Sarah wondered, *who is he?*

They left their winter home two days later.

Sarah again elected to avoid parading through a larger town, so they skirted Saint Joseph. Sarah counted the money they had left: $743.31. She stashed it in the money belt strapped around her waist. Guided by her compass, they set their course at northeast.

At least in theory.

Iowa seemed to Sarah to be one enormous and prosperous farm. Small rivers meandered en route to larger rivers. Cottonwood trees hugged their banks. Roads of dirt choked them with dust when dry and became mud puddles after a rain. They were laid out in mile-long squares as symmetrically as a checker board.

By sticking to the roads, no treks across plowed or planted fields, and by camping alongside one of the ubiquitous streams, they avoided offending farmers working the land.

Sarah saw no one regard Henry or Florenda with anything but curiosity.

Babe attracted open-mouthed awe from everyone they met. Offers to buy him were as predictable as the next morning's sunrise.

They had crossed into Minnesota without realizing it for nearly a day. There was no change in the pattern of farms neatly squared off by section roads, but ponds and small lakes began to appear. Fresh fish became part of their diet.

One evening, Henry shot a deer. He was dressing it out when a man wearing a farmer's bib overalls appeared behind him.

Henry whirled, stricken with apprehension.

The man sucked a tooth thoughtfully. "You're one them Negro folks I've heard about? Thought so. Often wondered what you looked like. Oh, them deer? Taste better come fall. Corn-fed by then. My corn. Blasted critters. While you're at it, you might wanta take a couple of 'em." He studied the sunset and made sucking sounds around his tooth. "Best not to let the game warden know you're doing it, though. Nice evening."

He nodded and wandered back toward a four-square white farmhouse. Henry dropped to his knees. He was quivering.

Sarah called a halt atop a bluff overlooking a substantial valley. They had come to a river with more heft than the streams of Iowa and southernmost Minnesota. Its valley was broad, a mile or more wide, suggesting that a truly mighty but forgotten river had scoured it out.

The troupe made its way toward a neat-looking small town nestled on the flats beside the water. While still a substantial stream, the river now flowing through the impressive valley was no more than eighty or ninety feet wide. "Minnesota River," a lad fishing from its bank told them. "That town over there? Granite Falls." He tossed a hook baited with a rind of bacon into swirling brown water.

The river narrowed to no more than forty or fifty feet wide

where it coursed through town. Water the color of stout tea churned across an outcrop of granite and stirred up foam like the head on a glass of beer. It seemed more a lively cascade to Sarah's eye than a waterfall. The sound soothed, a compelling invitation to dabble feet hot from the journey.

Although it was short of noontime, Sarah decided to camp in a park just downstream from the village. An excuse to preen, wash clothes, and relax. For weary muscles to recover. What was a day or two out of a journey with no timetable?

After lunch, Sarah stretched out on a blanket. Shade was tinted green by a riot of leaves on trees foreign to her experience. A soft murmur of water beside her, the commotion of the falls muted from their location two or three hundred yards upstream ... a modest nirvana ...

She slept.

27

Something brushed Sarah's cheek. She waved her hand before her face and hit another hand.

Her eyes popped open.

A man's head was silhouetted against a bright sky. Brindled auburn hair. A red plaid shirt. Broad suspenders.

He was sitting beside her, his legs stretched out before him.

"Sorry," MacPherson said, "but there was a mosquito on your cheek. I didn't mean to wake you."

She sat up abruptly.

"Your guards are on duty." He pointed. Henry, a fishing line in the river, faced them from his knees. Watching. Glaring. And Florenda stood ten feet away, her face frozen in mistrust.

"Where's Babe?" he asked.

"He's safe. We left him in a grassy field." Sarah's eyes narrowed. "Don't you understand the meaning of no?"

"I merely meant … he's usually with …" He rubbed his face with both hands. He peeked sidewise at her. "I've had a long month past, following your trail, missing a turn, doubling back, trying to catch up."

The man's facial hair had grown into a stubble, its color as nondescript as that on his head. He pointed toward a hobbled horse, a chestnut brown mare. She grazed on tall grass just outside the confines of the park.

"Nameless?" Sarah said.

"Ah, names. She probably had one before I bought her. Nobody mentioned a name. Now she's … I haven't gotten around to naming her."

"Of course not."

"What's this thing about naming an animal?"

"A name makes it unique. Important."

"But Babe isn't … you haven't sold …"

"Mr. MacPherson, you really must learn to speak in sentences."

He tapped his forehead with a fist and grimaced. "Perhaps we could take a stroll, and I'll … you have this effect on me. Make me blabber … perhaps I could explain."

"I prefer that you don't explain anything. Whatever you feel compelled to say, say it before my family."

"Yes. I see. Actually, I do, I need to explain to all of you, including … Jesus. Including Babe."

"On whom you have no fiduciary designs."

"No fiduciary … Sarah. Mrs. McAllfry, I'm a simple man. A lumberjack, ultimately. I stutter in your presence because … because you plain-out dazzle me."

Sarah stared at him. "What?"

"Oh God, I said it." He gulped air. "Hear me. Yes, I followed you because I had to find *you*. Not Babe. My quest to buy him … that's past anyway because I've deserted my post, so to speak. Paul expected me back weeks ago. I'm probably no longer employed by anyone. I wanted to tell you about me, hoping you might understand."

Sarah hunched forward, hugging her knees. She studied the steady, irresistible flow of water, its voice soft in the summer air. She turned toward him. "Are you hungry?"

He ducked his head. "Uh, maybe."

"If you want our trust, speak straight."

"I'm hungry."

She got up and prepared a sandwich of cold venison and a cup of coffee.

She pondered odd stirrings in her chest.

28

That evening, Sarah glanced at those circling the communal campfire. Its light flickered across members of the family, reserved and watchful. MacPherson sat at the focus of their attention.

"You wanted to explain," Sarah said.

"I'm called Jock by my friends," he said. "If this is going to work, you need to do that too. I was born in Ontario, Canada. I'm part Ojibwe Indian, about a half, probably more. My Scots blood seems to have dominated my appearance." He plucked a blade of grass and studied it. "Seems like a good thing if most of us end up a sort of inherited hash. Less likely to shoot each other on first sight."

He flicked the grass stem into the fire. "Living on an Indian reserve doesn't provide much prosperity. I attended school when it was available, but then a job with a logging company came along. I left home at fifteen. After Mom died, I never went back. Paul Bunyan took an interest in me—God knows why. He assigned me to a crew working out of Bemidji, Minnesota. We chopped down white pines like a farmer taking a scythe to hay. I learned the trade."

Sarah studied MacPherson. Firelight chased shadows across his features. Was he somber?

"A couple of years later," he said, "I met a woman, Lily by name. Down by Brainerd. We married up, just kids ourselves. Had us two little girls. Madeline and Renee. I worked the woods; she stayed in town and raised the girls. I spent summers with them, but winters I was gone. Logging camp. Winters are when loggers do most of their work. Swamps freeze, making access easier."

He paused, his gaze on some vision off in the darkness. "Winter is when a family breaks up. Lily and the girls just disappeared. That was sixteen years ago."

He leaned forward and laid a small log in the coals of the fire. It flared, eager tongues of yellow licking at the wood. He said, "Turned out I had ability at doing sums, and I learned the skills to be a timber appraiser. Assess the potential in a stand of trees on a new plot of land. I did scaling too, estimating available board feet in a pile of saw logs. Taking any wastage into account. I'm accurate enough that both seller and Paul, as buyer, wanted me. And I have the gift of gab." He glanced at Sarah. "Had it, before I met you. Paul appointed me to market the lumber our mills produce."

He stared into the fire, seemingly caught by the hypnotic effect of dancing flame, ever changing, ever the same.

Florenda said finally, "Did y'all find dat Lily and yo' girls?"

After a pause, he shook his head. "A person determined to disappear has no difficulty doing so." He closed his eyes for a moment. His voice was almost a whisper. "I wonder often, would I recognize my daughters if I met them on the street?"

Florenda moaned, "Oh, sweet Jesus."

Babe, standing behind Sarah, asked in code, "Why were you so bound to buy me?"

MacPherson turned toward him. "A yoke of oxen can outwork a six-horse team. For sheer pulling power, for ease of handling, for … call it durability, your kind are unbeatable. And you, my friend, are the most magnificent example I have ever seen."

Henry asked, "Where did you learn Morse code?"

"As a marketer, I need to communicate rapidly over distances. *Voila.* Telegraphy."

Sarah hugged her knees. "What are your plans?"

MacPherson raised his head and gazed across the fire at her. "I need to go to my office in Minneapolis and find out whether I still have a job. I know the trail along this river before us. I know the people—who to avoid and who to trust. I understand that speed of foot is not what oxen are known for, but I would cheerfully adapt to what is possible."

Perhaps it was some magic of firelight, perhaps some revelation of the man across the fire from Sarah, but she saw an appearance of yearning, a plea on MacPherson's face.

"And that is pertinent how?" she asked.

He sighed. "Given my druthers, I'd choose to travel with an unusual family I've come to know."

There the question lay.

In silence.

He rose without another word, collected his mare, mounted her, and rode downstream until darkness enveloped him.

Florenda finally said to Sarah, "Any more hunches, girl?"

Sarah went to her sleeping blankets and curled up on her side. Mosquitoes hummed in her ears, more than enough to roil her sleep.

29

Council evolved around the morning campfire.

"Well?" Florenda asked.

Sarah said sullenly, "Back off."

"Oh yassum, yassum, I's po' pusson what should hab her head 'xamined fo t'inkin' sorry feelin's 'bout a white—"

"Enough!" Sarah jumped to her feet. "And turn off the plantation jabber."

Florenda snapped, "Sit down. We agreed years ago that every voice was equal at council. Yo don't make all the decisions by yo' lonesome. I demand the chance to speak."

"So, speak," Sarah muttered.

Florenda pointed. "Sit!"

Sarah sat.

"What's yo' problem, girl? Nice man offer to show us the

way, place we don't know nobody or nothing about, and yo treat him like week-old fish guts."

"We can't trust … he comes out of nowhere … I'd be afraid he'd try to abduct Babe."

"We know well how Babe can handle that threat his self." She studied Sarah. "Land o' Goshen, he done got yo stuttering. Wake up. That man, he's took a shine to yo, traipsin' all this way after y'all." She burst into her most joyful laugh. "By grandma's old bloomers! I believe y'all afraid to admit it, but yo like him back." She slapped her thigh in high glee.

Sarah huddled over her knees sullenly.

Florenda snapped her fingers. "I hereby calls a vote. All who wants to invite Mr. Jock to join us, say so. To start things, I says it."

Henry peered past his eyebrows at Sarah, at his mama. He held up his hand. "Me." His voice was firm.

Babe rumbled in code.

Florenda looked toward Sarah. "That's three yesses. What's your vote?"

"You've already decided, so why ask me?"

"'Cause y'all as important as anyone else. That's why."

"Then I abstain."

Henry said, "That's not really a vote, Sarah."

Sarah jumped to her feet again. "Vote? All right. Yes, yes, yes. That makes it unanimous. Satisfied?"

"Actually," Henry said, "Your three and our three make six. That's a clear majority." He grinned shyly.

Florenda tipped Sarah's chin up and peered into her eyes. She smiled hesitantly.

Sarah tried to frown. A smile tickled for release.

Florenda's grin involved her full face.

Sarah threw her arms around Florenda. "You are all impossible." Her laughter was robust.

MacPherson stepped out from behind a tree. "On that note, may I add my vote?"

30

Florenda shook her head in wonder. *Sarah, that Sarah with all the answers, sitting across the morning cooking fire, seems uncertain. Hesitant. Indecisive. Because of the newcomer? I know people; I do. I declare, Sarah the Rock is smitten. What I don't see is whether anything good will come of it.*

Council now included MacPherson—"Jock" to everyone but Sarah. Unanimously, they decided to spend three extra days enjoying the peace of the Granite Falls Park.

MacPherson, Jock, moved his bedroll near those of the family. Weary muscles healed and sore feet recovered under the benign ministrations of the Minnesota River.

Henry caught a weird-appearing fish, one at least ten pounds in weight. It was long and broad, with a tail like half a crescent moon. Bristles surrounded a mouth pointed downward.

"Is dat a weird catfish?" Florenda asked.

"Sturgeon," pronounced Jock. "Don't be fooled by its appearance. They are a special treat. I'm good at cooking fish." While it cooked—great slabs of meat fastened to a cedar plank leaning above a bed of coals—he pontificated. "River sturgeons are survivors from millions of years ago. They can get as big as one hundred pounds. I've seen such from Rainy River, up on the Canadian border. Smoking them, salting them, we fed them to loggers in camp when they got tired of caribou meat and beans."

"Wow," said Henry.

MacPherson peered through his eyebrows at Henry. "'Course, along about February, the men hankered after fresh fish. Then my boss, Paul Bunyan, detailed several of us jacks to get us a mess of trout. Now, since ice on the lakes up north is three to four feet thick by that time of year, we had to modify our approach."

He leaned back, obviously waiting. Florenda sighed. "I'll bite. What yo do different?"

"I thought you'd never ask. We had two options. One was to have Bunyan bury the tip of his picaroon into ice covering a trout lake. Then he would simply haul it up on land. Problem with that was the damage to trees for acres around—that and a mile-wide four-foot-thick cake of ice threatening to start another ice age. So we favored the second option. We put on tree-climbing spurs, the kind a jack uses to shinny up the trunk of a tree he wants to limb before he fells it from the stump."

Silence. A waiting silence.

Florenda rolled her eyes. "All right. How dat let yo catch trout?"

"Ach, didn't I tell you?" Jock leaned toward Florenda, his gaze intent. "Up north, water in the streams and lakes gets really, really cold. Why, if you was to put your big toe into it for three seconds … tick, tick, tick … your whole leg would freeze—snap! Like that. It be common knowledge that ice don't thaw in the winter—no sirree, it thaws in the spring. So folks would have to let you sleep with that frozen leg sticking out a window till April or May, for fear it might otherwise break right off like a dropped icicle."

Jock looked at each of his companions as though about to tell a dark secret. "Now, those trout fish ain't dumb, you know. They ain't one bit more anxious to be in water that cold than your right big toe, so they grow a luxurious fur coat along about October, climb out of the lakes and streams, use their fins to hike up the nearest white pine tree, and make a nest of twigs and needles. There, they spend the winter, snug and cozy."

He beamed at members of his audience.

"We pick trout like apples off a tree and get a meal of fresh fish. Trout fur being in high demand in places like Paris, France, Paul earns a tidy income on the side."

Florenda joined in a group response. A groan is, after all, praise for a yarn well told.

She conceded that MacPherson's campfire culinary skills were not overstated.

That evening, as they sat around the fire, Florenda said, "I's curious 'bout why yo' ridin' all over de place. Tell us again how's come."

"I work for Paul Bunyan's timber production enterprise. As a marketer."

"Who dat Paul Bunyan?"

"As I said, he's the owner of …" MacPherson sat straighter, glancing around at the intent faces in the circle. A hint of a smile broke the lines of his face. "Do you want the absolute truth?"

Florenda shrugged. "From y'all, dat be a surprise."

MacPherson spread his hands to either side and whispered, "This must be held in confidence."

"A secret?" asked Henry.

"Of the highest urgency. I shudder to think what Paul would do if he knew I was revealing … but you are now my family. I'll start with his family. He was born out East in the state of Maine. He was huge, even at birth. His daddy made him a cradle out of red pine logs that were two feet in diameter."

"What?" asked Sarah.

MacPherson scowled. "Please don't interrupt. I may lose my nerve for telling. Why, whenever baby Paul turned over in that cradle, bedrock in half the state of Maine shook so hard that people ran into the streets because they thought there had been an earthquake.

"Paul's appetite was prodigious. Folks in the know claimed he grew by an inch an hour. His mama put the cradle by an open window, so his feet had room to grow overnight without kicking a hole in the wall of the house.

"He was weaned when he was two weeks old, on account of there not being enough dairy cows in the whole state to supply him with milk. Fortunately, Maine is gifted with moose and deer. Paul's papa was a fine marksman. He depleted the state and half of Quebec province across the Canadian border of game within a year."

Jock swallowed half the contents of his coffee mug. He

wiped his lips on the back of his hand. "Paul's papa was a lumberjack, born and bred. He naturally led the giant his son had become into the profession of lumberjacking. Paul had harvested every white pine tree in Maine by the time he was twenty. The Bunyans had heard about pine trees as thick as blades of grass in Wisconsin and Minnesota. Paul set up a logging camp in northern Minnesota."

Jock spread his hands far apart dramatically. "It was the *largest* camp in the world. In the mess hall, a server would set out from one end of a dining table on a Monday morning and finish his run at the far end by suppertime. He stayed overnight and then set off for home kitchen on Tuesday morning, serving the jacks on the other side of the table.

"The cookstove was so long it stretched from breakfast to supper. Cook greased the griddle by tying a twenty-pound ham on each foot. He would take off at a run, skating over the hot metal. Cooked the hams along the way, he did." MacPherson paused to drain his mug of coffee.

"How big is this Paul of yours, really?" Sarah asked, a grin on her face.

MacPherson rubbed his chin thoughtfully and leaned toward her. "Now there's the thing. Are we talking the man or the legend?"

"Are they not the same?"

"Yes, of course. All you need to do to confirm the truth in that is to ask Paul himself."

"I would welcome the opportunity."

"And I'll make sure you get it."

31

Fireflies speckled shadows at the edges of the Granite Falls Park. *Such beauty from a plain black bug,* Sarah thought.

The second night of their stay, around the inevitable campfire, Jock announced, "A special occasion tonight. I've given thought to my poor neglected mare. I'm going to have a naming ceremony, right here in your company." He got up and led the horse, still in hobbles, to stand near the fire. He took a branch of willow and touched her on the neck. "I hereby dub you … Petunia."

He beamed at Sarah.

She turned down her lips.

MacPherson's face fell. "Now what?"

"Are you poking fun at us? About names? Serious names?"

"Somehow I didn't think naming an animal would cause

such a fuss. Wait." He turned on Babe. "How did a magnificent creature like you ... your pardon ... end up called Babe?"

Babe rumbled in code. "Ask Sarah. She chose it."

MacPherson turned back toward Sarah, his eyebrows cocked.

Sarah felt her face flush. "It was spur of the moment. Whimsy. We just never changed it."

Florenda said sharply, "I calls a council. Sarah, what *is* yo' problem? A name for the man's horse is yo' idea, and a name is just a name. Don' make one difference to her, and if callin' her after a flower tickles Jock, so how dat yo' concern? Look at my name. It probably meant as a slap de po' stupid Nigra would never realize, but I take it, and I make it a name I proud of. Dat my thought."

MacPherson said hesitantly, "Maybe I was a bit flippant. I'll accept nominations—"

"No!" Sarah shook her head, nearly a shudder. "No. Florenda is right. I ... apologize."

"Land o' Goshen," Florenda whispered.

"And that," said Jock MacPherson, "what just happened here, is why I want to tag along with your family."

Florenda clasped hands with Sarah and Henry to either side of her. Henry gripped one of Babe's horns; MacPherson took the other and gripped Sarah's hand. Something approaching serenity passed from one to the next.

On the third night at the Granite Falls Park, they sat next to the fire, at peace. Sarah glanced around. The place was beginning to feel—what? Homey?

MacPherson studied Henry. "You appear lost in some world of your own."

Henry started and smiled. "Got to thinking. Nonsense."

"Want to share?"

"Oh, just … did you ever consider how elusive a minute is?"

"Come again?"

"If I say, wait a minute, there it is, by name. Yet I can't hold a minute in my hand. I can't see it or feel it against my cheek, not like a breeze. When it expires, I am no wealthier. I have seen no visions. It leaves no ashes to prove it came by, no *track* in time. And why is something that elusive part of a circle? So what *is* a minute?"

"God almighty," MacPherson said.

No one added any comment until Florenda sighed. "Since he able to talk, he ask questions like dat. Drive a person crazy."

Sarah beamed. "I say, Henry, keep asking questions no one can answer."

Another *minute* of silence ended when MacPherson began to hum.

Florenda asked, "What dat?"

He said, "Let me think. Ah. 'Clementine.' Know it?"

"No, but I learns songs real quick. Show us," she said.

MacPherson's voice was a baritone scrambling about for pitch, enthusiastically delivered.

> "In a cavern, in a canyon,
> Excavating for a mine.
> Dwelt a miner, forty-niner,
> And his daughter, Clementine.

Oh my darling, oh my darling,
Oh my darling Clementine.
You are lost and gone forever,
Dreadful sorry, Clementine.

Light she was and like a fairy,
And her shoes were number nine;
Herring boxes without topses,
Sandals were for Clementine."

The second time through the chorus, Florenda joined in. Her clear tones threw MacPherson's wandering pitch a lifeline. She hummed along with him when he sang the third verse.

"Drove she ducklings, to the water,
Every morning just at nine;
Hit her foot against a splinter,
Fell into the foaming brine."

"Ruby lips above the water,
Blowing bubbles, soft and fine;
But alas! I was no swimmer,
So I lost my Clementine."

The enthusiasm of their rendition of the chorus attracted a handful of Granite Falls folks, who joined in on the next chorus.

"When the miner, forty-niner,
Soon began to peak and pine;
Thought he oughter 'jine' his daughter.

Now he's with his Clementine."

Babe raised his head and joined the chorus with full-throated bellows. On the beat.

"How I missed her, how I missed her,
How I miss-s-s-sed my Clementine.
So I kissed her little sister,
And forgot my Clementine!"

A chorus of family and townspeople roared out the chorus. Babe jumped about and twisted his head in time with his bellows.

After the sounds had died down, someone from town hollered, "Do it again!"

So they did, adding five more verses.

Jock said, "Florenda, you have a wonderful singing voice."

"Dat's 'cause singing let my soul come outta hiding. Even when I's still a slave, dey couldn't lock it inside a me when I singin'."

MacPherson looked at her with slack-jawed wonder. "Until right now, I hadn't really thought about where you came from. Not the way a man should."

She smiled, her face luminous. "But now yo sees it here." She thumped her chest with her fist. "I can tell, Mr. Canada Indian Scotchman MacPherson."

Sarah looked across the fire at MacPherson. She thought, *Dear God, I "sees" it too.*

32

A bridge spanned the river within the village of Granite Falls. The following morning, family members, augmented by a horse named Petunia and led by Jock MacPherson, trooped across it before turning toward the East, downriver.

"I know the trail on the north bank of the river better," he said.

He offered Petunia to Florenda as a ride, but she demurred with a hearty laugh. "My feet are more used to walkin' than my sit down is used to ridin' no horse."

"Sarah? Would you like to ride?"

She refused without further comment.

MacPherson said, "In that case, I'll let Petunia carry your backpacks and join you on foot."

He tamed his long stride to match her own. They climbed diagonally up bluffs overlooking the river, quickly losing it from view in a welter of trees below. He sorted through feelings roiling in his mind. How to awaken warmth and responsiveness in his companion ...

Words from his usually glib tongue hid in awkward silence.

What did an educated, confident woman talk about? Or expect from a man? *Face it, MacPherson, from a lumberjack!*

He glanced around ... for inspiration ... for ... *Ah!*

MacPherson pointed up a ravine to their left.

"Birch Coulee. A bloody incident took place up that draw during the Dakota Uprising. More than twenty years ago. A bad time for both Indians and whites, that."

Sarah's eyes widened. "Are we in danger from hostile Indians?"

"No, no, there are no hostiles these days. Beaten-down Indians is the truth. They lost so badly that they were herded onto reserves too small for hunting and fishing, their ancestral way of life. Might as well call it prison. They have lived in terrible poverty since." He glanced at Sarah. "All the Indians were trying to do was keep from starving. And regain a remnant of dignity."

"Were your, uh, people involved?"

"No. My Indian relatives are Ojibwe. Or Chippewa, as white people pronounce our name. In fact, the Dakotas and Ojibwes are historical rivals. Were. Not really anymore. If anything has united us Indians, I guess it has been mistreatment by whites." They trudged quietly for a minute or two.

Sarah said, "You mentioned once that you have Scotch ancestors. How did that come about?"

He grinned briefly. "A lesson in terms, Sarah. Scotch is a

beverage, not the name of the people who distill it. Call us Scots."

They walked again in silence for a while.

He said, "The fur trade of 150 years ago brought Europeans to Canada and the northern states. My grandfather, of several 'greats' back in time, was one of those fur traders. He left his name as well as his bloodline among my Ojibwe relatives. Sometime I'll tell you how badly most Europeans treated my native ancestors. The French and Scots more often treated Indians respectfully. Married them, raised families together, didn't kill them like vermin. Still, even today we *Anishinabes*— we Ojibwe Indians—are often scorned for just being ourselves."

He walked for a full minute in silence before adding, "White. Native. My curse, if you will, is that having a foot in each camp, I see the point of view of each." He sighed. "Life is never simple." He squinted at the angle of the sun. "We'll need to cut down the bluff to the river soon. Water Babe and Petunia. Have lunch."

"You're our guide," she said.

They camped that night near the river. Henry caught three tawny, large-eyed fish that MacPherson pronounced to be walleyes. "Best fresh-water fish in the world," he promised. From her perch on a driftwood log, Sarah studied his technique. A dab or two of lard, a dusting of flour, salt, and enough pepper to provoke a sneeze from the cook. He again proved mastery of the art of cooking fish.

Florenda, Henry, and MacPherson joined Sarah around the fire that evening.

"Dat fish better den catfish," Florenda said.

"How did you learn to fix it?" Sarah asked MacPherson from across the fire.

"Cruising timber for prospective sales. Out for weeks at a time in wild country, you either eat off the land, or you carry a ton of groceries with you."

He got up and circled the fire to sit beside Sarah. "I'm cross-eyed from trying to see you through smoke and flames." He hunkered down on a log beside her. "May I ask you a personal question?"

Something frightening tightened inside her. Icy. "You probably will, no matter what I say." She winced at the sharp edges of her reply.

"Always on guard. I wonder why that is?"

"If ..."

If life is one trial after another, is there a choice? Learn from the porcupine.

She sighed. "Events have taught me to be cautious."

"Especially when dealing with men?"

She smiled wryly. "How do men typically approach single women?"

"My whole gender beats down your life?"

"It is hard to ignore experience."

He was quiet for a spell, as still as the log on which he sat. "Aye. Good advice. If I was to generalize about relationships from experience, I should be as cautious."

He stood. "I must see to Petunia." He nudged a fire brand back into the flames with the toe of his boot. With his shoulders hunched, he walked to the thicket where he had staked out the horse.

Babe levered himself to his feet and walked down to the river for a drink. Henry went to his bedroll and curled up on his side.

Florenda said softly, "Girl."

Sarah stiffened. "Be careful what you start."

"Bein' careful din't get me outta Possum Creek. I's sayin,' careful can leave yo lonesome as a polecat."

"I should have chosen to live under the foot of a Howie Longstreet? Is that your alternative to being lonesome?"

"God shut my mouf." Florenda jumped up. Hands on hips, she glared at Sarah. "Is yo as hopeless as y'all actin'? Makin' a two-person couple, girl, ain't some stupid game of sweet lil' belle sittin' quiet on her ass, waitin' fer a fella ta break t'rough all de thorn bushes she raise up. No ma'am, it ain't *nuthin'* like dat."

Florenda waved a pointer finger under Sarah's nose. "De woman, she spot de right one, she set all de traps God give us females to work wit', an' she no way don' quit till he catch her. Y'all talkin' crap. Dat my t'ought." Florenda strode to her bedroll and crawled into it.

Sarah stared into the fire. Where MacPherson spread his bedroll she could not see. *And, by God, I'm not about to find his hiding place.*

No!

No.

She wiped away a silent tear.

The turmoil in Sarah's mind, in her gut, affected her as nothing in her previous life had done. Basics—woman and man, and how did trust between genders survive emotion?

Her relationship with Jonas had been as spirited as a sleepy summer afternoon. Proximity, combined with lack of an alternative had led to their union. This truth she had conceded long ago.

Had her husband ever actually asked for her hand? *I cannot remember!*

She snorted. *Romantic twaddle.*

Still …

Florenda, with her earthy ways, had seen through her indecision. What Sarah felt now was terror. *To trust another is to surrender control.*

She pounded her thighs with her fists. A tear threatened to escape her eye. *No! I never cry!*

His approach from behind her was so quiet she did not sense his presence until he nuzzled her. She leaped to her feet and threw her arms around his neck.

"How can life be so complicated? Oh, Babe!"

Sarah saw daylight arrive with a hard-won resolve to speak to MacPherson. To Jock. She stirred ashes in the fire ring, found a spark, and persuaded it to freshen into flames. She set a knife to a slab of bacon.

The odor of frying bacon brought MacPherson out of hiding. He neither looked at Sarah nor spoke to her. Her half-formed courage shriveled away.

Between fatigue and her depressed mood, Sarah lagged to the rear during the day's trek. MacPherson led along the slight highland bordering the river, pointing out highlights to Henry, walking beside him. A broad shallow lake choked with reeds and myriad wild fowl lay to their left.

"Swan Lake," MacPherson announced. Once, he poked the youth on the shoulder, and they doubled over with mirth.

A risqué joke? *Men!*

They passed a grove of leafy hardwood trees. Jock led Henry off the trail to stand under one of them.

"Have you ever seen a hundred-dollar bill?" Jock asked.

Henry snorted.

"Take a good look at this," Jock said, patting a tree trunk nearly two feet in diameter. "That piece of lumber from roots to branches is a C-note in the raw. These trees are black walnut. The wood makes gorgeous furniture and paneling. I have a running contract with the man who owns this grove to obtain eight trees a year."

Henry studied the foliage arching above him. A light breeze rustled leaves softly. He ducked his head and trudged back onto the trail.

MacPherson trotted to catch up. "You don't seem impressed."

"What will you do once the trees have all been cut down?"

Jock turned back to point. "There are enough in that grove to last a good twenty years."

"Do you plant a new tree when you cut one down?"

"No. What for? Henry, those trees are at least 150 years old."

"So once they're gone, there won't be any more."

"That's the owner's concern." Jock matched step with Henry. "You seem upset."

"They look like they belong, growing there in that little

valley. I just wondered who planted those trees? And how will there be any more after twenty years?"

"Henry, business is business."

"Sarah didn't teach much about that. She spent lots of time on nature, though."

Thoughts churned through MacPherson's head. Be responsible for *planting* trees? Our *business* is to harvest what providence set aside for our use.

Dad blame it, that woman must be contagious.

Every time Sarah made eye contact with Florenda, she scowled or tossed her head toward MacPherson, far ahead. Or simply walked a little faster, leaving Sarah in the rear with Petunia and Babe—the horse oblivious to the pangs of being human, Babe placidly plodding at her side. Once he rumbled to her, "You are one very stubborn woman." He kept further observations to himself.

33

MacPherson chose to halt for the day about two in the afternoon. They camped on a river flat below the town of Saint Peter. At this spot, bluffs of hard, layered limestone rising above the river were more abrupt, the flood plain not as wide. The river meandered in broad curves within its valley.

MacPherson motioned to Henry. "We need supplies, and the town is interesting. There's a college here, a place we might consider for you to attend someday."

Henry's eyes widened. "Me?"

MacPherson squinted at Henry and stroked his chin. "The sponsors of the school are Swedish Lutherans. We might need to fix a small detail or two." He chuckled and gripped Henry tightly about the shoulders. "I've sold quite a bit of lumber in

Saint Peter and know a couple of the people deciding who goes to their college. We need to plan for your future."

His gaze skipped over Sarah to Florenda. "I am quite serious," he told her. "The boy deserves a chance."

He turned back to Henry. "Saint Peter was supposed to be the capital of Minnesota when the town was planned, but literally, a guy stole the charter and hid away with it until folks from the territorial legislature finagled a new one that moved it to Saint Paul."

Jock waggled an instructive forefinger. "See, Paul really did steal from Peter. As recompense, they put the state insane asylum here instead." With an arm across Henry's shoulder as they walked up a slight incline toward town, he said, "Some might dispute who got the worse of the deal, on the grounds that legislators are as certifiable as the poor souls here in the hospital. The difference is, voters haven't noticed yet."

Sarah plopped down on the trunk of a tree washed ashore in some previous high water. She had seen the result of her indecision. No, stronger. Rejection of MacPherson's tentative approach had sealed it. Easy, open, normal man-to-woman interaction—*name it, Sarah*—sexual attraction, so difficult for her to acknowledge. *Why?*

Bah. An inane question, because the why's of life choke off opportunity.

The way MacPherson now sees right past me shows how completely I lost my chance.

She did not try to convince herself that the reality was painless. She slumped on her log.

Florenda sat close beside her. "Want to talk?"

"I'm so confused. I'm exhausted. I don't know what I want anymore. I feel unreal."

Florenda hugged her. "Crawl into yo' blankets an' sleep. I's fixin' the camp. Shoo!"

Sarah stumbled to her bedroll. She was asleep in seconds.

Sarah awoke when Henry and MacPherson returned to camp. Supper cooked and consumed, everyone gathered around the evening fire. MacPherson nodded at Henry.

"You want to tell them?"

Henry ducked. "It's nothing definite. The college sits on the edge of that little bluff overlooking the river. Jock dragged me up there to ask about my going to their school. A man talked to me briefly."

"Admissions officer," said MacPherson, "interviewed Henry. The man was interested."

"He asked me questions about my formal schooling, which made him a lot less interested."

MacPherson waved a dismissive hand. "Pshaw. A detail."

"He said I'd have to have a certificate of some kind that proved I had been to high school."

"Or prove that he knows as much as those who have."

Henry shook his head. "It seems unlikely."

"It'll just require a little maneuvering."

Florenda dabbed citronella oil on her face and arms. She laughed, a merry chortle. "I ain't sure iffen dis scare mosquitoes away, or iffen dey considers it spice to go with my blood." She confronted MacPherson. "Mr. Jock, yo 'n' me takin' a walk tonight. In dat town y'all cotton to, or along de river?"

Jock said, "I'm tired, and we have a long walk tomorrow."

"We's goin'." She grabbed his arm and steered him toward the riverbank.

He asked, "Why do I feel a scold coming?"

"'Cause yo earned one. Why y'all treat Miss Sarah so rotten?"

He stopped. "Me? She treats … I've tried to … hold on here."

"Keep walkin', and don' yo stutter at me. Y'all need to unnerstan' dat lady. She live through de war as a Southern person, something a Northerner don' know beans about. She married, but her husban' had been shot up in battle. Leg broken, an' he healed up gimpy. Then he died, leavin' the farm to run by herself."

She stopped and caught at his arm. "She had to fight off a bastard what tried to rape her. Rescued Henry an' me, so the Klan got her in dey sights. Dat meant her scaredy-cat frien's ran like chickens before the fox. A bullet shot into her house; a cross burnt on her yard."

She resumed her slow march along the bank of the Minnesota River. "A whirlwind blew her house into kindlin'. Tooken near everythin' she owned with it, from her moo cow to her plow horse." Her voice lost its scolding tone. "It landed Babe onto her haystack—de only good part. She spent years teachin' Henry, bought books for him to learn from. After all dat, de Klan drove her off her farm and burned everythin' still standin'. Now y'all got yo' feelings in a bundle 'cause she *cautious?* Par-don me!"

MacPherson's voice was hoarse. "I had no idea."

"I ain't nowheres near done. Now yo sweet-talkin' my

Henry, big brother shit. Makin' like he got a chance in dat white man college. I done voted y'all into our family, but I ain't above unvotin' yo just as quick."

"You don't pull your punches."

"Hah! Yo ain't seen one itty bit how I punch when I's a mind to." She picked up a hefty stick from detritus along the riverbank. "Dis give you de idea? Foolin' wit' people's feelin's to gain somethin' fo yo'self—dat we don' allow. So, mister big-shot friend of yo' big-shot Paul Bunyan, what you gonna do 'bout dis mess y'all stirred up?"

MacPherson stared out across the gentle flow of the river. "You want the truth?"

"Truth never hurt."

"Hurt depends on which end of truth you're talking about. All right. You people have no idea what you have in that steer. You can name your price in any market. A circus? Any carnival. I could see him as the symbol for some national stock-feed company.

"I've made no secret of how Bunyan would regard the animal. Part of his legend is that he found a baby ox, blue from a fall of blue snow one winter, and that the animal and Paul became inseparable. The really spooky part? It is said that he named it ... *Babe*."

"Horse apples. Mister, iffen I have anything to say 'bout it, y'all are half an inch from bein' left behind when we leave here tomorrow. Babe ain't no *animal*! He my brother. He part of our family."

Florenda strode back toward the campfire.

MacPherson caught up with Florenda and restrained her by a light touch on her arm. "Listen to me. I admit that my initial goal was to obtain Babe, whatever it took. But that was before I traveled with you people. Saw devotion unlike any I've ever known. I even felt the edges of it around my shoulders." He faltered. "Up until now, my life hasn't provided much of that kind of caring.

"About Henry. I never met any Negro people before you and him. Never had a thought about what your kind might be like. Honestly, never a care to know. I'm uneducated; didn't finished grammar school. Still, I'm not dumb. I've discovered that I can interact with folks who boast of college learning and hold my own."

He picked up a small stone and skipped it across the dark water flowing past. "Given that, I feel no shame in admitting that I will never be on the same plane of pure ability as your son. That boy really is worth every effort we make to get him properly educated."

MacPherson paced a few steps. "Babe? He was a freak, a specimen, a property. A creature of destiny fulfilling a weird prophecy—until I dropped that prejudice and really listened to him. I came to realize that I was no longer humoring some bizarre animal. I was conversing with a mind every bit as sharp as I like to think mine is. As to Sarah …"

His voice broke, and he turned back toward the river. "I said the day I caught up with you that I was pursuing her rather than Babe. In some mysterious way, at that moment, my feelings overrode greed. I blurted out the truth." He turned back to Florenda. "She fascinates me."

Florenda regarded him, her arms tight across her chest. "How yo gonna convince her a dat?"

"I don't know, if she won't talk to me."

Florenda made a rude sound. "Yo big lumberjack tough man, can't show how y'all feel? Den sleep alone in de cold de rest of yo' life."

"What do you suggest?"

Her face was faintly visible in light from the fire. "Try gentle but persistent. She think she unattractive. Can't y'all find a way to show her dat she wrong?"

"I'll try."

"Bah. Triers is liars."

"I'll … yes, I will. Lady, I could use a hug."

Florenda backed away a step. "I don' give hugs for free. I's waitin' till I sees iffen y'all earn one. Unnerstan'?"

She headed back toward the camp. MacPherson rubbed his face. He sighed and followed her.

And ran smack into Babe's broad forehead.

Babe rumbled, "Pleasant evening."

When he returned to camp, MacPherson huddled by the fire until it burned out.

34

The next morning, MacPherson sat on a river-tossed log across from Sarah. "I want to talk to you," he said. And to the others, he asked, "Could we please delay our departure? I have things to tell Sarah. Private things. I've already waited too long to say them."

Babe rumbled in Morse, "I saw a patch of fresh grass downriver a ways." He disappeared into riverbank groves of cottonwood trees.

Henry said to his mama, "Maybe we could go into town. I can show you where the college is."

Florenda cocked her fists on her hips and stared at MacPherson with her stony-faced stare. "We'll be back in an hour. Suh!" She and Henry climbed the sandy incline leading to downtown Saint Peter.

MacPherson shifted his weight and rested his arms on his

knees. "I'm glad we have this chance to talk." He cleared his throat. "Alone. The two of us, that is."

Sarah peered at the ground. "Oh?"

He jerked off his cap and wadded it without mercy. "I'm a good stutter—that is, I'm *not* good with words when it comes to … being a lumberjack; you see, in winter camp, feelings don't often come up. Between jacks, I mean."

MacPherson drew a breath deep. "I'm trying my best now." He cleared his throat again. "Last evening, Florenda told me about what you have suffered through. I can't tell you how painful it was for me to realize how strong you have had to be just to survive."

He fitted his cap over his bent knee. "I told her the truth about why I followed the family. Clear across Iowa. After you, not Babe. She can tell you." He leaned forward. "Sarah, I want us to be friends. More than friends. I believe they used to call it—courting."

She raised her eyes from contemplation of her folded hands. "Why?"

"Because I find you … you are so … I think I'm in … that is, love. With you."

"I've been called a prune."

MacPherson slapped his cap across his thigh sharply. "Oh good God. You're gorgeous. Lively. Sparkling. So … capable."

"I have no dowry except a burned farm I can never reclaim. Less than a thousand dollars in cash and the clothes on my back."

"I can't afford a ring, and probably have no job anymore. Maybe that makes us even."

She smiled. A little one. "Probably so."

"I'll find something to do. I was wondering. Do you suppose it would be all right if I was to sort of, you know, kiss you?"

She nodded solemnly. "I have it on authority that the lady wouldn't object."

So he did.

And he hugged her.

And she hugged him back.

And Florenda and Henry walked down the incline from Saint Peter, grinning.

And Babe sauntered out of the grove of cottonwood trees. He rumbled, "What *is* this kissy business anyway?"

Florenda went to MacPherson. "Y'all want to collect that hug now?'

He did that too. With enthusiasm.

35

The wonders of her life arranged themselves clearly within Florenda's mind during the walk along the north bank of the Minnesota River. *I escaped from Massa's iron claw,* she thought, *like a butterfly coming free of its cocoon, with the support— and yes, the sharp prodding—of my improbable sister, Sarah. A sister whose guidance of Henry widened my own possibilities, because I was there to hear along with him. Call it an accidental education. How many former slaves had such an opportunity? Now, an escape from the enslavement of terror by Klansmen, once again with guidance from Sarah.*

It's like I crossed my personal Jordan River. I understand and accept responsibility for my own decisions. For a life in freedom.

"Lordy, Lordy," she said to the warm breeze caressing her cheek. "What a struggle it has been."

Florenda smiled at the serenity of the broad valley that so matched her mood, and at her traveling companions.

Sweet Jesus! Her soul soared.

With Babe's measured pace to set their speed, it had taken three days to reach the confluence of the Minnesota and Mississippi Rivers. Jock explained about a sturdy structure squatting on the north bank of the Minnesota River, just before it sent its waters into the larger river. It was a stockade called Fort Snelling, built to guard against Indian attacks.

When Florenda expressed concern, Jock hastened to explain. "In the seventy years it has been standing there, the fort has never had to close its gates, let alone repel attacks. Consider it a trading post."

Florenda was reassured, yet in an odd way reassurance made it seem less important.

They rested until morning in its shelter before heading north along the west bank of the Mississippi toward Saint Anthony Falls, nine miles upstream. Turbulence, a word Florenda had heard Sarah use, came to mind. An unending roar of impatient water came from the riverbed to their right, water in a commotion such as she had never seen or heard.

The river ran nearly one hundred feet deep in a gorge worn into a bed of limestone. For miles it was one continuous rapids thundering over rocks in an exuberant display of white water. Standing close on the bank high above made Florenda lightheaded.

It was late afternoon when they arrived at Saint Anthony Falls, with its encrustation of commerce—saw mills, flour mills, a paper mill, a textile plant, a plant generating electricity.

Florenda chuckled. MacPherson seemed energized. He swept his arm toward the west. "The city here is Minneapolis, built on what used to be part of the Fort Snelling military reserve." He turned toward the east. "And across the river is the city of Saint Anthony. The large seven-story building yonder is the newest flour mill, that of the Charles A. Pillsbury Company."

He pointed upstream. "My office is in one of those saw mills. We operate day and night, sawing white pine logs floated down the river from up north."

He waved a proprietary hand at a log framework enclosing the falls. Water rushed through a cataract beyond it. "Isn't that a sight? The falls itself is a sixteen-foot straight drop. Twenty-five feet more drop from the cataract. It's the only real waterfall along the whole Mississippi River."

Florenda squinted at the slight mist rising from the river. The falls of Saint Anthony stretched some 250 yards wide, bank to bank. The cataract below the falls was a three-hundred-yard jumble of broken rocks. Water poured between, over, and around them, tossing spray into the air. The roar made it necessary to shout to be heard.

In the basin of quieter water below the cataract a pair of islands divided the flow of the river. It narrowed to one hundred yards or less in width, once past the tumult interrupting the otherwise placid flow of Father Mississippi.

The family members lined up on the west bank of the river.

A jumble of logs, some three or more feet in diameter,

reared in a jam just above the precipice, and a random-appearing scattering of logs was caught among rocks of the cataract, evidently orphans of a sort.

Sarah said, "It reminds me of a giant's game of jack straws."

MacPherson took Sarah's hand. "This is what I've known all my life."

Sarah kissed his hand.

"Someone tried to put a harness on the Father of Waters," Henry said.

Babe rumbled softly in code, "I will never fully understand the activities of Two-Legs."

Florenda shook her head. "Dey done all dey could to make it really ugly."

Henry asked, "Why is the falls enclosed by logs?"

"Ah, that log frame is called an apron. It was built to *preserve* the falls. Erosion keeps undercutting the rock layers creating it. If it had been allowed to crumble into a cascade, much of the power would have been squandered. It's all about power to grind the wheat and saw the logs. Imagine—a continuous, unending source of power."

MacPherson sighed. "I'd better find out whether I still have a job." He trudged off toward one of the saw mills.

Florenda joined the others on the bank of the river to await his return.

Jock MacPherson's face was dour when he rejoined them. He was indeed no longer employed. "And Paul Bunyan just left on a train for Washington State to open a new logging camp. My sponsor won't be back for months."

Sarah and Jock became husband and wife a few days later. Since he didn't know whether he had been legally divorced, they settled for a mutual declaration of respect and love.

As matron of honor, Florenda held a spray of wild asters. She watered them liberally with tears during the brief rite. Henry stood tall beside Jock as best man. Sweet Jesus, Florenda realized, her son was nigh on to manhood! And Babe? If a huge blue ox cannot function as an authentic clergyman, his rumbled blessing sanctified the union in ways that were as holy.

36

The family rented a small house just north of the waterfall on the west bank of the river.

From neighbors, Sarah heard comments about a settlement of people of color located in the east-bank town of Saint Anthony. She decided to explore possibilities that someone there might help in finding a way for Henry to get into a college. She realized that she had exhausted her own ability to further his education, that he needed advanced tutors. He was ready for college.

Henry acknowledged a yearning to move on.

One day, Sarah, Florenda, and Henry set off on foot across a suspension bridge linking Minneapolis with the town of Saint

Anthony. "We'll just survey the situation," Sarah said. "Maybe meet a few people. Ask questions."

Arrived on the east bank of the river, Sarah turned back toward Florenda, who had not left the bridge. "Don't shuffle along behind me like that."

Florenda lifted her head. "I thought I was ready. Be responsible. But now I find dat I … I's 'fraid."

Sarah rejoined Florenda. "I've learned that when I'm afraid, if I put on a brave face I sometimes convince myself that I am brave. Chin up. Back straight. Proper diction. That sort of thing."

"What if we not allowed? I's never set foot in society."

Sarah's voice was gentle. "We have every right to be here. See the town."

"I won't know how to act."

"You don't have to 'act.' Just be the fine person you are. Freedom … remember?"

Florenda found a handkerchief and dabbed her eyes. She stood straight. "I do it for you, Henry."

"No, Mama, do it for yourself," he said.

Sarah linked arms with Henry on one side of her and with Florenda on the other.

Sarah knew the address of the family she had heard of: Mr. Ralph Toyer Grey and his wife, Mrs. Emily Goodridge Grey. "On Fourth Street. They are said to have been among the first people of color to settle in Minnesota. I'm hopeful that they can guide us when it comes to matriculating Henry in a college."

The home of the Greys was not imposing—a modest two-story place, white clapboard siding, set in a generous yard.

A fence bordered the plank sidewalk on which they stood. Shrubbery of some kind grew inside the fence. Along one side of the yard was a neatly tended vegetable garden. Sarah recognized potatoes, carrots, string beans, tomatoes, kohlrabi, and cabbages. A pair of apple trees grew at the far end of the garden.

They stood facing this display of domesticity. "This is where they live," Sarah said softly.

A woman rose from a position on hands and knees, where she had been hidden by the hedge. She stared at them impassively, but her eyes widened as she took in their appearance. Her complexion was as dark as Florenda's.

"Yes?" she said, her voice neutral.

Sarah said, "Oh my. Forgive us. I had hopes of meeting Mr. Grey."

"Mr. Grey is at work."

Henry stepped to the fence and bowed slightly. "It's my fault. Mama and Sarah have this notion that I should go to college. They thought to ask if you knew whether such was possible. We'll not interrupt your day any further." He bowed again before turning away.

Sarah shook her head impatiently. She put an arm across his shoulder. With her other arm, she encircled Florenda's shoulders. "Are you Mrs. Grey?" she asked.

A slight nod. "Yes."

"We are newly arrived from the South and thought that perhaps one who had succeeded in …" She sighed.

Mrs. Grey's voice was suddenly warm. "I was about to make some iced tea. Would you care to join me?"

She brushed garden dirt off ankle-length skirts and started for her front door. "Come."

They followed her.

The sitting room of her house was bright with color. Furniture was wooden, neither costly nor shabby. When she had seated her guests and served them tea, she looked around at them expectantly.

Florenda regarded her glass of tea with its icy condensation in awe. "I's never … uh, I've never tasted cold tea before."

Mrs. Grey said, "It's refreshing when it's hot outdoors. My name is Emily Goodridge Grey. Please call me Emily. And you?"

Sarah said, "We are Sarah McAllfry and Florenda and Henry Jackson, and we *are* a family."

Emily Grey set her chair to rocking gently. "A family. I can hardly wait to learn about *that*."

Each contributing, they told her how *that* came to be.

When the tale had arrived at the present time, Emily said, "You must stay for supper. I have plenty, and Ralph, my husband, will want to meet you. He is a barber, with a shop in the Jarrett House Hotel.

"Ralph and I are both from York, Pennsylvania. We moved out here in 1862 at a time when the Confederate Army was driving our way. My father had been a slave but was freed back in the 1840s. Ralph was active in the abolitionist movement, and it seemed wise for him not to be captured."

She looked at Florenda. "You understand better than I what the horrors of slavery were like. I will pray for your peace of mind. Now, I could use a hand with peeling potatoes."

All three family members volunteered.

The Greys were deeply involved in the affairs of the community, but neither was certain how to translate Henry's abilities into an acceptance by a college or university.

37

MacPherson became an employee of renowned miller Mr. Charles A. Pillsbury, although Jock had no evidence that the great man was aware of the fact. With MacPherson's usual enthusiasm for sharing his experiences, he explained the milling business to the family, from the viewpoint of a low-level employee.

During the first years of the milling business, flour had been stored and shipped in barrels made of wooden staves. At the time when Jock joined the ranks of flour packers, cloth sacks had become the rage. Each sack, of a size to hold 120 to 140 pounds of flour, was filled by snugging its mouth tightly around a chute delivering flour. The sacker controlled the operation by a foot pedal. Fill a bag. Tie off its mouth. Heave it onto a shoulder, and tote it across a dock to the open door of a cavernous railway boxcar to join a growing pile of others. Then back to the filling room—twelve hours a day, six days a week. During his brief tenure as an employee of Mr. Pillsbury, Jock filled sacks with premium white flour in the new Saint Anthony plant.

MacPherson dragged home in the middle of his shift one day. Blackened, bruised, and limping, he explained what had happened.

His job was a casualty of the latest flour-dust explosion, although his injuries were minor, and the plant, built to modern standards, failed to burn down.

MacPherson decided that Fate had rolled snake eyes, that his destiny lay in the North. It was time to leave Minneapolis with its "city" ways. Duluth beckoned.

Sarah and Florenda had found the culture of a city to their liking. They disagreed vehemently.

As man of the house, MacPherson decided the issue, as was proper.

38

Sarah had never ridden on a train. She had wondered occasionally what the experience would be like—speed along without an ounce of effort, sit on a comfortable bench. Perhaps even enjoy a meal while watching the countryside flash by, thanks to miracles of 1889 technology.

But this?

The family filed into the lone boxcar of a train headed for the frontier village of Tower, Minnesota. The train consisted otherwise of empty gondola cars returning north for refills of iron ore. After heated negotiations between MacPherson and the conductor, Babe was allowed on board.

"If that beast makes a mess, you clean it up," the man snarled.

"Barbarian," rumbled Babe.

The deviousness of a fate that had brought Sarah to the

dismal, drafty, rattling shack on wheels in which she stood left her too numb even to rebel.

The way Jock had explained how life had come to this ...

MacPherson had signed on to be an iron miner with a man-grabber outfit called the Mesabi Employment Agency. After weeks of no future jobs in Duluth, he had hired on for a stint aboard one of the cargo steamships plying Lake Superior between Duluth and Fort William in Ontario, Canada, more than two hundred miles away. A late August storm tossed the boat about so wickedly that MacPherson spent most of the trip in his bunk. "I ain't *never* been so sick in my life," he told Sarah upon his return, "nor half as scared. Up, sidewise, that boat bucked worse than any nag I ever tried to ride. When the boat docked back in Duluth, there was this Clem Stani ... some Slavic name ... holding out a pen. He talked me into joining the profession of iron mining."

Sarah plopped to a sitting position on splintery floor planks at one end of the boxcar.

The train jerked and clattered into motion.

One of the sliding doors of the car had been left partially open. Sarah monitored the countryside through which they rode courtesy of the window thus provided. At times, vagaries in air currents brought strangling clouds of wood smoke from the engine before streams of crisp, sweet air would dispel the stench.

The railroad tracks ran through country so rough there were no flat places. "Lessen you counts all those lakes out there," grumbled Florenda at Sarah's side. Tracks snaked around isolated rocks as large as the barn back on Possum Creek, under trees so tall and thick they cut off most of the sunlight, and across rivers and swamps that seemed to have no bounds.

The family clustered around Sarah at the end of the car. Once they had settled into the teeth-rattling rigors of the railcar, Sarah took stock of their fellow passengers. These came from a mixed barrel. One man was a heavily muscled Negro, whose scowl at them never lessened. A wiry white man with a peg substitute for one leg leaned against the end wall opposite them. An assortment of whiskered toughs, not a one of whom spoke English, huddled together.

Seated halfway down the length of the car, a middle-aged Indian man sat with his back against its vibrating side. The skin of his face and hands was the color of tannin-stained wood. His legs stretched out in front of him. He wore scuffed jeans, a lumberjack shirt, and a leather vest decorated with porcupine quills and colorful beads. Black hair was streaked with a few strands of gray. He wore it long, in a braid that fell below his shoulders. A small cloth bag of cigarette tobacco peeked from his shirt pocket. He watched the family with apparent interest.

MacPherson stood, balancing against the lurches of the car. He squatted near the man and offered an Ojibwe greeting: *"Ahneen, ay zhee 'ah ya yan."*

The man's eyebrows twitched, and he flicked a glance at MacPherson.

In English, MacPherson said, "I invite you to join my family and me at the end of the car—if that fits your schedule."

The man considered. *"Aye-yah.* It would be possible." He rose in a single coordinated motion and walked beside MacPherson to join the family. They stood and formed a circle.

MacPherson said, "My name is Jock. My real name—my Indian name—is *Mang Nagamowinini*. Loon Singer. I come from the Ojibwe band at Canadian Red Lake." He gazed into the distance.

The man said solemnly, "I am Ashawa Deerhorn, of the *Kitchi Onigaming* band on Lake Superior."

Jock said, "Onigaming, the Great Carrying Place. Grand Portage."

"I would meet your family."

MacPherson said with equal solemnity, "My wife, Sarah, is from the South. She is a teacher with such courage that she faced the devil and walked away victorious. Her sister is now my sister, a free woman who goes by the name Florenda. Her spirit soars with *Migisi*, the eagle. Our son, Henry, is going to be a doctor someday. He has been chosen by the *Manitou* who controls destiny. And this is Babe. He possesses wisdom bestowed by Thunderbird in person. He was born out of a great storm. He hears; he understands. He chooses to speak only in the language of a code."

"And you?" Ashawa Deerhorn asked. "You do not tell of you."

MacPherson stood straight. "I am a man of two nations. Of two natures. I seek to find which one is me."

Deerhorn nodded to each family member. "Matters of the spirit lie best hidden from the scorn of those who do not see. But ..." His face awoke in a warm smile. "Glad to meet you, everyone. What brings you on this luxury trip?"

The train grumbled to a stop in the village of Tower. Descending from the boxcar, Sarah wondered if the core numbness she felt was to be her destiny. She pivoted slowly, trying to absorb what she saw. This place that was to be their next home, this raw village, was so new it consisted of more tents than buildings. Streets of the reddest mud imaginable ran up abrupt little hills and along the shore of a sizable lake. A mile to the east, the town of Soudan was visible atop a rocky ridge. The opening to a mine shaft yawned from its crest.

Sarah was too numb even to cry.

39

MacPherson and Deerhorn went underground the next day. Descending into an endless hole just large enough to accommodate a rattling hoist was merely a beginning. At an incalculable depth, tunnels as black as midnight branched off. "Stars" were the lamps mounted on the caps of fellow miners. They walked along a confining tunnel that had been blasted through solid rock, the ceiling of which was barely head high. They were expected to push little cars on rails through clouds of red dust, load them with rough chunks of loosened iron ore, and trundle the heavy car back to the mine shaft for loading onto the hoist.

The process of fragmenting ore involved drilling holes in the rock of its vein. These were then filled with black blasting powder. After igniting a hissing fuse, the blast master trotted for an excavated shelter in the side wall of the tunnel.

A blast to threaten a man's ears, a stench of exploded rock now loosened in a heap—

Jock and Ashawa gasped and choked.

They looked at each other and tipped back their heads.

Unknowable tons of rock overhead.

MacPherson leaned against a rock wall; a dislodged shard landed beside his foot.

Breathing too tight to satisfy and dizzy from trying ...

As one, they trotted back to the descent shaft.

They made such a fuss that they were hauled to the surface before the morning was half over. MacPherson was chagrinned, sure, but for no amount of shame would he allow himself to be lowered back into earth's bung hole.

When asked, Ashawa gave Jock's point of view a hearty endorsement.

MacPherson led the way to a tent, where Florenda and Sarah were washing clothes in tubs borrowed from the Lutheran church.

"You have to understand," Jock said earnestly to Sarah.

"That solid rock squeezed my throat closed," Ashawa explained.

Jock broke in. "All our lives, the sky has been our ceiling."

"Outdoors, where breezes talk to the trees."

Jock said, "Where even at night *gisiss*, the moon, chases away darkness."

"Where even the dark cloud *nitaganakwad* cannot hide the stars for long," Ashawa said.

"We were dizzy. Dangerously dizzy."

"Ready to pass out," Ashawa agreed.

"It's darker than any grave. What if no one had ever found us?" Jock said lugubriously.

Ashawa nodded. "Easy to forget us, we being new on the crew."

"Are you a drinking man?" MacPherson asked Ashawa.

"Not I."

"Me neither."

"Bad medicine. So the elders claim."

MacPherson nodded. "I've heard the same. But ..."

"But ..."

Jock said to Sarah, "We'll be at the Iron Trail Saloon."

"In case you need us." Ashawa broke into a trot.

MacPherson arrived first at the tavern.

Seated at the bar in the Iron Trail Saloon, Jock MacPherson poked Ashawa Deerhorn with an elbow. "Here comes that fellow," he said, "Clem What's-His-Name from Mesabi Employment."

The man stalked into the Iron Trail Saloon and directly to Jock and Ashawa. He gripped shirt fronts of both men and pulled them off their barstools. Because of his Slavic accent, neither Ashawa nor Jock understood most of Clem's words, but looks required no translation. The man was unhappy.

Clem went behind the bar, where he held a whispered conversation with the burly barkeep, one punctuated by pointing fingers and unrelenting scowls aimed at the ex-miners. The pair shook hands, and Clem left.

Jock and Ashawa turned attention to the important issue of consuming whiskey in as efficient a manner as possible.

The bartender leaned his elbows on the bar. "Gentlemen, I don't believe I heard your names."

Jock addressed the barkeep with a sweeping gesture at Ashawa. "My associationate think he's name Deerhorn."

"I damn sure my name Deerhorn," Ashawa said.

"Aha! Impossible, my misguided frien'. There isn't not any such thing as a *deer horn*. Deers gots *antlers*."

"So, *Anishinabes* not think up antler. Not every Indian lucky enough to graduate out of fourth grade like you. For that matter, antler no damn good for anything else, but horn, now. Play taps with antler? Hah!" He spat at a spittoon—and missed. *Oh well.*

The barkeep poured more Jim Beam. "I hear you gents are from the mine."

MacPherson said, "I weresn't not what a man would call 'fraid."

"Absolutely not." The barkeep filled Ashawa's glass again, saying, "You're getting low." He reached behind him for another quart.

Ashawa raised a wobbly index finger. "Ain' no one more willing to wark. Werk? You know."

Mr. Friendly Barkeep nodded. "Plain to see." Another refill materialized. "Got a place to live?" he asked them.

MacPherson shuddered, spilling a bit of his whiskey. "I didn' not stay down in that bung hole long 'nough to …" He dried a tear with the heel of his hand. "Got no money buy place."

A belated memory from his far youth prodded MacPherson. *Wha's name he was? Duggan—bar tend that joint; narrow point view 'bout paying for drinks* … Caution reared a groggy head. "'Course, we hab plen'y money, pree' soon."

The barkeep smiled. "Yes, you will, so I'm told."

Ashawa reached across the bar and groped for the man's arm. "Wha's yer name?"

MacPherson turned to Ashawa. "Barkeeps always name Duggan. I tol' you and tol'."

Ashawa patted the barkeep on the arm. "You a pince … a plinz …"

Ashawa slid off his stool onto the floor and began to snore. When Jock leaned over to see what had become of Ashawa … he … tipped …

40

MacPherson wondered if he had died.

Slurp. Splash. Tunk. Splash.

Was the clamor coming from within his head? A pounding in his temples suggested that his skull was about to explode.

Slurp! Splash! Thudding footsteps. Bangs like railcars coupling, echoing one after another …

Racket from hell's back door. A pounded steel drum when your head is about to split like a dropped pumpkin. The noises came from somewhere outside his head …

A scratchy voice, from the region of MacPherson's feet. "Watch it, Eight Ball. Sink us, and you'll be in hock for the next ten years."

There was a reprise of pounding feet, a grunt, and more ghastly trotting footsteps going the other way.

It started all over again.

MacPherson opened his eye—one eye; the other lid seemed welded to a rough wooden surface. He lay on his stomach. *Easy—don't want to give innards ideas about reversing course.*

What he saw was not informative—an unpainted wooden shack, weathered to a vaguely white hue. Behind him, out of his line of sight, booted feet stomped past before returning at that hellish trot.

I'd raise my head if the effort wasn't so unthinkable.

Someone kicked his foot. Not gently. "Your buddy's awake. We're almost to the landing. If you have to puke, do it over the side. Hop to!"

MacPherson groaned and levered himself to a sitting position. He was facing the stern of a flat-bottomed, square-ended barge about twenty feet long and a dozen wide. A floating wanigan. A crude cabin of a sort occupied the center of the boat.

A tall, stringy-strong–appearing man dressed in work clothing was poling the barge. Slurp. Splash. Tunk. Pounding footsteps when he retraced his steps.

Another man sat in the stern. He appeared to be sixtyish. A fringe of hair on its way from brown to gray ringed a pate that was bald and sprinkled with age spots. His eyes glittered behind squinting lids. He wielded a stick as hefty as a baseball bat. He slapped his palm with the stick. "Strong drink is an abomination before the Lord," he said.

MacPherson blinked. "Where the hell are we?"

"Thou shalt not use strong language, nor take the name of the Lord in vain." He banged the gunwale of the wanigan with his cudgel.

MacPherson squinted at the man. "Who the hell are you?"

"Marvin Richards. I am now your employer." He pulled a paper from a pocket. "I bought your contract from Mesabi Employment, signed and sealed, Mr. Jock MacPherson—the one you welshed on back at the mine. Saved you from some trouble, I did, giving you another chance. Let it be said that Marvin Richards is a just and godly man. Work honestly, and you will be paid. After you have earned your contract, of course."

Richards whirled toward the tall man walking back and forth on the narrow side deck of the wanigan. "Watch out for those rocks!"

The man—*Eight Ball, was it?*—eased the barge through shallow water strewn with large boulders.

MacPherson lurched to his feet. He leaned against the rough planks of the cabin built into the center of the wanigan.

Richards waggled his club.

"I still don't know where we are," MacPherson growled, "or where we are headed."

"We're approaching the western end of Lake Vermilion."

MacPherson squinted past the shack. A narrow, shallow, winding arm of water stretched before them.

"If you entertain ideas of tossing the ax, forget them," Richards said.

"I don't go in for ax throwing."

"Desertion, I mean. Be aware that we are on the extreme western end of thirty-mile-long Lake Vermilion. Walking back to Tower is a major hike through dense forests, with the sheriff waiting at the other end."

We'll see about that, MacPherson thought. "When we reach the end of the lake?"

"We walk. You are about to become a lumberjack."

"Become" a jack? Huh. "Where's my friend?"

"On the other side of the cabin from you."

MacPherson edged around the end of the shack. He peered past its corner.

Deerhorn sat with his back against the wall of the cabin. He waved weakly at MacPherson before suddenly crawling to the gunwale and retching.

"Good boy," said Richards. "Into the lake."

MacPherson plopped onto the deck, legs extended. "I have a wife and family back in Tower," he said to Richards.

"Did have." The man smiled coldly. "A magnificent ox is tied up on the front of this barge. I have bargained for use of the beast this winter in camp. Your wife and two Negroes occupy the cabin behind you, along with a load of supplies."

"Sarah's here? I have to talk to her." MacPherson crawled on hands and knees. He fumbled at the latch of the door opening into the shack.

Richards smiled triumphantly. "Judging by comments your wife and the Negress made earlier, I doubt you'll want to hear what they have to say."

An upwelling … MacPherson crawled urgently to the gunwale beside Deerhorn and joined him in communion with the lake.

Sounds made by Eight Ball behind him where he plodded on his endless journey magnified the headache ricocheting about in MacPherson's head.

41

MacPherson stood next to Babe at the front of the wanigan when they reached the spot where Lake Vermilion gave out. Half a dozen men awaited them. There were no roads. Wheeled vehicles would have bogged down within yards of departure. Three large sledges would carry the material stored aboard the wanigan. Three teams, four oxen each, would power them. The men, human pack animals, carried everything ashore: Kegs of nails. Crosscut saws, axes and steel felling wedges. Carpenter's tools. Barrels of flour and sugar and cured meats. Bales of blankets bundled in canvas. And a great iron cookstove. Anything left over would go into packs on their backs when they departed the lake.

The stove occupied one sledge, tools and building supplies a second, and the third bore food supplies. By nightfall, Deerhorn and MacPherson had sweated away every drop of whiskey.

Then they faced their personal court of last appeal: Sarah and Florenda.

Richards, Eight Ball, and the other six lumberjacks gathered around one fire. MacPherson and Deerhorn collapsed onto logs before a second fire, tended by the family, a discreet distance removed.

Her face bleak, Sarah handed MacPherson a bowl of beef stew while standing at the maximum distance, allowing for the transfer to occur.

Florenda's scowl cut deep lines in her face. She set Ashawa's bowl on the ground, three feet out of his reach.

The women retreated to the other side of the fire. The eloquence of nonverbal language left little doubt as to the size of the problem Ashawa and Jock had created for themselves.

Henry glanced back and forth, settling on a rock halfway between two such obvious camps. Babe chewed a cud placidly.

Silence crept around MacPherson and Deerhorn, along with curlicues of evening ground fog.

MacPherson cleared his throat.

Deerhorn belched politely.

"Good stew," MacPherson said.

"Aye-yah," said Deerhorn.

"Been thinking."

Deerhorn gave a solemn nod. "Happens."

MacPherson scraped his spoon around the bottom of his bowl. "It's probably a good thing for a man to get stinking once in a great while."

Ashawa cocked an eyebrow. "How, good?"

MacPherson waggled an index finger. "Glad you asked. See,

a real bender reminds a man how unsatisfying the experience really is, and how miserable he feels the next day ain't a bit more enjoyable. Tend to forget."

"Probably be easier to remember now. At least for a while."

Jock placed a log on the fire.

"Ever consider the nature of a contract, Ashawa?"

"I'm not even sure what a contract is."

Jock again waggled his finger. "Think of it as being like a treaty."

"White man crap, huh?"

Jock nodded. "Easy enough to sign treaties, but they hardly ever turn out good for us *Anishinabes*."

"There you go. Should've stuck to not signing stuff."

MacPherson raised his voice. "Be good if the ladies understood this whole thing is the same kind of mistake."

"Aye-yah."

"The ladies" jumped off their logs and boiled around the fire. Florenda pushed Sarah off balance with a solid hip check to stand over MacPherson. The fire in her eyes outdid the flames behind her.

"Y'all! When I left Possum Creek to get away from trouble, I never bargained for endin' up in a pickle at the North Pole. We trusted yo, Jock MacPherson. I nominated y'all to join the family. Yo' worse than a cottonmouth water snake, 'cause they don't pretend they yo' friends."

Ashawa said, "She talked as good as you just now."

MacPherson said, "She forgets to use her plantation accent when she gets riled up enough."

Sarah shoved Florenda aside to tower over MacPherson, squatting on his log. "Go north, you always said. To your Paul

Bunyan. To a man who isn't here. To a job you didn't have. To Duluth, where you were sure to find work. To be a miner or some damn thing. I had a better future back on the farm."

"Sarah, you cussed."

"Damn right!" She shook her fist perilously close to MacPherson's nose.

The ladies stomped to the opposite side of the fire. Sarah's face loomed above the flames like a sprite on Halloween night. She waggled a finger. "Y'all can sleep out in those woods you're so fond of."

The ladies marched to their bedrolls.

Ashawa said, "There might be advantages in being single."

Henry hunkered down on the same log serving as MacPherson's seat. "Think she'll get over this?"

MacPherson shook his head slowly side to side. "Thing about women, son, ya can't always tell." He sighed. "There is nothing as chilling as the displeasure of a wife convinced she's been wronged." He turned to Henry. "I can sort of understand why Ashawa and I ended up in this fix, but how come the rest of you are here?"

"When Sarah heard that you were out-cold drunk on the wanigan and headed for a logging camp ... I've never seen her so angry. She yelled and cried and swore—"

"Swore, then, too, huh?"

"Words I didn't know she knew."

"Jesus."

"Way beyond that, Jock. She tracked down Richards, grabbed the front of his shirt, near spitting in his face, and demanded that he release you two from your contracts. Richards started waving that club of his around. She latched onto the business end and yanked it out of his hand. He still wouldn't unsign you, so she insisted that the rest of us accompany you and Ashawa."

"She did that? I wonder why?"

"At first he had a laughing fit over the idea. That got Sarah all the madder. About then, Babe wandered by, curious to see what the fussing was about. When Richards spied Babe, his eyes got bigger than baseballs. 'What is that creature?' he says, his voice all squeaky. I pipe up, 'Our friend Babe.' Richards says, like in a daze, 'How much for him?'

"Sarah gets a funny look on her face. 'He isn't for sale,' she says, 'but he might be for lease.' Babe starts asking questions in code, and Sarah tells him to hush up."

Henry tossed a stick onto the fire. "I'm not sure how she did it, but by the time Sarah finished with Richards, he had agreed to lease Babe, cash in advance, and allowed that Mama would be camp doctor."

"Doctor!"

"Before she was freed, she was the one person who tried to fix fevers and cuts, sprains, even broken bones of the other slaves. Richards has no real doctor for his camp. Sarah will be an assistant to the cook, and I'm Babe's official handler."

"Jesus."

"You already said that."

42

Marvin Richards turned out to be foreman of the logging camp. He had a special harness rigged up for Babe and hitched him to the sledge holding the huge stove.

Henry took a position beside Babe's left shoulder. Richards stood nearby. He growled, "All right, boy, let's see what that beast can do. Giddy him up." He flicked Babe's back with a long willow whip.

"Don't do that," Henry said. He stood quietly; Babe did not twitch.

Richards applied the willow whip more vigorously. Henry grabbed it out of his hand and threw it aside.

Richards confronted Henry. "You, boy—you're supposed to drive this beast. Do it!"

Henry said, "My name is Mr. Jackson. Babe is not a beast. He will obey only me. Those were the terms of our agreement."

Richards's face turned cranberry red. "If he doesn't perform, he's staying behind, boy."

"Mr. Jackson."

Through gritted teeth, Richards said, "Mr. … Jackson."

"He'll 'perform.'" Henry stood directly before Babe and rubbed his broad forehead. "Ease into it. My understanding is that we have a long trek."

Babe leaned forward enough to test the harness. He nodded. "Good. Let's show them."

Babe walked, muscles taut against the harness, and the sledge slid over gravel and forest detritus as fluidly as though over snow.

Fifty-seven miles is not far, something veteran woodsman Jock MacPherson would have sworn to before that first week in September 1889. Babe and the other oxen plodded along a forest trail scarred by ruts from what were obviously previous crossings. Climbing rocky ridges, through vast swamps where muskeg trembled beneath them, over a few precious sandy spots, around lakes, and across shallow streams where tea-brown water seeped between the endless trees, the safari followed the trail. Mosquitoes, vicious little black gnats, and deer flies were constant companions.

On the third day, they reached the Tower and Crescent Lake Lumber Company camp that Marvin Richards had christened Jericho.

Haggarty was head cook of the operation. If he had another name, Henry never heard it. He wore a flaming mustache, its ends curling into tight corkscrews. When Babe and Henry delivered his new stove, Haggarty fussed over it like some lovesick swain over his lady of the hour.

When introduced to his newest helper, Henry swore the man's mustache straightened out like Babe's horns. Haggarty recovered quickly and bowed to Sarah.

"I make the best cup of coffee in Jericho. Help yourself. After that, I'll expect you to keep the pot full."

Six other cutting locations lay around the hub of Richards's headquarters at Jericho: Nind, near the Chippewa Lake Indian reservation; Cusson and Ackerman's Corners to the north; and Togo, Greaney, and Lost Lake to the south.

Supplies continued to arrive at ten-day intervals, including hay for the stock from Koochiching County, sixty miles to the north.

MacPherson and Deerhorn were two of fourteen jacks assigned to erect the Jericho camp. They first built Haggarty's cookshack. MacPherson swung an ax and manned a crosscut saw to help clear a spot. The felled trees were trimmed to become walls or were split into rafters. He wielded a hammer and handsaw while calluses toughened his skin. A log bunkhouse— the first of two such buildings, each large enough for twenty men—came next; Haggarty and Richards would bunk in the cookshack. A mess hall, twenty feet by thirty, was attached to the cookshack. A horse barn would shelter ten Clydesdale horses and the oxen. A shack for the saw sharpener snugged against the blacksmithy.

Next was a long, narrow building partitioned into four twelve-by-fourteen rooms. One was to be Richards's office; one was a commissary, stocked with chargeable goods for the men. One room became lodging for Florenda and Sarah. The last was a medical dispensary—"Dr." Florenda's, in which she was to improvise.

The final project, begun in the middle of October, was a second twenty-man bunkhouse. Finished two months after MacPherson's arrival, it awaited a final contingent of twenty men to fill it.

The leaves of fall had drifted to the ground when the last spike was driven.

43

Henry ended up in one of the bunkhouses.

The bull cook for Jericho camp was a brute named Carlson. He was Haggarty's second in command. As was customary in logging camps, this gave him authority over the bunkhouses. He assigned beds and rode herd on the men to clean up once in a while.

A bunkhouse was a shedlike building, thirty feet long and twenty feet wide. Its ridgepole height was about ten feet, down to six feet high at the side walls. A bench called the deacon's seat ran the length of the place, centered and interrupted halfway by a woodstove. Bunks ranged ten to either side. Those nearest to and parallel to the bench were called side-loaders. Another five placed at right angles outside these beds were named muzzle-loaders. They were preferred because a man could get away from the endless bickering and groans of card players occupying the deacon's seat.

As the youngest peon of the group, Henry was assigned a side-loader next to the door, farthest from the stove. He decided that between the scent of wool clothing hung over ropes to dry each night, unwashed jacks, and bean farts, a breath of frigid, clean air scored as a benefit.

To the uncomplicated men given to working in a logging camp, Henry's race seemed, at worst, a passing curiosity. Some wanted to know whether his skin color rubbed off. A few commented on his accent but good-naturedly. His youth and inexperience were fair game for ribbing, but he sensed that he would have received the same had he been white. Certainly, to Henry's perception, Ashawa was treated no differently than any of his age group.

Henry's relationship with Babe caused far more interest. That he talked to Babe and that the animal obeyed even complicated requests won respect, touched with superstitious fear.

Henry's heft had caught up with his bones. Working alongside the other jacks showed him that he was nearly as strong as most of the others, but logging required skills that came only with the doing.

Babe's assignment was to drag individual logs from the cutting fields to a central collection spot beside the river—the landing. Any time he was needed, Henry worked with Babe (who refused to move a muscle unless the lad was at his side). Logs to be skidded needed first to be cut and trimmed. Babe's work was often confined to three or four days a week.

Henry was expected to become a real jack the rest of the time.

As he watched others go about their jobs, Henry's respect for the skills logging required grew apace. A team working a two-man crosscut saw learned each other's strengths. Take Shag Peterson and Petr Starnovich. They threw a saw back and forth like a couple of fine square dancers. The blade seemed to fly of its own account, with the men merely guiding it.

Pat Dion agreed to try Henry as a partner, but the boy promptly got the blade caught between stump and tree when he wasn't quick enough.

Marvin Richards aimed an Old Testament scowl at Henry. "Most valuable things we got—horses and saws. Break a saw, and you walk back to Tower and fetch another."

Still, working with Babe developed not only skills but—he had to call it—friendship. Henry realized that he had never had a true comrade like Babe.

Life in a bunkhouse was, of necessity, intimate. By unwritten law, a man's bunk was his castle. Inviolate. Henry realized that scuffles were a rarity. Bickering was constant, but it was as though physical conflict was a line not to be crossed.

Henry quickly learned that one of his most important functions was to serve as the butt of good-natured teasing. The greenhorn of the crew. Yet in the process, the crew became a team. And he learned that, to a man, those inarticulate, rough-mannered, uneducated, casually profane men would have stood up to the devil for each other. For him.

Evenings, the three or four hours before everyone retreated to his bunk, the men played cards, sharpened equipment, mended torn clothing, and told stories.

One night in late October …

From his spot beside the door, Henry's view was the whole reach of the bunkhouse. Some men sat on the deacon's seat, others on side-loader bunks. Conversations rumbled and grumbled, a baritone background.

Henry opened his senses.

Winds up north are seldom quiet, as though they have secrets to whisper and not enough time to tell them all. A building as crude as the bunkhouse had many a crack or crevice for a breeze to explore—a whistle, a soft moan to rise and fall like a distant siren. Tireless, the voice of the wilderness.

Does it speak to me now? Henry wondered. *Will it someday?*

Henry's bunkmates came to one of those odd silences that punctuates any conversation.

Petr Starnovich straightened up from his perch on the deacon's seat. "There 'tis, boys. Damn! One's out there."

Henry craned to listen. *What?*

A tree branch with a bit of heft, carried by the talking wind, landed on the roof overhead.

Rat Root Mooney said, "By gar, I believe we got us a *argopelter* on the prowl."

Sven Svendsen said, "Ja, den vee need send some vun out dere; scare dat monster him away before he t'row a whole tree, ja sure."

Petr said darkly, "Remember poor Hans? The time he wolunteered to see vat vas? Never sawed him again, no sir. Chust the ax he tooken wit' him, claw marks scratch into da steel, da bit chewed smack in two. So now, who dare go out dere?"

Bob Maxeiner said, "Vut if he be a *wampus cat*, wit' dose big tooths and claws? Vut den?"

Rat Root jumped to his feet from the deacon's seat. "Quiet! I think I heard ... on the roof? Lord help us if he finds a loose board up there."

Henry shivered.

A swirl of wind. Whooo ...

Josef Stark said, "Dat sound like a hungry *hugag*. One came dat close one night, he did. I wrestled him all de way to de ground. Den I pick-ed him up by de tail—"

"You telled us, t'ousand times," muttered Dave Schmidt.

"Oh ja, dem *hugags*," said Bob Maxeiner. "Dey always wailing liken dey got de heart brokens. I 'member vun time, I vas late coming back to camp an' a big female *hugag* caught me out in de open. She grab me in dat hug what crush a grizzle bear's insides, ja, and she cried all over me. Her tears froze until ven dey finded me, it tooken ten days to thaw me out."

Josef Stark said, "Gott im Himmel, I vas more closer to croaking den you!"

Rat Root Mooney said, "Bad enough. Still, not bad like a *hodag*, all spikes and horns and railroad-spike teeth." He shuddered.

"Somebody need go out there and see for sure," muttered Frank Horner.

"Ja, sure. Only I vonder who?" Sven said.

As one, nineteen men turned toward Henry. Rat Root said, "We can't expect him to go unarmed. Ham, get the *glawackus* whacker."

"The *glawackus*? My God, do you think it possible?"

Hamilton Simons reached under his bunk and came out

with a club to rival Richards's. He handed it to Henry solemnly. "Start swinging the moment you get out the door. They're so quick. If you wait until you actually see one …" Ham jerked his thumb across his neck.

By God, Henry thought, *Simons rubbed away a tear … from his dry cheek?*

Aha!

Henry took the club with a show of reluctance. "Uh, fellas, I'm probably not the one you want to have face this creature."

"You closest to de door," Sven said.

Rat Root nodded solemnly. "An' you don't show as good in the dark. Excepting yer tooths. Don't smile."

"It may yust be de vind," Maxeiner said. "But maybe not."

Henry stood and brandished the cudgel above his head. "Open the door, Richard!"

Dick Farnhorst pulled the door open, and a gust of wind swirled a cloud of fallen leaves into the bunkhouse. Like a spooked herd of buffalo, the men scattered before them toward the other end of the building.

"*Leech leaves!*" shouted Banjo Tom. "Them bloodsuckers'll drain a man's blood and marrow in seconds."

Josef Stark grabbed Banjo's arm. "Vas marrow ist?"

"Dutch, only a *leech leaf* knows, but it's important."

Josef "Dutch" Stark shrieked in a credible tenor. He jumped onto his side-loader.

Arms waved in frantic circles as the men swatted at any leaf to come near them. Henry swung his club with enthusiasm, demolishing two of the invaders. When the leaves settled onto the floor, his bunkmates made a foot-stomping production of dispatching any of the remaining bloodthirsty vermin.

Henry went to the open door and stood as straight as a statue of Stonewall Jackson, sword … well, club … aloft.

"I'm ready!"

He swung the club in swooping arcs and marched into the night. As the door slammed shut behind him, he heard a rasping *sotto voce*, "Hold de door, so's de fearsome critter can't get in."

Sniggers leaked through rough planks of the door.

Henry walked around the bunkhouse, banging its sides lustily as he went. He brushed the building's one window with a branch from a pine tree, lying loose on the ground. He bellowed, "Take that! No, you don't! Agghh!" He grunted as though lifting Babe off his feet. Someone scraped at frost on the inside of the window. Henry crouched beneath it and swept up an armful of dry leaves, crunching them, moaning and groaning. He hoisted himself onto the roof and shuffled noisily across it, from one side to the other.

"Come down here, you scurvy coward!" he shouted. "If I have to climb up there to get you, I promise no mercy."

Henry dropped quietly to the ground, sneaked back to the door, and waited, the club on his shoulder. A minute passed. Maybe two.

Then …

The door opened an inch and then a foot, and a pair of whiskered faces peered around the jamb.

Henry pushed back into the bunkhouse, handed the club to Ham Simons, and sat on the edge of his bunk. Henry stretched. "No monstrous, flesh-eating *hugag*. No *hodag* either."

He waited.

Finally, Rat Root said, "What was all that racket?"

"That? Oh, I just wrestled a Texas cottonmouth snake. Only

a baby, less than thirty feet long. Maybe forty. Seems it followed my scent all the way up north from Texas. Being a water snake, he couldn't keep up with me on land. I told him to head south before he freezes. Had to persuade him a mite, but he's gone now. Probably."

"Forty feet?" Ham Simons muttered.

Rat Root said, "You, uh, talked to him?"

Henry nodded. "I talk to animals, you know. Babe. Moose and deer when I'm hunting. Helps them to die happy. Makes the meat taste better. It's important to talk to snakes, especially those really, really poisonous snakes. Especially those really *big* poisonous ones. After discussing it quietly—somewhat quietly; no trees knocked down or damaged—he and I compromised. I promised not to tie a knot in his tail if he agreed to keep those six-inch fangs of his sheathed."

"Six-inch tooths?" an anonymous voice whispered.

Henry yawned. "See y'all in the morning."

He turned over on his bunk and then raised his head. "A caution—he may be a little sluggish because of the frost out there, but he's still right peckish. How would you like to crawl on your belly for hundreds of miles, and all for nothing? If you see anything about a foot, foot and a half in diameter and fifty, sixty feet long, looking like a debarked white pine, poke it with the stoutest pike you can find before you go close, but be ready to run. They don't actually spit their poison, more a lightning strike, up to twenty feet or so. Well, figure thirty feet to be safe. Safer. Sort of safe. G'night, boys."

A silence lasted five seconds. Maybe six or seven.

A snigger. A chorus of sniggers. Roars of laughter, and those rough-hewn loners, those magnificent fellows, pulled Henry off his bunk to have a rousing, back-thumping, shoulder-poking festival.

How else are real men allowed to express affection for each other?

44

It happened a couple of nights later.

Henry lay on his bunk, half asleep. Winter skulked just beyond an icy horizon, ready to pounce. Restless winds of the North Country had died away to a profound silence. The temperature plunged like a stone dropped from a cliff. Air, clear and cold, sharpened the brilliance of the stars.

Toivo Latvila came into the bunkhouse, his beard white with frost from his breath. The man of few words nodded at the jack named Eight Ball Schwindlehurst. "It has started," he said.

Eight Ball grabbed his jacket. "I'm coming. Anyone else?" His words went unanswered.

Latvila stopped beside Henry's bunk and said, "Maybe you like to come?"

Come?

Henry shivered in the chill loosed when Eight Ball started

to open the door. "What am I missing if I say no?" He waited for a chorus of sniggers from the rest of his bunkmates.

"Ice singing tonight," Toivo said.

"Ice singing? Sure." Henry rolled his eyes.

Eight Ball shrugged. "It's not for everyone, Toivo. Let's go."

They slipped out the door into the waiting stillness of a frozen forest.

Henry glanced at Francisco Plunk in the muzzle-loader next to his bunk. "Whatever the joke was, they didn't try very hard."

Plunk said, "No joke. Dat real. Only happens when it cold gets really fast."

"One of your what? A terror like *hugag?* Singing ice. Well—"

"If you want to hear, have to go now. Won't sing again all winter." Francisco turned over onto his side.

Not a prank? A trip into ear-nipping cold? All right, I should check on Babe anyway.

A dusting of snow reflected just enough starlight that Henry could see faintly. He heard crunches of woodsmen's boots off to his right—Latvila and Schwindlehurst. He called to them, and they stopped.

"You decided to come," Eight Ball said. "You'll be glad you did."

Toivo Latvila led the way through a dense patch of forest that lay outside the contract cutting area. "Half mile," Toivo said.

Henry stopped. "Wait. Is this some glorified snipe hunt?"

"No snipe," said Eight Ball. His voice sounded solemn.

So, singing ice should be more believable than snipes? Henry nearly turned back to the warmth of the bunkhouse and its very human odors. The bickering over cards. Then, the pure sanctity of air breathed for the first time and the odd vision provided by will-o-the-wisp starlight stilled his concerns. He trudged after his comrades.

The men came to the shore of a lake. Round, it looked to be about a mile in diameter. Ice, still bare of snow, had already sealed it for the season.

Eight Ball's hushed voice was barely louder than a whisper. "Minnesota has thousands of lakes, most of them carved out by glaciers. Ice Age times. With some, the ice never sings. We're lucky with this one."

Henry's comrades found a convenient log and sat facing the expanse of new ice. After a moment, he joined them.

Silence swallowed their very breathing. A minute passed, then two. Henry cleared his throat and said, "Fellas, this has been grand, but when does the show begin?"

Toivo's voice was hushed. "Quiet. Listen."

Sit on a frozen log, staring at an anonymous lake covered with ice? Listen to absolute stillness? All right, it's peaceful. Call it meditation.

Then …

A humming began, as light to the ear as the touch of a springtime ray of sunlight is to skin. The sound came from the dimly visible lake before them. Abruptly, its pitch soared and strengthened, until Henry felt it in his bones. Ripples of sound, shapes of sound, reminded Henry of the sinuous curtains of light that graced a northern lights display. Harmonics of harmonics danced up and down a scale from deepest base tones to ethereal whispers of music in a range disappearing above an ear's ability to hear them. Always plaintive, it was as though nature shared some deep anguish and was speaking of a singularity known only to the deep forests. From the left, from the right, directly before them, and again—and on without pause. The chorus was never boisterous, ever plucking at the edge of awareness.

Eight Ball whispered, "Sometimes you can feel the ice when it sings; it quivers under your hand. Just don't freeze to it."

Henry knelt on ice beside the shore and touched his knuckle to its surface. The lake vibrated to the sounds surrounding him.

"What is happening?" he whispered. Any tones louder seemed a profanity against nature.

Eight Ball sighed and responded in kind. "Don't know. Indian friends believe it is the lament of all their ancestors who have drowned through time. Me? I don't worry about explanations. Some things are meant just to be experienced."

Time became an immeasurable dimension. The tormented weeping of freezing water touched something so deep inside the core of him that Henry could give it no name. Tears—homage—streamed down his cheeks and froze where they lay.

The three jacks sat in thrall to such an improbable gift of nature.

The sounds faded finally, like last wisps of a dream.

Eight Ball said, "After that, I can almost believe there is a purpose to life."

"God's whispers," breathed Toivo.

Why not? Amen.

The first real snow fell on Halloween night. To Henry, it somehow put an exclamation point to how isolated the Jericho camp was. The men could not expect to see Tower again before May.

45

Judging from snow's brief appearances in Texas, Henry expected no surprises when it began to fall in the North Country. He awoke that first morning in November to sight of snow two feet deep and still falling in a white deluge. Before the week was out, it had piled up into drifts ten feet deep.

Nature revised Henry's expectations of what a snowstorm could do.

Forty lumberjacks settled into the routines of a logging camp, carrying Henry along with them. He found new respect for his bunkmates when he watched them in their element. He focused all his energy on learning the skills that would make him acceptable in their eyes.

Work was from dawn until dusk, with Sunday the only day off. Then, camp foreman Richards gathered everyone into the mess hall, where he insisted on reading aloud from the Bible. That ended one day in November. Francisco Plunk, who used the muzzle-loader next to Henry's bunk, announced during Richards's Old Testament reading, "*Mon Dieu*, the man sounds like a duck." Forty jacks sniggering in unison made short work of the solemnity of Exodus.

Isolation from society did not mean isolation from all of life's scourges. Bedbugs and gray backs—lice—appeared almost before the men had settled in. Despite the poverty of Henry's childhood—and due to the diligence of his mama, Henry acknowledged—such freeloaders had been unknown to him.

He decided that bedbugs took a heap of getting used to. Where they came from was never settled, but they prospered in the hay mattresses and pine boughs of the bunkhouses. The men burned the old and brought in new; they stripped and scrubbed with lye soap created by Sarah. Bull Cook Carlson boiled their clothing. If it slowed the beasties down, it couldn't have been for more than a night or two.

Lice were sly, Henry realized. He couldn't always tell by looking at a man whether he was a hotel for the miserable critters. Like everything else in Jericho, the men shared gray backs.

Rat Root Mooney announced the first gray-back derby of the winter in early November.

Eight Ball explained to Henry: to race lice, each jack captured a specimen from his own head. It was considered unsportsmanlike to use another's. The critters entered in the race were placed in the center of a frying pan, which was then heated over the bunkhouse woodstove. Lice as sluggardly as a jack on Sunday morning quickly developed an interest in running. The winner was that louse first to the edge of the pan. Its prize was a return to the head of its owner. The rest ended up in the fire. Bets were paid off in the currency of a logging camp—Copenhagen, precious snuff.

Another Sunday diversion was dancing. The mess hall was cleared of tables for the occasion. The practice had always been to designate half of the men as female. As the youngest, Henry was first chosen. John Savage played the fiddle. His music resembled the braying of a donkey, but it kept more rhythm than not. Quiet Toivo Latvila, the camp saw filer, burst out of his Finnish shell on dance evenings to stomp his feet and wave his hands elegantly. The moment the music stopped, he reverted to being the silent Finn. Henry liked dancing with Toivo. The man's grace made Henry feel as though he knew what he was doing.

Henry's status as the greenhorn acknowledged to be the clumsiest jack in camp left him far down the social scale—until the day Richards sent him out hunting for fresh meat.

Henry had not fully appreciated how much he had learned from Sarah about stalking game. He brought in a deer within the first three hours. Eight Ball Schwindlehurst, Ole Oleanson, and Pat Dion returned in late afternoon with a brace of rabbits.

Francisco Plunk asked that night from his bunk, "Was dat

deer more'n luck? Eight Ball told me he tramp all day an' all he seen was tracks in de snow."

Henry grinned. He understood.

Eight Ball was a genial chap. He had been a schoolteacher until a thirst for whiskey had become more compelling than that for teaching.

Henry explained to him, "Don't chase the deer. Find a trail, make a blind or climb a tree, and then wait for them to come to you."

Henry cornered Richards one day. "I'll keep us supplied with deer, moose, and fish from the river if you free me up occasionally." The day he shot his first moose, Babe dragged it into camp. To say that Richards came to respect the youth seemed contrary to his religion. Nevertheless, Henry became the official hunter.

46

Henry pondered. His basic sensitivity to the feelings of others was especially fine tuned in his relationship with Sarah. Something was driving the MacPhersons apart. He decided that the reasons included an element of South versus North. Call it South adapting to extreme North. Add in stress resulting from the mining fiasco with its barroom sequel, the *kitchi giwashkwebi*, to borrow an Ojibwe phrase for a historic drunk, a term loaned to him by Ashawa. Exile to Jericho seemed to have confirmed for Sarah that life had whirled out of control, consequences that she was not shrugging off. Henry's affection for her and his respect for Jock meant that the coolness between the two adults felt personal to him.

Logging camps were conceived as bachelor institutions. Florenda moved her bedroll into the infirmary, leaving room for Sarah and Jock to share sleeping space. Oh, Henry heard no recriminations. What passed between the MacPhersons was an awful politeness, more chilling than sharp words. If Henry had put more stock in his mama's Southern Baptist sweet Jesus, he'd have prayed for them. Still, when the time to celebrate Jesus's birth rolled around in late December …

In the odd way of weather up north, on December 23, it warmed up into the midthirties—sixty degrees warmer than it had been two nights before. Dance night moved outdoors to the open space in the center of camp. Sweet air.

Henry helped eager jacks shovel off every trace of horse shit. Stomping feet compacted snow into a polished veneer. Clyde Prommersberger brought a twelve-foot white spruce tree and stuck it into a snow bank. Strings of popcorn and dried high-bush cranberries hung from its branches. A dozen hurricane lanterns surrounded the dance area. John Savage tuned his fiddle (roughly), and Rat Root Mooney came out with a harmonica.

Dancing began. Savage's fiddle heated up, inviting foot-stomping rhythms. Grotesquely coy "female" jacks mimed their visions of feminine coquetry, matching rough-shod gallantry by partners. Rat Root punctuated agonized wailing from his harmonica with shouts of "Hoo, hoo, hoo!" and "Eeyow!"

Henry felt something compelling about mindless stomping around in an exuberance of animal spirits. Call it relief from the drudgery that is logging, with its forced isolation. It was a time to forget the discomforts of camp. He freed his very soul as though opening an iron gate.

As he swung in some vague rendition of an allemande left, he spied MacPherson standing by himself, outside the ring of lanterns.

Jock's face was frozen in gloom, even as he watched the rest of the men comport themselves.

Then …

John Savage's scratchy fiddle slid far off scale. Rat Root Mooney ended a "hoo, hoo," one "hoo" short. Prancing jacks collided into an amorphous mass when the music stopped.

John Savage's voice rang clearly in the still air. "I'll be damned."

Florenda and Sarah stood just outside the ring of lanterns. Sarah wore her dress. The dress. The only dress she had brought with her from the farm. She had coiffed her hair into a coil atop her head.

And Florenda? In a way, from the point of view of a son, Henry had never thought of her as a *woman* woman. He'd never considered what she might look like to others or how she might interact with a man.

Mama?

She had made cornrow braids of her hair. Her old plaid shirt—her grungy cotton shirt—was … alluring? *Analyze, Henry,* he thought. Three top buttons were open, and the body of the shirt somehow was drawn taut, artfully emphasizing that she had a figure of the kind a man's eye is drawn to faithfully. Such features were admired in girls swimming alongside in life's stream, but his *mama*? Unlike Sarah, Florenda had brought no actual dress to Jericho. She had stitched a pair of flour sacks together, colored them with broad, vivid, horizontal stripes, and wore them as a skirt.

The men murmured approval.

Florenda pulled Sarah determinedly into the circle of light. She announced in a clarion voice, "Y'all, the ladies are waitin'."

Not a jack stirred. Henry wondered if they even drew breath. He understood. After listening to conversations as they swirled around the bunkhouse, he realized the dilemma these tongue-tied roughs faced. Loners almost to a man, they dealt with normal appetites at the whorehouse in town. There, a woman was just that—female. But how should they address a woman who was far more, yet still so clearly a woman?

Toivo Latvila broke the spell. He marched up to Florenda and bowed. He offered his arm. Florenda smiled. Henry had never seen the look that shone on her face right then. Call it ... coquettish? His mama?

Florenda bobbed her head and accepted Toivo's arm like a society lady at a ball.

Rat Root Mooney stuck the harmonica in his pocket and bounded into the circle before Sarah. He bowed until his nose barely cleared the snow.

"Begorrah, young lady, I'd be most honored."

Sarah glanced at MacPherson, skulking in the gloom beyond the lanterns, and curtsied a quick bob.

Dancing began with renewed vigor.

John Savage finally took a ten-minute break. Jacks, those unlettered, humble woodsmen, found some excuse to be in the neighborhood of Sarah or Florenda for a question, a comment, or a silence as eloquent as any paean.

Henry searched for MacPherson and spied him just as Jock spun on his heel and headed toward the room he still shared with Sarah.

As he disappeared into gloom outside the circle of lamps, he stopped abruptly and stumbled back a step and then another. A force propelled him.

Babe, all ton and a half of him, pushed against MacPherson's chest with his broad blue forehead. His horns gleamed wickedly in the light from the lanterns. Babe herded the man implacably. A butt with his head, a turn of one horn to head off an attempt to slide away, a quick turn with the other, and Babe deposited Jock before Sarah.

Staccato rumbles came from his throat and chest.

MacPherson sputtered, "You have no right—"

More rumbles. Henry laughed out loud when he translated. Jock said, "Don't you call me—"

Sarah turned away quietly.

By well-calculated *chance*, Henry arrived next to her, and again by pure chance, he tripped her when he tried to move aside, such that out of courtesy he wrapped her in his arms to keep her from falling, when by oddest chance he himself tripped, propelling her straight against MacPherson's chest.

Some might call it reflex, but guided by whatever impulse, Jock tightened his arms around Sarah's shoulders, and by whatever odd reflex came into play, Sarah slid her arms around Jock's neck, perhaps for stability.

When she seemed to loosen her arms, by the oddest chance of all, Florenda squeezed past Petr Starnovich and tripped also, plastering herself against Sarah's back, holding her in place. Just for a moment, just for a precious moment, just …

Jock and Sarah looked at each other from nose-tip distance. She began to cry and so, by God, did MacPherson. They clung to each other without one iota of help from family, and Henry doubted that they were aware of anyone else.

Someone began to clap and then another. It took only a breath or two more before that bunch of tough, uneducated, hard-bitten, profane, unwashed bachelors burst into roars of approval. Backs were pounded and eyes wiped ... the cold, mind you. Jacks don't cry. *By God,* Henry confessed to himself, *I'm a jack too!*

He let the tears freeze on his face.

Florenda began to croon. Henry had heard the lilt of her singing all his life and had wrapped himself in its comfort when she chased away life's terrors. In the quiet, cold air and the hush of his suspended breathing, the sound of her voice plucked aside aspirations of maturity, and Henry recaptured the safety of her arms and breast as when she had held him tight. A peace surpassing all understanding flooded his chest.

That night Florenda filled the crisp, still air with magic. She sang "Silent Night," "It Came Upon a Midnight Clear," and "Oh Little Town of Bethlehem." She shared Southern croonings without words, as plaintive as a prayer for hope in a sea of despair.

Without noticing—perhaps without anyone being aware— everyone circled up behind the lanterns, leaving Florenda alone in the middle of the cleared area. Forty jacks and the family, including Babe, held hands—well, horns in Babe's case.

Henry smiled. There was a thing about his mama. She was never solemn for long.

She turned slowly, scanning those in the ring around her. A twitch of her shoulders and of her hips and then her feet broke free, and she began a tantalizing cakewalk strut. She threw back her head and laughed. "It a *birthday* party! Sweet Jesus declare, be happy. Dat mean *yo*." She pointed at dour Marvin Richards, standing aloof from everyone else. "An' y'all." It was a spinning, sweeping invitation, her arms flung wide.

She marched up to Toivo Latvila and held out her hand. She called to John Savage, "Mr. Fiddler Man, play us a lively tune."

Savage fiddled as though he had suddenly been gifted with talent. Jacks stomped in unison. Babe bobbed his head and bellowed with the authority of Gabriel's horn. In the middle of that charmed circle, Toivo and Florenda twirled and strutted and waltzed and two-stepped and swung in gravity-denying circles. They promenaded in a grand parade before gliding to a finish in each other's arms. Toivo smiled, his entire stoic face involved. He held a bow before kissing the back of Florenda's hand.

Henry had never loved Mama as much as he did right then.

When at last the lanterns were extinguished, and the men wandered off to the bunkhouses, Babe remained, standing quietly. He made no attempt to fathom the symbolism of the evening, but he understood and resonated to the cheer emanating from his Two-Legs comrades.

A lone figure remained in the clearing, one kneeling in the snow ...

Babe edged closer.

Richards shouted at his God. He screamed scriptures denouncing the debaucheries of Sodom and Gomorrah; the fleshly sins of Jezebel; the evil of Salome, the whore of Israel, who coveted the head of John the Baptist; the treachery of Delilah. He called down divine wrath onto the black demon descended from the loins of Ham, who had aroused lust in his men—they, simple clods of clay. He wept and threatened and pleaded … and pinched his legs tightly together in a vain attempt at containment.

Watching silently in the star-speckled darkness, Babe stood as a guardian between the rest of his intimate herd and the foreman. He did not leave his position until Richards finally stumbled into the cookshack to collapse on his bed of despair.

47

The seventh day of February that year of 1890 was so cold that when a man spat, tobacco juice froze before it hit the ground. Ashawa felt sharp pain in his nose if he drew breath too rapidly. He pulled a muffler across his face, leaving only his eyes showing. Snow crunched under foot, and if two icicles were banged together, they rang softly, as though they were formed of metal.

A team of four Clydesdale horses pulled a dray loaded with sixteen-foot logs, each between two and two and a half feet in diameter. The load loomed twelve feet high above the driver, who walked beside the dray. Ashawa Deerhorn held reins in his hands.

The angle of decline in the trail they followed wasn't much by Jericho standards, but forty-eight-below-zero temperatures made judging friction uncertain. Ashawa pulled back on the brake handle of the dray to slow its descent. An ominous squeak told of runners losing traction to run ahead on their own. Ashawa dug in with the brake to keep the dray from riding onto the horses.

Unseen by Ashawa, a boulder stuck out of the snow off to the side of the track. The right-hand runners of the dray rode over the top of it. A dozen logs creaked and groaned.

Behind Ashawa, Pritch Connor screamed, "Jump! Ta hell outta there!"

Ashawa looked up to see the load tipping his way. He leaped to his left, floundering through waist-deep snow. The dray's side poles snapped with sounds like rifle shots.

He didn't quite make it; a log pinned his right leg against a rock.

Casino was the lead horse. He nickered twice and tossed his head. He pranced in his harness. Pritch Connor floundered through snow and used a peavey to roll the log off Ashawa's leg.

Then pain hit.

Ashawa stuffed snow into his mouth in a vain attempt to stopper a scream, a groan. He lifted his leg. It flopped between his ankle and his knee.

He knew the kind of trouble he faced.

Pritch and Rat Root and Petr and John Savage and Banjo Tom picked up Ashawa as tenderly as would a mother her newborn. They carried him on a toboggan and skidded it into Florenda's dispensary.

Florenda looked at Ashawa's leg and blanched. "Sweet Jesus."

"He's in pain, Doc," Pritch said.

She covered her mouth with both hands. *Doc? I ain't no real doc. Dear God, my pride done trippin' me up.* She leaned against the wall.

Henry edged into the cramped dispensary. He steadied his mama and gave her a quick hug. He turned to the men, who were stricken as mute as the trees they cut down. "Outside. Give Mama room." He herded them into the open. "Pritch and Petr, pound together two sawhorses. Banjo, fetch Sarah. John, tell Richards I'm going to need that laudanum he has locked up somewhere. Also, the plaster of Paris we toted in last fall." He surveyed their anxious faces. "Mooney, you are going to help us fix his leg. Stay here. The rest of you, scat."

The men scattered. Henry went back inside the dispensary. "Mama, we're going to need your bedroll for after we're done. Let's get his pants off. Cut off, likely." He took Florenda's shoulders and smiled at her from close range. "We gonna do this, Mama. You'll see." He kissed her forehead.

He squatted beside Ashawa on the toboggan. "Y'all have to know this is going to hurt. We won't make it worse than we have to, but there it is."

Ashawa nodded. "I'll do my part."

"Good, Uncle Ashawa. Ah … do you mind if I call you uncle?"

Ashawa's face showed a glimmer of a smile. "An honor."

Henry located his precious *Gray's Anatomy* book. "I want to study."

An hour later, after a sizable dose of laudanum, Ashawa had dozed off. Rat Root Mooney and Henry lifted the toboggan onto the sawhorses. Deerhorn's leg had swollen to half again its normal size. Bruised and abraded, there was no open wound, no splinter of bone protruding. Florenda had ended up cutting his pant leg along the seam. Henry decided to use Ashawa's grimy long-john underwear legging as an under pad for the cast he was going to make.

Haggarty brought a bucket of hot water from the cookshack when Henry sent word that he was ready. He made a squishy paste of plaster of Paris and then dipped a dozen yard-long strips of towels and flour sacks, torn three inches wide, into the goop. He gathered a handful of plaster and strips.

"Uncle Ashawa, now comes your part," Henry said. "This is going to hurt. Mama, I want you to hold Ashawa's ankle the way I showed you. Pull down on his leg. Hold it steady and straight. Mooney, I want you to lift his thigh off the toboggan, with the knee bent just a little, and hold it until I say quit. Ready?

"Let's go."

The unlikely crew of Henry, Florenda, and Mooney captured Ashawa's leg in a cocoon of plaster and torn-up flour sacks. They propped up his leg in a sling of canvas suspended from the ceiling. The cast looked remarkably professional. Ashawa dozed away in a God-given cloud of laudanum.

The problem reared its head the very same night, when Ashawa's need to piss became a crisis. He snarled, "I'm getting out of this contraption."

Florenda held out an old can. "You's usin' dis, like I tol' yo."

"Over my dead body."

"Yo din't kill yo' body. Yo jes' bust a stem. Use the can."

"I won't let no woman watch me do that."

"No? Well, I got big news fer yo, Mr. Deerhorn. T'ain't no treat watchin' yo pee. I tells yo one thing fer sure. I ain't changing no wet bedding."

"I got to go really bad."

She gave him back the offending can. "I tells yo one more thing. I birthed a son, so I's used to how a man do it. Get busy."

After he finished and handed over the brimming can, Ashawa muttered, "You docs are as grumpy as damn wolverines."

A smile broke up the grimness of Florenda's face. "Fine. I be yo' Doc Wolverine. But y'all, now—yo stubborn as a Southern mule. I likes my animal better." She laughed from her belly, and Ashawa finally joined her.

Maybe it was his laudanum talking.

The plan was to transport Ashawa back to Tower three or four days later. Babe insisted that he would pull the toboggan. Richards was actually inarticulate over events. Rambling threats seemed to include everything but imminent hanging.

The issue became moot on the day they had planned to leave. During the night, it began to snow. And snow. It was impossible to work on the job, and travel was unthinkable. The people of Jericho were as marooned as the Robinson family of literature. Snow piled onto the buildings of camp, and activity shifted to shoveling off roofs in danger of collapsing under its weight. "Doc" Florenda Wolverine was stuck with her patient.

Ashawa wriggled his shoulders and hips, seeking a more comfortable fit with the toboggan that still served as his bed.

Florenda dragged the only chair in the dispensary to sit

beside him. "It time to settle somethin'. We cuts yo' hair down to de scalp."

"No."

"Yes. I been po' all my life, but one thing I can't never abide is lice." Her shiver was a shudder. "Yo stay in my place; yo gets rid of yo' hair."

"Then I move out today," Ashawa said.

"What talk is dat? Yo can't move outta dat sling."

"Who says?"

"Henry says, an' he got the book what shows yo' parts. Only way to get shet them lice bugs is by goin' bald fer a while."

Ashawa struggled to sit up and then grabbed the sides of the toboggan. He plopped back. "I won't cut my hair. A man is a man because of his hair."

"Like ol' man Samson? S'pose I shaves off those bushy sides, leavin' yo' braid an' a stripe down de middle? Mebby we can get rid dem lice from dat part."

"A Mohawk cut? But I'm not an Iroquois."

"No, more's the sorry. What yo are is one pain in de ass. Y'all choose—bald or a Mohawk." She snipped the air near Ashawa's ear.

Before Ashawa realized, she had skinned his head bare.

"Imagine dat," Florenda said. "My hand done slipped."

He grumbled and snorted, saying finally, "I have a cousin who claims to be half Seneca. I'd've gone with the Mohawk."

"Fine. When it grow out, y'all give it a try. Lean over the side," Doc Wolverine said brusquely.

She doused Ashawa's shiny head in kerosene from Haggarty's supply, searched for nits, repeated the kerosene rinse, shampooed it with a bar of lye soap, and dried it with a soft flour sack.

"I declares yo fit to share my room," she said. "Now, I's blowin' out de candle."

He heard her crawl between blankets in the far corner of the room.

48

The men dropped by to see "Doc Florenda" from time to time. Ashawa had a firsthand seat to watch her practice her art. Rat Root Mooney developed an abscess on his butt. Ashawa flinched and turned away when Doc lanced it.

On his way back outdoors, Mooney rubbed Ashawa's scalp bristle against the grain and yipped a non-Indian's version of an Indian war cry.

Ole Svendsen stepped on a hot coal that had escaped the stove. He squinted at Ashawa. "Is you dat's? By gar, she scalped you close."

Florenda gave Ole a half ounce of petroleum jelly. She winked at Ashawa. "Dat soothe his mind while things heal."

Banjo Tom cut his shin with an ax while splitting firewood. She stitched the five-inch wound, to Tom's vociferous admiration.

He said to Ashawa, "How you gonna keep warm?"

After he had departed, Florenda asked Ashawa, "Why he called Banjo? He don' play no music."

Ashawa chuckled. "His shape. He's skinny like a pole up top; round like a banjo when you get to his butt."

"Dat kinda cruel."

"It's accurate."

Then there was Horace Hanson—Horse's Ass to his comrades. He didn't jump fast enough, and the limb of a falling tree struck his shoulder. Florenda merely snorted when Ashawa pointed out the poetry in his nickname. On the assumption that something might have broken, she borrowed a dish towel from Haggarty and fashioned a sling.

Concentrated on his own misery, Horse's Ass merely raised his eyebrows at Ashawa's appearance.

Between such emergencies, Florenda tended to Ashawa. She rubbed his back when the skin became irritated, brought his meals, doled out laudanum, and served as a human crutch when the time came that he could tolerate the pain while hopping about his prison.

And they talked.

Long, dark evenings invited talking. A candle guttered on the small table in one corner. *Save the wax drippings so Sarah can make another candle*, Florenda thought. She tended the small woodstove that held winter's mighty grip at bay. She sat on the floor, her back against the wall opposite Ashawa's toboggan/ cot. He lay on his back or sat up while dangling his good leg.

One night Ashawa asked, "You were a slave?"

Florenda said, "Yo wants to know … why?"

"My people been treated bad enough. Killed just because

we were where another person wanted to be, pushed onto reservations, our traditions ignored. Yet being straight-out owned by someone, that didn't happen. Even when I put my mind to it, I can't imagine what it would be like. I have trouble with the idea of owning Babe, as though I could own his soul."

"Do y'all see Babe as havin' a soul?"

Ashawa pondered. "Ain't ever put the idea to a test. But yes, I see him as an unusually large person."

"Halleluiah, sweet Jesus. Yo see real good."

"You don't have to answer my question. It's none of my business."

"Then I's tellin' yo." She clasped her hands and tightened her fingers into knots. She looked toward the candle as though mesmerized. Her resonant contralto tones suddenly became a hesitant whine, childlike.

"It twenty-five years since gov'ment say I's a free person. Massa Munson, he owned de plantation, along wit' Mama, my two brothers, my sisters, an' me." She wiped her cheek with the back of her hand. "A while after the war ended, two Union soldiers come by, one dem a lieutenant. Dey checkin' to see we been freed. Massa, he gather us slaves in front his big house. He march back an' forth, shoutin', shakin' his fists at us, his face all red. 'Y'all wan' yo' freedom? Think it so easy? Yo got it now, wit' outten me havin' a say. So y'all get outta the houses I been givin' yo to live in. No more feedin' y'all an' yo' brats. No more free clothes. Out, out, out. Yo been usin' my things. I's a generous man, so I givin' yo the clothes on yo' backs, but try to take one stitch more an' I calls down the sheriff on all of yo worthless scum.'

"That's how I left. A fifteen-year-old slave girl without a

thing he allowed me to call my own, walkin' down a road to places I'd never seen or heard of. White people lined up 'long side de road, dere faces so twisted with hate dey din't look human. Spittin'. Throwin' rocks an' horse shit. Hollerin' at us. Chased by dogs. My brother shot dead when he tried to grab a few cobs of corn for us to eat. We din't dare try to bury him …"

She wiped both cheeks with the heels of her hands. "They was twenty-five of us when we started. We realized we needed to split up; we too much like an army. I had my skill. Missus Munson taught me how to sew, fancy work or heavy duty, like canvas."

She paused, smiling. "Missus Munson the onliest one treated me like a person. Massa Munson beat on her too, whenever he din't have a slave at hand to hit. I t'ink about dat—no one emancipated Missus Munson.

"She gived me her very own ivory-back hairbrush a week before we freed. She musta known what was comin'. I determined not to leave it behind, so I waited till dark and sneaked back to our shack to git it. Dat, at least, the massa din't git from me!"

Florenda lapsed into silence. She held her head high. Light from the candle held steady. It brushed her ebony cheeks, and shadows chiseled her features into a sculptor's dream.

"My God," Ashawa breathed, "you are a beautiful woman."

Florenda froze; then rose to her feet in a single abrupt movement. Her eyes flashed in the wan light, as though light originated from within them. Her breath came in ragged pants. "Go to sleep, you *disgusting* man!"

She fumbled her way to the door. She ran into the icy breath of a northern winter night, running until the cold penetrated her anguish. She curled up alongside Babe in the barn. He lifted clean hay with his horn to cover her where she slept, finally, against his flank.

49

During the week that followed, Florenda tended to Ashawa with diligence.

Except …

Ashawa pondered the difference. She had scrubbed her words and actions of any warmth.

They sat in silence at their accustomed places, he on the edge of his pallet; she opposite him on the floor against the wall. A fire crackled cheerily in the little stove that kept thirty-below-zero winter at bay. Light from a single candle bravely held back darkness; held Ashawa's gaze until its flame swelled to become all that he saw …

My people, he thought, *the men of my people so value stoicism. The very face of bravery, honored above most other virtues. Yet this new—stoicism?—in my nurse, leaves me feeling as chilled as would the nighttime cold outside the cabin. Bah! The woman is merely another symbol of life's instability. Now you got it, now you don't.*

Times change, and the traditions revered by my ancestors are stomped into the mud under boots of uninvited hordes from across the sea. How to keep to tradition in a world where there is talk of carriages that run by some contained fire or by electricity?

That force itself such a mystery—invisible within fine wires, yet with the strength to operate huge machinery. A birch-bark canoe becomes a relic when massive boats made of steel float, defying all logic. Birch-bark wigwams or lodges of skins and poles disappear from traditional odenas, the villages of my people, replaced by ugly cubicles made of flat, planed boards.

This woman Florenda. Her gently chiding warmth lifted my spirits. Brought a smile to my lips. I can't deny that I became dependent on it. When she abruptly turned as cold and unyielding as ice sealing Jericho's river, I felt abandoned.

And what did I say to trigger it?

"My God," I'd said. "You're a beautiful woman."

Fury so unexpected, of an intensity to scald. Does a man ever understand a woman? In the way two men who hunt together or share a beer understand each other? He snorted softly. Does a woman really know what a man wants? Does she care? *Kitchi Manitou,* for what purpose do a man and a woman both exist? Surely, you could have figured out a simpler way for the people to perpetuate themselves.

He punched a fist into the other palm.

Her voice startled him out of his revere. "You upset?"

"You spoke to me."

"Yes."

"Why?"

"It been too quiet."

"Oh."

"Do yo want it quiet?" she asked.

"Not this quiet."

"Good." She arranged a pillow of blankets between her shoulders and leaned against it. "What you like to talk about?"

My God, not sparrow chatter, he thought. *Think.*

He said, "You talk different at different times. Like now, you're talking almost regular."

She laughed, the kind that made an answering smile inevitable. "You've noticed that I do that?"

"Jock told me once that if you get riled up, you talk regular, and other times you talk plantation."

"He has it backward. The way I talk usually depends on what effect I want to make."

He shook his head. "Now you're mocking me."

Her face became troubled, and she shook her head. "Oh no, I would not do that to you. It goes back to what we discussed last week."

He winced. "I'm sorry if I offended you. I really didn't mean anything."

She smiled, and it was warm and relaxed. "I know. About talking—hear me. I can speak as well as Sarah when I want to. She's given me years of practice. Let me tell you what my explosion was about.

"When you are a slave, your daily existence is at the whim of people who consider you to be an expensive form of stock animal. Kill one of us, and neighbors or the sheriff shrug, merely wondering why waste an investment? None of them has any concern that someone like me has thoughts, feelings, abilities. They wouldn't care if it did occur to them."

She snorted. "Show initiative, and you get labeled uppity. Not good! Walk with a shuffle, let your lower lip sag, look down and say 'yassuh' when anyone talks to you, and the river flows quietly. Dumb nigger; everything normal. I bother to maintain the façade only up to a point.

"I'm intelligent, the worst possible thing for a slave to be. I'm also stubborn, and eventually I fight back. In Possum Creek, that could get you whipped, even lynched."

She leaned across the space between them and touched fingertips with Ashawa. "You didn't deserve the reaction you got when you asked me about being a slave. Most of the time, I lock those horrors in the deepest dungeon of my soul. Your simple, honest remark reawoke, *on that instant*, every terror of what my life had been. I could scarcely breathe. My heart battered my chest."

Her voice rose, taut. "Panic! Run from the hounds! Men in white sheets swinging bull whips and nooses. Wild-eyed hatred and filth screamed loud, and not a one to care when my beloved husband is spitted on the sword of a *gentleman* for accidentally getting mud on a woman's skirt! Oh, oh, sweet Jesus! How can you allow such a thing to happen?"

She huddled, her face in her hands. Ashawa slid awkwardly off his bed and hopped across the room. He collapsed beside her, and gathered her into his arms.

She clung to him and sobbed. "Ashawa, why do humans treat each other that way?"

The candle burned out before Ashawa released her to lie back on her blankets, asleep in a near coma.

50

Another evening.

Florenda felt a sense of comradeship like a warm blanket, softening their conversation. During a lull, she said, "You never tell about yourself."

Ashawa shrugged. "What's to tell? I'm just a thirty-eight-year-old *Anishinabe* with an obsolete past and a future going nowhere."

She frowned. "That's unfair. I've told you about my past. What you said makes me feel naked for saying so much."

He shook his head, a quick jerk. He sighed. "What do you want to know?"

She watched him solemnly. "Are you married?"

"Not church married. I spread blankets with a woman years ago, but she left one day. A guy from Canada, I think mostly because he had a way to get whiskey."

He rubbed his face. "I'm from the Grand Portage band of the Ojibwe tribe. Or Chippewa, as whites say it. That's a reservation on the north shore of Lake Superior. They tell us that Grand Portage … *Kitchi Onigaming* … is the oldest continuously occupied town in Minnesota, because of the fur trade a couple hundred years ago.

"It was the place where voyageurs traveled by canoe to bring a winter's catch of furs from as far away as the Canadian Northwest Territories. There they met the large British fur company cargo canoes. Trade goods were exchanged for the furs. My parents, their parents, back even further were born there. I was a fisherman on *Kitchigami* … Lake Superior, until—" His voice broke.

He sighed. "*Kitchigami* in November is treacherous. I fished with my brother James for a living. It was a calm day, but James looked out across the water, up the hills, and sniffed the air. 'Going to storm,' he said. 'We'd better not go.'

"I was cocky-young; he, my overcautious big brother. I complained that we'd lose fish in the net if we missed a day. I said, 'I'll row both ways—'" Ashawa tapped a fist in the other palm. "He gave in." His face twisted. "We were about two miles out from shore. We hoisted nets loaded with trout. I crowed about our catch, until James said, 'Drop the net! Head for home. Now!'

"I looked over my shoulder. A storm front, with clouds dark and swirling, roared over the hill above Grand Portage Bay. Within two minutes, it slammed into our boat like the fist of *Manitou*. I pulled on the oars with all my strength, trying to head into that monstrous wind, but I … I couldn't hold it. We broached and flipped over. We wallowed in waves suddenly crashing around us. The boat floated upside down and waterlogged. James came up on the other side from me. The water in Superior is always cold.

"We clung onto the boat until we were numb. The temperature dropped like a stone. My hands, covered with ice ... James looked across at me. His head was ice-capped ... he looked almost peaceful. He said, 'Honor our father and tell Mama good-bye. Be good to her.' Then his hands slid off the boat. He smiled at me and just ... disappeared. Eventually, my other brother spotted me and dragged me ashore.

"James was never found. Lake Superior doesn't often return those it claims. After that, I drifted without a compass." Ashawa smiled wryly. "Ended up a miner for half a day. A jack."

Florenda's cheeks were awash in tears. "Have you forgiven yourself for James?"

"I ..."

"You should. I believe James did."

He hunched over. He stiffened with a sob ... and then another. A wail forced its way past clenched teeth.

Florenda sat beside him on the edge of his pallet and cried along with him.

51

One evening, Ashawa said, "This cast stinks. I believe it's getting loose too. Maybe we could take it off."

"Tomorrow," Florenda said. "It's been six weeks. I wonder how long it takes for a bone to heal."

He waved his cast around. "It doesn't hurt anymore." He plunked down beside her on the floor.

She rested her chin on one hand. "Does your name mean anything in Indian?"

"Nothing special. I have an Ojibwe name, chosen by ... well, you people call him a medicine man. I'm told that there was a ceremony when I was a baby. All very solemn. He meditates, offers tobacco as a sacrifice, prays, and dances and sings until the spirits advise him. He—or they—chose *Wawashkeshi Eshkan*— deer horn in English. I've only heard you called Florenda. Do you have a special name?"

She said softly, "A slave is called whatever Massa want to call her."

He inspected her closely and touched her cheek.

"What?" she said.

"I dasn't say what I'm thinking."

"I give you permission."

He shrugged. "No matter; it's true. You are a beautiful woman." He held his breath.

She looked past his shoulder, gathering thoughts and harnessing feelings. "I was fourteen that day. Hot like it gets in Texas. I wore a light dress. Missus Munson had given me tasks indoors, a kindness because of the heat. Massa Munson called to me from his office—'Come here, you.' He close the door, circle around me, looking. Looks that feel like groping. He … he grab my breasts through the dress. Pinched until dey hurts. He touch me like dat all de time when Missus not close by. 'Take it off,' he say.

"I pretend dumb, but he knock me against de desk. He yank de front of my dress an' rip it down de middle. It fall 'round my ankles. I cryin'. 'Yo can't do dis,' I say. 'I's only fo'teen.' He say, 'Yo *nothin'* but my bitch slave. I do what I wants.' He rip off my underwear, grab my hair, pull me to my knees, an' unbutton his pants. 'Suck,' he say and yank my head against … I bit him, I did, an' he yowl like a kicked cat.

"Dat's when he say dat, jes' after he rip off my clothes. 'My God, you a beautiful woman,' he say, 'an' my own bitch slave.' After I bite him, he's say … he say, 'I's teachin' yo,' an' he hit me in de face over an' over, jes' before he … he rape me on de floor."

Her eyes focused on a horror out of a past of hopelessness, and she was beyond tears. "Missus Munson, she heared me scream. She march in de room like General Robert E. Lee arrivin', an' she point a shotgun straight at where he pants s'pose to be. She toss me a robe an' tol me go in de hallway. Out there, I hear a bang like thunder, an' she follow me.

"'He gonna live,' she say, 'an' lucky I's not a better shot.' For jes' a few seconds, she look me straight an' … an' … she hug me an' say soft an' warm, 'You like a daughter, child, but … ' She pat my cheek like she meant it. 'Use cold rags on the swelling. Now, get yourself to de quarters an' stay outta sight.'

"I worked in the fields after that—pickin' cotton, hoein' the kitchen garden. He never look at me that way again, but my brother, my mama, he beat them, nagged and cursed at them, found a hundred excuses to fault them. I wished—how I wished—that I had never fought back, 'cause he crippled my brother, the one he called Rastus."

Ashawa gathered her in his arms as gently as though she were fragile. She held for a short while; then pushed against his chest.

"I need to know something." She scooted back tight against her wall. "You, Mr. Ashawa Deerhorn, do you want me?"

He opened his mouth and finally said, "More than I know how to say."

She pointed to the toboggan. "Sit up there. Now!"

He struggled to his feet and sat on the edge of the toboggan. "Look, I apologize."

"Hush."

She stood, her gaze intent on Ashawa.

252 | ROGER A. MACDONALD

Light from the candle in a corner lit her face from the side—smooth, without expression. She unbuttoned her shirt and let it slide off her shoulders onto the floor. Her woodsman's pants and a pair of worn underpants joined it. She turned slowly, and soft light took intimacies as it caressed her form. She teased a blanket loose from her bedroll and draped it around her body and over her head. She was transformed into a medieval monk. She knelt on the bedroll.

"I'm here," she said from inside her cowl. She bowed her head and waited.

Ashawa slid off the pallet to kneel before her. He eased the blanket from around her face. Her eyes were closed, her features neutral.

"What do you want?" he whispered.

"Someone to care. Someone to care enough to see me as a person. At this moment, someone to just lie here beside me. Hold me in trust. Let me finally rest."

"I swear that I will do those things."

She lay back on her bedroll.

Ashawa got to his feet; he dragged his blankets off the toboggan and spread them beside Florenda's. He blew out the candle. She turned toward him in her cocoon of blankets, and he covered her with his. He kissed her gently on the forehead. She was asleep within a minute.

"Ashawa."

Midnight dark. Sleep barely crept into the wings. His lady beside him—that much he recalled.

"Are you awake?" Florenda asked. She took his hand and

guided it to her breast, open to his touch. She loosened his shirt and belt. "We really must get rid of this cast."

She rested on his chest, her breath warm on his face. "You beautiful man, I swear I will be for you … oh … my. Oh my! Sweet Jesus, *oooh my* …"

52

Henry lounged on a bench beside one of the dining tables. He scanned the room.

The mess hall was thirty feet long by twenty wide, an extension of the cookshack. This he remembered from the day in September when he had helped stake out its dimensions. Four tables, each sixteen feet long, were made of rough-hewn planking. Seating five to a side, with one end of the table against the log wall, access was from the opposite side of the room. Split-log benches of a similar length served as seating.

Supper had been a relaxed occasion. Even Richards seemed to damp his need to control, and he ignored the raucous, profane conversations swirling about his head. Haggarty dished food onto metal serving plates: beans in some incarnation, the meat of the day, stored onions and carrots, and wild rice. Rice, obtained from Indians at Chippewa Lake Reservation, thirty miles north of camp, was their staple starchy food. Precious potatoes were a treat reserved for Sundays or holidays. Dried fruit, apples and plums, served as dessert of sorts. Sarah refilled the serving dishes as needed.

This evening, Henry had chosen to share a table with his mother and Ashawa. *There's something about Mama.* He contrived to wait out the meal until their tablemates had departed.

Henry then said to Ashawa, "Uncle, I watched you walk in here tonight. Your limp is nearly gone."

"I'm fine." He glanced at Florenda. "I had a good doctor."

Florenda and Ashawa sat shoulder-to-shoulder, nudging each other, smiling at nothing.

What? Henry leaned across the table toward Florenda. "What is it, Mama? You look … really happy."

Ashawa and Florenda looked at each other, smirked, and Florenda … giggled. They held up hands—Ashawa's left and Florenda's right—with fingers interlaced.

Henry cocked an eyebrow. "Tell me."

Ashawa said, "We will share our blankets for the rest of our lives. I'm glad you know."

Florenda reached across the table and took Henry's hand in her free one. "We hope you approve."

"I …"

Ashawa extended his free hand, a question on his face.

Henry gripped it firmly. "It's just that … oh, I'm glad for you, Mama, but … y'all won't be lynched because you're with an Indian white man?"

"Son, we not in Possum Creek no mo'."

53

A restlessness seeped through Jericho. Henry felt it like some perceived aura radiating from the experienced jacks. March spent its days, snow settled, and when he listened closely, he could hear water flowing under the ice of tiny rills feeding the river. Some days, a stirring of air was warm to his cheek.

April was the month for log drives on Minnesota waterways.

A light breeze carried a cloying scent of pin-cherry flower perfume from ubiquitous shrubs growing in every clearing. Ice on the river turned dark before breaking up to sounds of deep-throated thunks when floes ground against each other in flight downstream. The swollen river inched higher in its bed. Jacks, shod now in the cleated boots of log-drive men, lined up along its banks with peaveys and picaroons in hand. They waited for the call to put logs into the water.

Minnesota's white pine trees were the chief targets of northern loggers. Eight Ball told Henry that the largest of them, three feet and more in diameter, were at least three hundred years old. A few that the men cut down were more than four feet across at the stump. In rocky terrain, felling a single tree of such size, getting it to the ground without its shattering by an awkward twist, a hang-up, or landing on a piano-sized boulder, could be the work of an entire morning. Skidding a sixteen-foot-long log with that much heft was a task, even for Babe.

Eight Ball explained the process to Henry. Logs awaiting commitment to the river that flowed past Jericho would be rolled into a network of interconnected rivers. It caught Henry's imagination—logs floating down creeks swollen to seasonal freshets, to rivers, to larger ones, and finally to the Big River. The Mississippi. The very name, according to MacPherson, was loosely derived from the Ojibwe words *kitchi sibi*. Mighty river.

These were logs Henry had helped to create!

But …

The thought again pricked at his pride. *Who will plant the next great white pine trees?*

He asked Marvin Richards one day. The foreman regarded Henry as though he was daft and stalked off without a word.

MacPherson walked next to the landing and craned his neck to inspect the man-made mountain of logs looming above him. He touched the end of one that was more than two feet in diameter. Its bark was dark, but the knot-free wood itself was white enough to explain how the species got its name. *How many such logs would it take to build a house?* he wondered.

The piles of logs waiting beside the river were winter's harvest. Each log of the precious supply bore the imprint "C L & T Log" hammered into both ends—the property of Crescent Lake and Tower Logging Company. Hundreds of thousands of board feet of prime lumber, the logs faced a two-hundred-fifty mile swim before arriving at mills beside Saint Anthony Falls in Minneapolis. They would be money in the bank once they arrived.

MacPherson hefted a logger's pike and joined Richards on the riverbank. When he glanced at the foreman, he frowned.

Richards paced in tight little circles, as skittish as any gray back on the hot griddle. He muttered, "Today. No, no, no! Tomorrow?" He seized MacPherson's arm. "What do you think? Too late?"

Jock said, "Well …"

"Dunderhead! It isn't for you to decide. Keep your advice to yourself. But really, today? Tomorrow? Oh, God of Abraham, send a sign."

"Sir," said Jock, "there is still ice downstream in a couple of places."

"Ice? Ice? What does ice have to do … are you suggesting that we should wait until tomorrow? Shut your mouth! You are merely a hired hand. Is the water level still rising? God. My decision … but if we wait until tomorrow, and the flood stage passes before we … don't try to mislead me. Paul Bunyan may think you have talent"—Richards seized MacPherson's shirt and screamed up into his face—"but you'll notice who he left in charge while he's out West. Me, fella, not you. Get out of my sight."

Jock pried Richards's hands loose and backed away. He went to stand on the far side of the landing, hidden by a mountain of logs.

He heard, "MacPherson! Where the hell did you get to? You provoked me into strong language, you nitwit. I asked you a question. God above, why am I burdened with worthless help?"

Jock jogged into the mess hall and poured a mug full of coffee.

Richards declared the morning of April 8 to be the time.

MacPherson said, "Sir, scouts report ice is still thick in the Devil's Chute Rapids. If logs get hung up there—"

Richards swung at MacPherson, a blow MacPherson easily sidestepped.

"Get them into the water!" shrieked Richards.

Ole and Homer looked at MacPherson, eyebrows cocked.

Jock shrugged and turned his back.

The men swung sledges and knocked wedges free. Great logs stirred, responding to gravity. They broke bonds of ice formed from winter's snow and tumbled over each other in a monstrous game of leap frog. Water splashed as high as willows lining the opposite banks. Piles of logs floated free in the spring current and headed downriver.

Only the most experienced jacks earned the privilege of riding the logs hurrying away from Jericho. To shouts from shore by those chosen only to watch, fifteen men in sharp-cleated boots guided logs with long-handled pikes. They rode the heaving logs proudly, confident in their skill.

Jock MacPherson was one of the select crew. Prodded by a tension in his gut, he trotted across jostling logs, moving faster than they in their courses downstream. He peered ahead anxiously.

A smooth flow of logs changed abruptly. The log Jock rode caught up with ones ahead of it, slamming into them and riding up over one. Ominous screeches of tortured wood grinding against others of its kind filled the air. Around the next bend in the river ... what Jock saw confirmed his fears.

For two hundred yards, he ran across crowding humps, the spikes of his cleated boots digging into the bark of logs beginning to stack up, until he reached the Devil's Chute Rapids. A sixteen-foot log lay crossways to the flow of water, caught against two boulders. Another pair of great logs had wedged into an opening between other boulders that was large enough for only one. Logs backed upstream, coming to a stop despite the wild force of water ...

The logjam occurred less than a mile downstream from Jericho. A field of boulders—remnants of a glacial esker, worn by the river to a hundred-yard obstacle course of scattered two- to four-foot rocks—was enough to choke the drive. Ice had frozen deeply in the Devil's Chute Rapids during the winter past—rock-trapped ice that had not floated away with surface ice.

Despite the efforts of MacPherson and the other jacks to guide logs through Devil's Chute, a giant more than four feet in diameter slammed into the modest rapid, and stopped. Too broad and too heavy, it slid on top of ice lurking beneath the current to become a plug that was more than flowing water could move. Within seconds, other logs jammed against the new obstruction. Logs piled upon logs, filling the width of the river and its depth as they built up—logs sideways to the flow of the river; logs forced high into the air, crunching, shredding, and splintering. Others pushed ashore onto the banks.

Upstream at Jericho, unknowing, men tipped more logs into the river.

Ashore, Jock MacPherson jogged across a bight of land back to camp. He cornered Richards against a remaining pile of logs. "A jam! Stop putting wood into the river."

Richards stared blankly. "It's drive day."

"They're piling up. Order the men to …" Richards's vacant appearance registered on MacPherson. He ran to the men rolling logs into the river. "Stop! A jam. A big one."

Richards landed on Jock's back, nearly driving him to the ground. "Get the logs in!" Richards screeched. "The river'll go down!" He seized a peavey from Hans Jorgenson and rolled a log toward the river.

MacPherson grabbed burly Arne Iokala by the arm. "Sit on him, tie him up if need be, but stop him."

"Jock, he's da foreman. I can't—"

"You can. I give you permission. Do it."

"Oh ja, all right, den." Arne wrapped Richards in his arms and carried him, kicking and bellowing, to the mess hall. "Sir, you maybe want a cup of coffee? Ja, good."

MacPherson relieved Richards of his set of keys and opened the shed where blasting supplies were kept.

Sarah followed him, her face twisting anxiously. "Dynamite? What are you going to do? Jock! Tell me."

He held Sarah by the arms. "A bad jam can ruin our whole winter's work. We have to loosen it before it crams in too tightly to ever let loose, while the water is still high enough to float the wood. Dynamite is our best chance."

"But why you? Jock, I'm afraid!"

"You saw the shape Richards is in. He's gone crazy. Who else is there? I've ridden log drives for twenty years. I have no choice." He kissed her hard and then trotted off toward the rapids, where so much hung in the balance.

"Jock!" Sarah wailed.

The river ran seventy feet wide at the point of the jam. From river bottom to the top of the jackstraw pile of logs was about twenty-five feet. Tons of uncertain logs awaited some signal. Jock studied them from the top to the water's surface and side to side. He picked three spots but needed one more. He fastened half a dozen sticks of dynamite in each of his chosen three places, inserted blasting caps, and stretched out a connecting line of fuses.

Richards smiled at Arne Iokala. "Thanks for the coffee. I believe I had a faint spell, but I'm all right now."

"Yes sir, Mr. Richards, I din't want to do it, but Mr. MacPherson, he told me to hold you."

"Yes, yes, the proper thing. But now I need to take charge of the drive. Can't let the river get the best of us. Oh, where did this MacPherson fellow say he would be?"

"He took some dynamite. To da jam."

"The jam! Of course. I'd best check on things. See if there

really is a jam. The river is running high, but that won't last, you know."

"Mr. MacPherson tell me you should stay here, Mr. Richards, sir."

"Who? Oh, that strange fellow. I'm relieving MacPherson of command now. You finish putting logs into the river."

"Well, if you say I should."

"I most certainly do. Carry on, Andy."

"Arne, sir."

"Yes, yes. Of course. Finish your coffee." Richards scurried out the door.

Arne refilled his coffee mug.

Sarah burst into the mess hall. "Arne! I saw Richards leave— he got away."

Arne stared at her placidly "He says he all right now. He going to help Jock wit' the jam."

"Help? *Help!* You fool. I have to ... Jock!"

Enough snow remained in the woods that a path created by running feet was clear. Sarah sprinted after Jock. Her legs ached, and her breath tore at her throat. She arrived at the site of the jam half faint from exertion.

Men lined up along both banks of the river. A giant's haystack of helter-skelter logs loomed above her. Out on the river, twenty feet away from her, Jock knelt near the base of the pile, readying a fourth bundle of dynamite.

Out of the corner of her eye Sarah caught a flash of movement, a lean form scrabbling like a spider over logs of the jam. Richards?

What ...?

Water roared through and around the jumble, drowning

other sounds. The scratch of a match being lit. The hiss of a burning fuse. Shouts of men jumping, waving their arms, and pointing. Sarah's screams.

The explosion of eighteen sticks of dynamite shook the ground and, for their brief moment, covered the roar of the river.

Time distended in shattering detail for Sarah.

The limp remnant of the man who had been Marvin Richards landed well downstream of the jam. He disappeared in the rush of tea-colored water.

Jock MacPherson jerked erect. Sarah saw surprise on his face. For a second of precious time, he stood straight, looking directly into Sarah's eyes. He saw her; she knew that he saw her before he leaped toward shore, barely twenty feet away, running over logs suddenly shifting up—and slamming back toward him, dropping him into water briefly exposed.

A pair of logs rose out of the water like breaching whales and clamped Jock's right leg between them at knee level. A tumble of other logs rammed against them ...

The jammed-up logs came to rest in some apparent new equilibrium of forces at the Devil's Chute Rapids. Once more, the roar of a river dominated the sounds of nature.

A man twenty feet away, still half alive, lay stretched out on the rough bark of a white pine log.

Anatomy did not allow for the space left to Jock's leg.

Sarah dropped to her knees and screamed.

Henry arrived at the site of the jam, followed shortly by Florenda. They knelt beside Sarah, a huddled icon, unmoving.

"Sweet Jesus!" Florenda hugged Sarah with all her might. "Can't someone pry those logs apart?"

Leino "Tikki" Tikkinen shook his head. "No, ma'am."

"Babe could," Florenda said. "He as strong as ten horses. I'm going to get Babe."

"Ma'am, I've seen what Babe can do but not this. Two locomotives couldn't pull them apart, not with all them other logs piled together."

Henry walked to the edge of the jam. "Tikki, I believe what you're saying. So there is only one other way to save Jock's life. Cut off his leg out there."

"Whoa, now. How that gonna happen?"

"I'll be damned if I just sit here and watch him die by degrees for lack of trying."

"Might be that dynamite loosened things up. He maybe go in the river like that bastard Richards."

Henry said, "Then we'd best get at it. Could you and some of the other men carry Mama and me out there to where he is?"

"No disrespect, Henry," Tikki said, "but you planning to use a crosscut saw?"

"I'll need a few supplies from camp."

Twenty minutes later, Florenda said, "I ain't been this scared since I runnin' from Howie Longstreet. Pick me up, Mr. Tikkinen. Let's get dis over."

Tikki elected to carry Florenda piggyback. Rat Root Mooney and Pigskin Petersen guided Henry, one to either side, with a firm grip on his arms. Eight Ball Schwindlehurst carried the supplies Henry would use.

Eight Ball said solemnly, "I dipped into my secret stash of Mr. James Beam's elixir. Got old Jock flying with the wild geese. He won't remember what we're up to." Then he half muttered, "I hope."

Henry said, "You're a good man, Eight Ball."

"Ah, now. Ain't many hold to that opinion. Here we are, Doc."

Doc? By Uncle's Manitou, Henry thought, *may I fool whatever gods decide such things into allowing that I'm more than I am.*

Henry crouched on a log awash with icy water, as close as he could get to Jock's leg. Florenda straddled a log opposite him, clamping with her legs. "Sweet Jesus, there's nothing left of his knee."

"That may help us, Mama. We won't have to cut through bone. I remember from the anatomy book. There are some blood vessels—big ones. I have to find and tie them with that fish line. Then, I want you to sew up his muscle ends and the skin. Make him a good leg."

She nodded. "Get started before I lose my nerve."

Tikki said uneasily. "An' you best hurry 'counta this jam might be gettin' ready to let go. The log I'm sitting on quivering."

It took them three and a half minutes to separate Jock from his crushed leg. "I can finish sewing the skin on shore," Florenda said.

Tikki helped Florenda climb aboard his back again, and the other three men picked up Jock, lighter now by half a leg.

"We'll be back for you in a minute, Henry. Stay put."

They clambered carefully to shore and laid Jock on the ground.

The jam let loose with a roar of rushing water and *basso profundo* grinding from hundreds of logs abruptly shifting.

Surging water flung logs into a welter of bounding porpoises. Henry clung to a log with arms and legs as it joined the rush downstream. Just before the thunder of water drowned out all other sounds, he heard a scream, a mother's anguish, and a shout from Tikki: "Hang on, Henry! Don't never let goooooo."

The determination that allowed Florenda to survive her last year of slavery steadied her hand. She sewed cold, blanched muscles and skin into a flap covering the shortened end of Jock's thigh bone.

Huddled on her knees in cold mud, Florenda only dimly noticed that Ashawa had set out along the bank of the river, searching, probing with a pike pole.

Twenty jacks stood in a cluster a few yards away from her. Inarticulate as bashful adolescents, they mumbled their concern ("The boys is lookin' downstream"), offered hope ("Tikki and them others ride a drive all the time, so probably Henry'll be all right"), and leaped to man the handles of a litter made of a blanket and two poles when it came time to move Jock ("Lemme help, Joe").

Sarah practically dragged Florenda by a rope around the waist when she, at first, had insisted on staying beside the rapid. "He won't be returning here." *He's miles away by now.* "He probably will come tramping back to Jericho in the morning. Florenda! I have to see to Jock. Come!"

Sarah held onto sanity by the grim set of her jaw.

Sarah made the decision to transport Jock first to Tower and then to Duluth. Babe insisted on carrying him. His harness was adjusted and padded to accept a gurney atop his broad back. Jock, still sedated by Eight Ball's last bottle of whiskey, was tenderly strapped onto it. Toivo Latvila volunteered to travel with Sarah.

They left just before dark, with Sarah plodding at Babe's left side and Toivo walking on his other side. They would not rest short of the village of Tower.

During Ashawa's absence, searching downriver for Henry, Eight Ball took Florenda under his wing. He fed her like an unwilling infant and wrapped blankets about her when she ignored the cold. He sat beside her for all of that first night ... waiting.

The candle burned down to a nubbin.

It began to rain.

Rain continued into the dawn, a gray pall. The rains of April in the far North are as cold as a miser's heart. Late that afternoon, the men not assigned to shepherd logs to Minneapolis straggled back to camp. Tikki shook his head at Eight Ball. They had found neither Henry nor Richards. Haggarty brought bowls of steaming fish chowder. The men ate because they had to.

The gray April day dipped below the horizon. Rain dripped from clouds hovering barely off the ground. Hope sputtered, bled out by the steady hemorrhaging of time. The following morning, Ashawa returned. He collected Florenda from Eight Ball and took her into their blankets. They clung to each other, too numb even to weep.

On the fourth day, rain turned into snow. Hope now bore a cold shroud of white.

54

The biblical images of Hades that Sarah had retained from her youth depicted it as fiery hot. She revised her own definition of *hellacious* to include the trek from Jericho to Tower—a dark, dank, frigid, seventy-seven miles of plodding torture. Babe set the pace, a maximum of three miles an hour. If he was tired, he didn't show it. As for Sarah, she willed herself to become an automaton. Guided by a hand on Babe's horn, she slogged in darkness as complete as that Jock had described while underground in the mine. She reacted only to Jock's occasional murmured request: for a sip of water, a lump of maple sugar, a suppressed groan when Babe stepped into an unseen pothole.

At Toivo's insistence, they stopped every hour or two for a five-minute rest to drink water or cold coffee; to choke down venison jerky or a cake of cold fried wild rice.

All earthly hells do finally end. Twenty-nine and one-half

hours after starting, they stumbled down the muddy streets of Tower. Sarah collapsed like a falling tree. Babe—even mighty Babe—dropped to his knees, his nose resting on the ground. Toivo lay down flat in the mud and began to snore.

A dozen pairs of hands, recruited from the Iron Trail Saloon, lifted MacPherson and carried Sarah and Toivo into the Miner's Hotel. They brought bales of hay and a tub of water to Babe, where he knelt when he could not regain his feet.

The next morning, Sarah dragged herself on board the lone boxcar in a train of loaded ore cars, headed south for Duluth. Her feet were swollen clubs, aching but oddly numb at the same time. Toivo Latvila supervised a motley group of stretcher bearers as they carried Jock into the railcar.

Sarah hugged Latvila with all the strength she could muster when he prepared to leave. Her words of thanks dissolved into tears.

"You'll do," the laconic Finnish man said. He waved for as long a time as she could still see him, as the train pulled away.

Babe lay on a bed of straw carefully scattered by Sarah.

Jock slept.

55

Saint Andrew's Hospital was a just-completed red-stone block, four stories tall. It sat on a spacious lot at the corner of East First Street and Eighth Avenue East, a few blocks from the business section of Duluth.

Saint Andrew's, the hospital as an institution, had begun in 1881, with a few beds located in a flat above a busy blacksmith shop.

A sprightly young physician with the personality and physique of a happy elf took charge of Jock MacPherson's care. "I'm Dr. Moyer," he said. "Sam Moyer. Tell me what happened here."

So, Sarah did.

"You're saying that a nineteen-year-old ex-slave boy—"

"His mama was the slave."

"Son of a slave, having no medical training, amputated Mr.

MacPherson's leg while sitting on a log immersed in ice water up to his knees, on the face of a logjam threatening to let go any second, 165 miles up in the wilderness, and performed what is a completely presentable piece of *surgery?*"

"He had a copy of *Gray's Anatomy,* which he studied before he began."

"And how did he happen to have access to an anatomy text?"

"He wants to be a doctor—has since I first had him as a pupil. Wanted—" Sarah exploded in grief too long delayed.

Dr. Moyer leaned toward Sarah and waited. When she had regained control of her tears, he said, "Past tense?"

"The … the men carried my husband to safety after Henry finished, but Henry—he was still out on the jam when it … it let go, and he was swept away. The river was full of huge logs and water of barely melted ice and snow. There seems no chance he will have survived."

The physician sat back. "As the Book says, the Lord giveth and the Lord taketh away."

Sarah looked up from her vigil beside Jock's hospital bed.

The woman who entered the room was slender, even wiry. She wore a black dress that resembled the habit of a nun, but … Sarah couldn't put her finger on what was different. She wore her hair in a no-nonsense trim.

Sarah waited expectantly.

"I am Sister Margaret, a Lutheran sister."

Sarah dipped her head. "I didn't know there were Protestant nuns."

"Just 'Sister.' I'm the administrator of Saint Andrew's Hospital. I'm told that you own the huge cow out on our front yard. You must remove him immediately, or I shall have him exterminated."

Sarah jumped to her feet. *"What!"*

"Shot. A brute like him? He will destroy our lawn. And what if he takes after passers-by? He isn't even tied up."

Sarah strode to the front of the hospital, trailed by Sister Margaret. Out on the lawn, Babe faced a sheriff's deputy, who held a rifle pointed squarely at him. A crowd of twenty or more gawkers stood in a wide arc behind him. Sarah ran to throw her arms around Babe's neck.

The deputy waddled to stand at Babe's side from twenty feet away. He again sighted his rifle. Sarah marched up to the pudgy man and jerked the gun out of his hands. She ejected its ammunition before handing it back to him.

"Your name, Officer?"

"I'm Deputy … you can't do that!"

"Name?"

"James Witherspoon, deputy sheriff of this here county. Lady, that there steer is the biggest, meanest-lookin' animal I ever seen."

"He's a pussy cat."

"Look at them horns. Could spit a man through and through."

"I'll tell him not to." She walked back to Babe and muttered into his ear. "Help me out here. Would you play some of those games you and Henry—" Her voice broke. "We've had enough tragedy in this family. Behave."

He rumbled in code, "What do you want me to do?"

"First, apologize to the deputy over there."

Rumbles came from deep in Babe's throat. "I'm sorry he's such a jerk."

"Babe! I can't tell him that. Do it."

She walked toward Deputy Witherspoon, one arm across Babe's broad neck. "My friend wants to apologize for making a bad first impression. Don't you, Babe?"

Sarah had to smother a laugh. Babe nodded and knelt on his front legs. He managed to look repentant! More rumbles.

"He says that he will gladly give anyone who wants one a ride around the block. No charge this time, but in the future, he will charge fifty cents—proceeds to go to the hospital."

Murmurs came from the crowd, which was still growing in size.

"What a hospital won't do to make money," someone said.

"I don't know. That's one awful big beast."

"Don't be a sissy. I dare you!"

A lean, tweedy chap sidled up to Sarah. He held out his hand. "Arnold Grover. Reporter, *Duluth Herald*. Neat trick. I read Morse code and heard what you claimed. I want to know how you do it, all without moving your lips."

Sarah sized him up. "You were watching the wrong pair of lips."

Babe obliged with a coded reprise.

She left the reporter scratching his head.

To Sarah's limping perception, the days plodded by in anonymous shades of gray.

After a spike in Jock's temperature, Dr. Moyer released a pocket of pus from the stump of his leg.

"Conditions were not ideal for an operation," he said wryly.

Jock's temperature returned to a baseline of 99.6 degrees. The stump was red, swollen, and obviously tender. The doctor gingerly inserted a drain of rubber tubing. Bloody serum oozed out in a steady trickle.

"Let's put some ice around the stump," Dr. Moyer said one day. "Try to cut back on the heat radiating from it."

Throughout the week, Jock hovered in a nether land of restless somnolence. He muttered incoherently. During moments of awareness, he clung to Sarah's hand. On the seventh day, he failed to rouse or respond to a touch or a pinch.

Moyer sat in a chair across from Sarah. Her breath caught. *Is he about to deliver bad news?*

He took her hands in his.

"In every serious illness, there comes a moment when a person seems at a tipping point, almost as though deciding whether to continue the fight or whether to cross over. Mr. MacPherson's stump looks remarkably healthy now. Swelling and inflammation have subsided, and the wound is barely draining anymore."

Sarah struggled for understanding. "If that's good, why is he still so bad?"

The physician leaned back and steepled his fingers before

his lips. "In my practice, I am convinced that I have seen some people decide to live, while others decide to die. That decision determined the outcome of the illness. I have an eerie feeling that your husband might be at such a moment. What kind of person is he?"

Sarah closed her eyes. Dr. Moyer waited.

She sighed. "He is a robust person, both physically and psychologically. If I were to choose a single word to describe him, I'd say 'doer.' He goes at life with such vigor and regards a challenge as an opportunity—or he did, before." She closed her eyes for a moment. "If I had to guess, I'm afraid that he might regard loss of his leg as loss of what he values most. Independence, activity. He would not like being waited upon."

Dr. Moyer turned to gaze out the window. "Then I hope my conjectures are nothing more than fantasies confined to my own imagination."

In the morning, when the doctor made rounds on Jock, he sat beside Sarah. "He's no worse than last night."

"But no better," she said woodenly.

"Not suffering, not in pain."

"That sounds too much like the opening phrases of a death notice."

He sighed. "Sugaring the truth never makes it easier. I wish I knew—"

She smiled sardonically. "Wishes sound a lot like sugar."

He nodded. "Guilty. What we need is for someone or some event to break through to Jock." He stood, putting a comforting hand on Sarah's shoulder.

56

Amelia Squinteye touched an Indian-brown finger to the cutting edge of her ax. *Sharp enough.* She laid the whetstone back on its shelf.

She walked outside her cabin and surveyed the tiny lake at her doorstep. Still ice-bound, it would soon melt open. Suckers would gather, scores of snouted fish, each two to four pounds of succulent stupidity, crowding the creek that fed her pond. Prods awakened by the season brought them to crawl all over each other for the honor of spraying roe and milt into the gravel of the tiny stream. Did their groins ache? Memory of times when she had followed nature's call as blindly brought a wry smile to thin Ojibwe lips. Ten years? No, by God, nearer fifteen since the kid lit out on her own.

Her eyes flashed with the poignancy of her thought, her dark velvet eyes deep in the sockets of a face weathered to fine crinkles and soft brown skin painted browner still by years of sunshine. She stood straight, as she always did, confident with a sureness born from doing for herself woods-style; of coping with whites and schizophrenic governments not of her choosing; of surviving when family wandered off or drank whiskey or beer until they could no longer recall the distinction between men and dogs.

Amelia's lakelet nestled in a shallow valley. A meandering stream less than three feet wide fed it. Willow brush and reeds confined it. In places, demarcation between bank and stream was a matter of arbitrary definition. It was shallow and murky, draining as it did another of the endless swamps. Then, an exclamation of surprise, it widened into the lake that Amelia considered her own and the Federal Forestry Department called "pond 217, also known as Muskrat Lake, 3.15 acres, more or less."

Brook trout were available to the patient fisherman. Amelia knew well how to catch what she needed—from the lake, at first light of day, or from the stream, creeping on hands and knees a full ten feet back from the water, with a slender willow pole tipped with two feet of fish line, held far out before her. She knew not to jar the bog muskeg on which she sprawled to drop a hook baited with a worm into eight inches of water. From under overhanging muskeg, a streak of rose-and-blue speckled energy darted. An instant later, breakfast flopped on the bank.

Two or three times a year, Amelia walked the sixty miles to Cusson or Koochiching to exchange furs for flour, salt, and coffee; perhaps a slab of bacon.

Amelia survived.

When the relentless white government bought out the

Indian holdings, she refused to sell. A battle was joined—the United States of America against one Amelia Squinteye of the Minnesota Ojibwe tribe. It was the rush of a river against a granite boulder in its path.

The USA was unaccustomed to losing Indian wars. Still, the battle turned out to be a Little Big Horn affair. Oh, the USA won in court. Four years before, Federal Marshal Olaf Wilson had set out to serve Amelia with eviction papers. The July day was steamy hot. There were no roads, and Marshal Wilson was from Minneapolis. He lost his way within fifteen minutes. What with swarms of black flies, mosquitoes, deer flies, and wood ticks, Amelia's eviction notice ended up in a musty file in a basement storeroom of the courthouse in Koochiching.

Amelia went placidly about her business, at home in her log cabin, one room square and slightly at the lop but snug enough.

Amelia Squinteye shouldered her ax. It was never too soon to begin gathering a supply of firewood for the next winter. She stretched her muscles. The activity would do her good. She climbed the slight ridge defining her valley—rocky ground where maples and birch trees grew.

She began to chop.

The eternal winds, messengers of the forests, brought news of an event. The dull thud of a distant dynamite blast punctuated its soft conversation with tree branches. Curiosity stirred Amelia, and she decided that her wood supply could wait.

She strode down the far side of the ridge toward the river. Muffled shouts reached her—excited, anxious calls.

The roar of a river in flood now filtered through the trees. Something more—logs battering each other in the hurrying water sounded a train of bass thunks.

The crazy tree assassins are at it again.

She nearly turned back in disgust, but momentum, winter's-end ennui, and "Oh well, what the hell?" kept her moving.

She stood on the bank of the river, watching the dark brown backs of pine trunks hump past. Their numbers thinned out, and the voices of the men balanced atop them faded into distance. Here and there, a log had been stranded, caught in an eddy or thrown onto the bank in the first frenzied rush.

She turned away, irked with herself for wasted effort.

At first, she could not locate the eerie sound. A deer groans in mortal pain just before it dies. She became a hunter on the instant, stalking, ax at the ready. She stepped across an orphaned log that had been tossed onto the river bank.

A man lay behind it, his left forearm pinned under it. Blood oozed from small cuts to his face, his scalp, and through tears in his clothing. He sprawled on the mud of the riverbank, eyes loosely closed, unseeing.

Amelia leaned her ax against a tree and squatted beside him. He breathed raspingly in irregular snorts. She tugged on the log; it did not move. She used her ax as a lever. The log rolled off his arm, teetered, and dived sluggishly back into the river.

He was dressed in the clothing of a tree murderer. A most peculiar white man, his skin was black. She rubbed at his arm. The odd color did not rub off. His blood was red, his eyes brown when she lifted a lid—although the white parts were off-white—and his teeth gleamed.

He had to have come from the camp farther upriver. She had spied on the place several times during the winter, hidden among trees still standing. She had seethed at the devastation being visited upon *Manitou's bikwawa*—God's forest.

She stood and scanned the river in vexation. Brown, frothy water now carried only a few straggling logs. The other men were far downstream. Her day had been wasted. Justice had been served in a way, a broken tree taking its killer with it. *Slaughter trees far in excess of a person's need.*

She prodded him with her boot. He did not twitch.

What the hell? Leave him. Not my concern.

She shouldered her ax and strode stolidly up the back side of the ridge. Movement to the right, a mere flicker, caught her eye. She turned aside to investigate.

Fresh tracks in the remaining snow revealed the presence of *Maingan,* Brother Wolf and his harem, three females. Peace reigned between Amelia and the wolves. They had no designs on her, and she never put them into the sights of her rifle.

A wolf does not attack a man. This she knew. Still, it was springtime, after a winter when a normal amount of game had been thinned by the camp hunter.

The scent of fresh blood would be in the air.

The black white man was as vulnerable as a man could get.

It began to rain—cold, dreary, penetrating. She looked back toward the river. *Maingan's* yellow eyes regarded her steadily from a thicket of high-bush cranberry bushes.

She turned toward the riverbank. She cursed in Ojibwe and English and in languages not yet invented. All the way back to where the man lay, she reviled this intrusion into the serenity of her life.

He still breathed but had not moved otherwise. She sighed. When she grasped his left wrist, it crunched under her grip. She winced. Broken. She took the other wrist. It was solid. She pulled him to a sitting position, floppy and spineless. She knelt beside him. He fell across her shoulder. She grunted with the effort but stood with the same strength that carried deer from the forest.

Amelia plodded steadily up the gentle slope toward the top of the ridge. She rested once, leaning against a tree. The downslope was easier.

Inside her cabin, she knelt beside her bed frame, built low in one corner as a projection of the cabin itself. She sat the man down, wet-rag limp, and laid him flat, lifting his legs onto the bed. She peeled off sopping clothing and unfolded the blanket on the foot of the bed.

He was just a boy—slender, tall, muscled from the work he had been performing but still a youth.

His flesh was as cold as meat left outdoors to cool. She could detect no pulse in his wrist, and when she squeezed his hand and the skin of one leg, the blanched-out areas failed to regain a normal color, remaining a ghastly gray shade. *Is he dead?* None of his injuries seemed severe enough to cause death. *So is it the cold? Probably.*

What if he dies anyway, after bringing him this far? A waste of time and energy.

And what can I do with a white man's body? Any man. To simply leave him … no, damn it! … leave it, a carcass, as food for Brother Maingan, violates something deep inside my gut. She shuddered.

Damn the man! Damn fate. Damn her inquisitiveness. Damn!

A stove—fashioned from a fifty-five-gallon steel barrel tipped onto its side, provided with squat legs, with a door cut into one end—sat a few feet from the bed. She sighed and fed sticks of birch and a couple of maple to an already hot fire. *Don't burn down my home.*

She covered him with another blanket. He was too chilled for it to help.

He did not twitch. She found a pulse deep in the boy's neck and compared it with her own pulse. Less than half as fast, mere flickers. His breathing was a barely discernible sigh—quick, shallow sips of air. He was as cold as ever. *Must be cold to the core of his body.* He needed warmth so desperately. *How?*

The decision was obvious yet so revolting. If she really did all a person could do to save this life …

She stood straight in the dignity of being a person and bowed to the morality of being *Anishinabe ikwe* ("woman of the Ojibwe people"). She listened to whispers brought down to her by instruction of her parents in ways of the People: Failure to share with those most desperately in need is a failure of the soul.

A decision once made? Act.

She opened her shirt and let it drop off her shoulders. She undid her woodsman's woolen pants and stepped out of them. Sweating from the excess heat in the cabin, she slid under the blankets that were covering him.

She gasped. His skin was as cold as that of *nibowin*—of death itself. She gritted teeth and hugged him with as much of her body as she could. She willed the boy to accept her living warmth. She monitored his pulse—no need to warm a corpse.

Gray light coming through her cabin window died gradually. The boy's pulse seemed no faster. She shivered for both of them.

Darkness showed through the window. The boy's skin didn't seem as cold. Was she adopting his temperature, or was he accepting hers? She raised her head.

His pulse abruptly began to jump and skip and then settled into a rate … She checked her own again. They were almost the same.

He took a deep, shuddering breath. She raised up onto her elbow.

His breathing became more regular. A muscle in his face twitched.

She stood and shrugged into her clothing again.

She wiped blood and dirt from his face, his arms, his hands. His nakedness stopped her momentarily. In his stupor, he lay as openly as a baby. She had forgotten what sight of a man could do to a woman. She dropped the blankets over him, clucking at herself irritably, at fancy and memory, over a white man, even one so oddly blackened.

Bah!

He now slept deeply, even snored, but she sensed that it was a healing rest.

She sat cross-legged before the open door of her stove. Contemplating. Wondering over what she had done.

57

In the morning, Amelia ate breakfast.

Rain played steady music on the roof of her cabin. The air felt heavy, and at times smoke backed down the stovepipe, acrid and eye-stinging. She stirred the fire and persuaded the draft to flow up its accustomed way. She took off a sweater in the resulting heat and opened the outside door a crack. Rain noises entered the place, fresh-sounding.

She heard rattles from the man's chest when he breathed, as though he needed to cough. He groaned. She went to stand beside the bed. He turned his head restlessly, licking his lips. He moved his left wrist and yelped, a frightened puppy sound.

He opened his eyes. They were vague, puzzled brown chips, peering here and there. They located her, and his gaze ceased its restless searching.

He croaked, "Who are you?"

She grunted and pulled her chair across the hard-packed dirt of her floor to sit beside the bed.

"*Nind awassab oshkinjigoma.*"

He blinked. "Oh."

She shrugged. "White people say that Squinteye. I let them call me Amelia."

A tiny grin may have twisted his lips. "Names are like mercury, hard to hold on to."

She twitched her eyebrows. "What is your name?" she asked.

"I think I have one," he said. He wrinkled his brow. "Yes. I'm called Henry. My papa's name was Jackson, so I guess that makes me Henry Jackson." He moved his left arm and cried out softly. He cradled his wrist in his right hand and held it over his face. "Broken."

"*E. Aye-yah.* Yes."

He lowered his wrist carefully to the bed at his side. "Where am I?"

"My house."

"Which is where?"

"My lake."

"Of course." He closed his eyes.

She asked, "Are you hungry?"

He opened his eyes again and studied the split-log ceiling overhead. "I believe I am."

"I have *wabooz naboob.* Rabbit soup." She stood, collected a bowl from the corner of the single-room designated kitchen, and returned to ladle a steamy mixture of meat, wild rice, and onion from a pot warming on the stove. "Sit up."

She watched the boy struggle to sit up while holding his wrist with the other hand. He tipped to one side before collapsing back onto the bed. Amelia clucked in annoyance, set the bowl on the floor, and pulled him to an upright position on the edge of the bunk. He steadied himself with his good hand.

When he seemed upright to stay, Amelia held the bowl while Henry spooned *naboob* into his mouth. He coughed and sputtered, but more soup ended up inside him than not.

Amelia tossed Henry a wad of sphagnum moss. "Clean your face."

He wiped his chin and lips; then studied the material. "I need a splint for my wrist. Could you get me a few finger-sized sticks, fourteen or fifteen inches long, and more of this stuff? A little fish line too."

She broke her willow fishing pole into pieces. He winced at her action, but she said, "I'll cut another one when I need it."

A cushion of moss, half a dozen willow wands, some fish line to bind them snugly ... Amelia and Henry fashioned a splint for his wrist.

He lay back on the bed and waved it experimentally. "Better. Thank you, Amelia, of the unpronounceable *Anishinabe* name."

She brought her chair to sit facing the stove. She opened the door set into the end of the barrel, fed it a couple sticks of birch wood, and stared into its cheery blaze. "You know what we call ourselves."

"Uncle told me." His eyelids closed. "He and Mama are married."

Amelia rested her chin on her fist, searching the flames murmuring inside the stove. She asked softly, "How much else did Uncle tell you?"

Henry snored quietly.

Amelia arranged blankets into a bedroll and stretched out in front of the stove. *What have I gotten myself into? Is a black white man as rabid as most of the regular white men? A mere boy, although from his appearance grown strong. I can cope.*

She put her ax at hand, closed the stove door, and turned onto her side.

Rain beat steadily on the roof.

58

aylight, when it came, was merely a gray extension of darkness. Dim light oozed through cracks around the door and through the glass of Amelia's only window. She rolled up her sleeping blankets from their place on the floor and put the ax next to the wood box. She stirred ashes and fed tired coals with teased birch-bark wicks. Yellow flames awoke to lick the strips of papery white bark into curling black shreds. She added more bark, a splinter of dry wood, a small stick. The fire grew robust enough to crackle. The stove door clanked solidly when she closed it.

Amelia took the pissing can outdoors and squatted under the fickle protection of the eaves. She sluiced urine into the brush. Indoors, she silently handed the can to Henry. She looked aside when he slid it under the blanket.

The Henry Jackson swung his legs over the edge of the bed

and tried to sit up. Sweat appeared on his skin, which was as gray as the day. He groaned and fell back.

"You all right?" Amelia asked.

He closed his eyes. "I must be one solid bruise."

She inspected the man's battered face. It was puffy, lined with livid scratches, and lopsided from all the swelling. Stubs of curly, wiry facial hair grew out of scabs beginning to form.

He raised his head again.

"I have fish," she said, "and bannock fry bread. I'll make coffee."

"I was going to dress. My clothes?"

Amelia collected his clothing from twine suspended above the stove and laid them beside Henry. Having proved that he could not do the job alone, he allowed Amelia to dress him.

A flat sheet of metal had been welded to the rounded top of the woodstove, a platform for cooking pots and pans. Amelia used it to fry fish and bannock cooked in beaver fat. She solved the problem of keeping Henry in an upright position by propping a worn Duluth backpack full of furs behind him.

Amelia's coffee attracted notice. She poured turbid licorice from an old coffee can used as a steeping pot. Henry dealt with momentary queasiness until he located "the other can" sitting beside the door.

He sipped. Divine edict could not have allowed him to drink any faster.

"More coffee, Mr. Henry Jackson?"

"Uh, no thanks. I would like to know where we are. Besides your house, your lake."

"It is away from that camp of yours, I bet three or four miles through the woods."

"I need to get back. People must be worried about me."

She pointed at the ceiling. "Through all that rain?"

Sound can be as much perception as physical law. The steady pounding overhead was no different from the drumming that had filled the night. Still, for a time, Henry had tuned it out as a factor in his life.

She said, "Can you walk?"

He hunched forward, tried to stand, and winced when a spasm froze him in place. "Maybe not right now."

"I can't carry you four miles. Part of the trail is across bogs that will be underwater. I think we wait."

"Can't we at least send word?"

"How?"

"Yes, I see. Maybe I should lie down again."

That evening, Henry lay on his side in the bed, a captive of the storm's monotonous tempo on the roof. Amelia sat cross-legged on the hard dirt floor. The stove door stood open, a golden square cleaving the darkness. Darting gleams of yellow light caressed her cheeks and her hair—black streaked with gray, strands smooth across her scalp and braided down her back, falling to her waist. She wore faded woodsman's trousers. Her woolen shirt claimed ancestry to a plaid. Sure brown fingers threaded strips of rawhide into the oval frame of a snowshoe. She hunched her shoulders in the absorption of her work.

The woman's shadow was a thing alive when light from the stove pulsed with restless, random motion. Light and shade flitted across the logs of Amelia's shack. A modicum of imagination gave them cryptic meaning. Imps. Dancing haunts. Writhing, beseeching forms reaching toward him from a world of childhood fantasy nearly forgotten, charmed into beauty within the mind of a man. Tears trickled down his cheeks.

Amelia grunted and stretched her shoulders.

"How do you manage here?" he asked softly.

She swiveled to face him. Her eyes now hid in the shadows of their sockets. "I hunt. I fish. I trap. A few things I buy with fur money. I make do."

"Alone?"

"For a few years. My people went away. Town and lights. Beer, whiskey. Department of Interior, *Micaduc* gov'ment come by. Hassle me." She smiled bitterly. "I wouldn't go."

"Mica—what?"

"Big white gov'ment. 'You Indian, move over here to some other damn place. *I'll* tell you where you want to be. We come in peace ... and will blow out your brains if you don't let us help you. Stupid Indian, do like I say. No one like you can tell where she want to live!'"

"I see."

"I doubt that a damn bunch."

"No, for a damn dumb Indian, you're very eloquent."

Suddenly, the iron in Amelia's spine melted. She threw back her head and cackled. Her eyes sparkled. "Maybe black white men aren't exactly the same."

Henry smiled as widely as new scabs allowed. "I know some regular white folks who aren't either."

Amelia rolled out her bedroll before the stove. She turned evening into night by closing its door.

Henry lay in comfortable darkness, pondering on his hostess. He was amused by the varieties of tone and inflection that passed for English among those he had come to know. Amelia's voice is … *Call it lilting*, he decided. She stressed unexpected syllables, and its music rose and fell at unpredictable places. *Rather appealing. There is some resemblance to Uncle Ashawa's style of speech but with tones unique to Amelia.* Imitating it might be hard to resist.

Wind joined pelting rain, telling of the aloneness of every creature with ears to hear. The stovepipe thrummed gently, heated air hurrying up its length to join the tumult outside.

Breathing sounds quieted.

Henry said softly, "Mama was once a slave."

"Oh? Oh!"

"Other regular white people helped her."

Silence.

"Good night, Mrs. Squinteye."

"Good night, Mr. Henry Jackson."

59

Morning wore an April shroud. Gray wetness pried at the cabin's every opening. Henry's wrist throbbed with sullen persistence, and he could barely turn over on the bed.

Amelia poked at fish sizzling in a cast iron fry pan. She used a spatula to snare a piece of fish turning as brown as her nimble fingers.

"Two?" she asked, glancing over her shoulder at Henry.

Henry consulted hunger. "Yep."

Today, she brought her chair to sit beside the bed instead of hunching over the wobbly table in a far corner, as she had done the day before.

She set a tin cup before him. "Willow-bark tea. For pain. There's more if you need it."

The quiet time of their meal felt companionable.

"It's time to walk," Amelia said tartly. She pulled on Henry's right hand. Sweat dotted his forehead from the fierceness of his effort, but he stood. Legs that had clutched his log, legs pounded by others on courses as mad, barely allowed it to happen. He lost his balance and staggered forward in fiery agony when his muscles rebelled. He tottered and gasped. The strong arms of a woods person caught him and eased him back onto the bed.

He held out his hand.

"Once more."

He managed his first steps.

Henry dug a watch out of his pocket. "It's no use," he muttered, "gone. Full of water and bent out of shape."

"What do you want that for, Mr. Henry Jackson?"

"So I know when to be where."

"Why?"

"That's the way the world runs. Schedules. On time."

"Hah."

"I hear doubt."

She shrugged. "I tell time by whether it snows, if the sun is up, if my belly growls, if I have to piss. Who cares?"

"Telling time your way, I've been gone for three days. I don't doubt that Mama and the others think I'm dead. I know the rain out there is miserable, and I hardly know how to ask this. Could you … would you walk over to the camp and tell them I'm alive?"

"No."

"I'd be glad to pay you."

"No!"

"Couldn't you use the money?"

She bounded to her feet. "I have no need for more money."

His voice became a whine. "But I can't ... myself ..."

"Yourself! Look at you. Sleep on my bed. Eat my food. Smell up my home with blood and pus and piss. You crash into my life, disrupt everything I do. Maybe you not so different from other white men, like I wondered."

She stormed out of the cabin.

A pout is a magnificent thing. Brooding on the edge of the bed, Henry fed it misunderstandings and hurt feelings. With pout-style resolve, he thought, *I'll show her.* He staggered to his feet—and sprawled onto the dirt floor of Amelia's home. He could not even crawl.

When she returned, she lifted him under the arms and dragged him to the bed.

They did not speak for the rest of that gray day.

The gloom of day succumbed to night. Henry struggled to his feet. One step. Shuffle. The other foot. His feet did not keep up with momentum, and he dropped to his knees. Amelia caught him and kept him from crashing full length. They knelt beside each other, he panting from his efforts; she supporting him stoically. Together, they stood again. He pushed at her, pique still hot within him, and wobbled sideways toward the rumbling woodstove.

She grabbed him. "Are you determined to break something else?"

"I'm *determined* to do this myself." He wobbled, feet spread far apart.

She stomped to the door and flung it open. "Fine. Good

travel. Don't fall into the river, and keep an eye out for Brother *Maingan*."

"Brother who?"

"The wolf and his pack. He showed interest in you before and will have your scent. *Boujou*. Good-bye."

"A wolf?"

"And his harem."

He backed up to the bed and plopped down. She slammed the door and stood before him, her arms crossed on her chest. Her voice was grim. "We need to get you walking so you can get out of here."

"In a minute. Are you not afraid of the wolves?"

"No."

"But I've heard they're fierce animals."

"Have *you* no understanding of the creatures of the forests? I respect *Maingan*, as he does me. We each hunt and take what we must to live. I thank the spirit of every creature I use, whether for its fur or for its meat. Now, get up. We walk."

"I'm not in the mood right now."

"Yes, you are."

She pulled him to his feet and threw his arm across her shoulders when he nearly fell. She propelled him forward; he gasped and stumbled ahead.

On the fourth day, Henry awoke to the oddity of silence. No rain hammered the roof overhead. He levered himself to a standing position and cracked open the door. "Oh, God."

Amelia peered past his shoulder. "Snow. No wonder it quit raining. Maybe six inches."

Henry flopped back on the bed, sullenly.

For the tenth time, Henry dropped forward onto his knees. "I don't understand it. My legs won't … maybe I do need your shoulder."

They walked a while, and sat a while longer.

She asked, "Are there other black white men like you?"

"Where I come from, we outnumber, uh, regular white men."

She asked, "You are married man, Mr. Henry Jackson?"

"No, no."

"Why not?"

"Mama and Sarah are the only women … we've been on the move. No single girls. A logging camp, an iron mine."

"You said your mama was a slave. Did she like it?"

"*Like* it … good God. A slave has … had … no choices in life. Bought and sold like chickens or goats. Could be whipped anytime Massa felt like it. Killed as casually. Work harder than a mule and live in shacks worse than a sty for pigs. Yo' mama or papa could be sold and sent away, yo' sister raped, and de sheriff jes' laugh it off …" His voice broke.

"If your mama didn't like being a slave," Amelia asked, "why didn't she just quit?"

"Quit? You don' unner'stan'! Look. A runaway slave was hanged or shot by anyone who caught him. Called it *making an example.*"

Amelia studied Henry intently. She said, "I'd be interested to hear more."

So Henry told her, talking halfway through the night—about wanting to learn, and Klansmen, and water moccasins, and about a teacher who sacrificed her career for love of someone different from her. About a longhorn steer who dropped out of the sky, who learned right along with Henry about words and doing sums, and about a world unimaginably vast that was just out of sight beyond the horizon. About logging and the greatest logger of them all, a man named Paul Bunyan, whom Henry had yet to meet. About cutting off a leg to save a life because "I didn't know enough to know I couldn't do it."

And about his most secret plan. "I'm going to be a doctor," he said.

"My God, I believe you will."

"Good night, Mrs. Squinteye."

He heard a smile in her voice, a gentle smile. "Good night, Dr. Henry Jackson."

Amelia closed the stove door. Silence settled over the cabin, a good silence this night. Maybe snow had scrubbed the air, taking anger and bitterness away.

60

The fifth morning dawned sunny and clear. Snow on the ground shrank rapidly under its rays.

After a breakfast of pounded venison patties, Henry walked across the cabin floor with the support of his relentless guide. Twelve steps toward the east wall. A reversal next to the stove, like a great ship turning around ponderously. Twelve steps west.

Henry asked, "Mrs. Squinteye, where is your husband?"

Her voice was a monotone. "I never had a husband."

"But you said, a daughter."

"I was born right here in this cabin. Mama, Papa, and me. I was as free as any creature of the forest. And happy, so happy. Papa trapped furs, and we lived as I do today. Off the land. *With* the land. One day, when I was about ten, some white man canoed up the river and climbed over the ridge, bringing a piece of paper. 'Your place been annexed by the US of A to be part of a national forest'—some damn thing. 'You got a piece of paper what says we can't do that?' he asks. 'No? And I see you got a young one. She in school? Not a white-man school? That gotta change.'

"Later, two sheriffs came by and dragged me off to go to Indian school in South Dakota. I was kept there for five years, long enough for me to know I wanted no part of white-man schools or anything else white man. Long enough for me to get pregnant when I was fifteen years old."

They made two more circuits in a somber silence.

Then he asked, "What happened to your family?"

She helped Henry to the bunk. "Papa just died. You get to be a doctor, Mr. Henry Jackson, you study and see if a man can die of a broken heart. Mama found booze. She's down in Minneapolis or some damn place. I named my daughter Trillium, like the little flower that grows in the forest each spring. She found … she like booze too."

Tears brimmed in Henry's eyes. "I'm really sorry, Mrs. Squinteye. I always thought our lives were hard, Mama and me, but we found people to care about and who care about us. I wish for you …"

She stood before him, wonder on her face. She touched his cheek. "You sweet boy." She kissed his forehead. "If you want, I'll walk over to your camp tomorrow and let people know you're here."

He considered. "No, I believe by tomorrow, I'll be able to make it. With your help?"

She nodded and went abruptly to the door. "Firewood." She turned back. "Why don't you call me Amelia?"

That evening, Amelia went to the corner and retrieved her bedroll. Their lamp—the open door of the stove—glowed orange and yellow. Flickers of light draped her figure when she squatted to spread out the bedroll.

Henry said, "Could we walk one more time? I believe the soreness is less."

She stood silently, and they resumed their walking embrace. One trip, two, three, another. He tightened his arm across her shoulder; she bumped against his side. They stopped before the stove. He stared down at her in wonder—at the gleam of yellow light on copper skin, at the round of her breasts. Had he not noticed before? The vitality of her body awoke awareness in his arm and his hip where they touched.

"You're beautiful," he said.

She sighed and turned to face him. She gripped his upper arms. "How old are you, Henry?"

"Uh, twenty. Well, almost. Nineteen. Mama says I was born in the summer, but she didn't know about names of months."

She patted his chest. "Go to bed." She pushed gently, and he sat.

"I think I'm in love with you," he said.

She knelt on her bedroll. "I'm thirty-eight, old enough to be your mama."

"But you're not my mama. And I feel like I want to make love to you."

"Henry ..."

"But I can't"

"You can't?"

"You'd have to want to too."

She sat back on her haunches. "You ask? Don't demand?

I'll be damned." She stood abruptly. "Make room beside you." She opened her shirt, letting it slide back off her shoulders, and dropped her woodsman's trousers.

"Mrs. Squinteye—"

She leaned over him and kissed his nose. "For God's sakes, I'm Amelia." She stretched out beside him.

"Uh, Amelia, I don't know what to do."

She stroked his cheek. "I'll show you."

So, she did.

61

The sixth day dawned cloudy and dank. Henry picked at his breakfast—freshly caught trout, floured and fried; bannock fry bread and a lump of maple sugar; and a cup of coffee.

Amelia sat in her chair beside the bed. "What's wrong, Henry? My cooking unsatisfactory?"

"No, no, no, it's about last night."

"Yes?"

"I feel that I violated your hospitality."

Amelia put her plate down on the floor. She placed her hands on her knees and leaned toward him. "Don't destroy a nice memory by talking it to death. I'm a woman. I've had damn few chances to enjoy what that can mean. You graduated, Henry. You're a man. Now hush up and eat so we can get started for your camp."

Four miles is a comfortable stroll. Slogging through snow and slush and mud and bog water made a lie of such a thought. Amelia supported half of Henry's weight, but his savaged muscles screamed for relief before they had gone halfway. His patient crutch struggled through brush to give him the path and hopped over fallen trees and rocks. When they reached the halfway point, Henry knew he could not make it. At the three-quarters point, long past a chance to return, only grim refusal to die kept his feet moving.

On they plodded.

At last, Amelia gasped, "Through that ... gap in the trees ... your camp."

They faced each other. "Amelia! Come with me. I want you to meet Mama, Uncle, Jock and Sarah, and Babe. You must see Babe."

She shook her head. "You know ... how I feel about ... tree murderers. You, I forgive, but ... be a wise *mashkikiwinini*." She grinned. "A medicine man, Dr. Henry Jackson." She kissed him on the forehead and turned toward her cabin.

"Amelia, please."

She waved without looking back. He watched until she disappeared into a welter of trees.

Be a wise doctor? He made a vow, silent but soaring.

When he turned toward the rude buildings of Jericho camp, his legs nearly betrayed him. He was standing unassisted! He edged one foot forward, then stopped, clutching at a sapling beside the trail. He moved the other foot. Muscle quivers subsided.

Henry shuffled slowly toward the opening between the trees, into the clearing.

Eight Ball Schwindlehurst first spotted Henry. He stopped, feet apart and hands extended. "By gar, it's you! I thought my DTs had come back." He turned and bellowed, "Yo! The camp! A ghost has come to visit."

Sounds of running feet announced a stream of jacks. Uncle Ashawa, grinning, waved his hat. Mama stumbled in her haste, her hands extended. "Sweet *Jesus*!" She hugged Henry with the passion of faith restored.

Eight Ball brought Henry up-to-date with camp news. Because no one had walked as far as Tower, there had been no word as to Jock MacPherson's condition or if he had even survived. Richards's body had not been discovered. Haggarty assumed control of breaking camp.

Horses and oxen were assembled, ready to set out for Tower. Reusable equipment weighed down the same drays that had brought it to Jericho. The buildings stood empty, already relics doomed to decay in the humid terrain. A few mature white pines stood alone in a shattered landscape.

"Seed trees," Eight Ball said laconically.

A sad acknowledgment of the power of greed, thought Henry. A gesture to soothe a collective conscience.

62

Sarah nodded to Dr. Moyer when he arrived to make afternoon rounds on his patient. He raised his hands in a question.

She shook her head. "No change. Still …" Her voice caught and she bowed her head.

Sounds of running feet came from the corridor, punctuated by the brisk tap, tap, tap of a following pair of shoes.

The voice of Sister Margaret came to them. "Here now! You three! Visiting hours are not until this evening. I insist that you—"

Florenda stood in the doorway, her eyes wide with concern. Ashawa peered over her shoulder. Henry stood beside her. Behind them all, the diminutive figure of an outraged hospital administrator hove into view.

Dr. Moyer stepped back against a wall, his eyes bright with interest.

Sarah leaped to her feet. "Henry! You're alive! You're here! You ... what happened? How did ...?"

Tears blurred her image of Henry when she gathered him into a feminine bear hug. They clung to each other.

"Sweet Jesus did it," Florenda said.

"With a major assist from Amelia," Henry said, his voice tremulous. "Let me see Jock."

Sarah, Florenda, Ashawa, and Henry clustered around Jock's bed.

Sarah realized what was troubling Jock! *Survivor guilt over who is chosen to live and who to die.*

"Henry," she said urgently, "tell him you are here. Tell him how you escaped the river. Tell me! Touch him while you do. He must hear you."

Henry sat of the edge of Jock's bed. He took Jock's hand in his. "It's me. Henry. Here's what happened. When the jam let go ..."

Behind them, Sister Margaret marched through the doorway, her face grim. Dr. Moyer blocked her way. "This is essential," he said softly.

"Infractions of visiting rules are bad enough. That man is *sitting* on the patient's bed!"

"Yes, yes, Sister. Doctors do break a lot of the rules of conduct, don't we? You see, that lad with his wrist in a homemade splint is the *surgeon* who saved our patient's life."

"But ... he's a Negro. And just a boy."

Moyer nodded. "Astounding, isn't it?"

"I am obligated to report this to the hospital board, Doctor.

I confess I am surprised, even a little disappointed in your cavalier—"

"See that? I'll be damned." Moyer brushed past Sister Margaret and stepped to the edge of the bed.

Jock MacPherson coughed, muttered, and opened his eyes. He looked at Henry, touching his face with one hand and then with both. He grinned suddenly. "You need a shave." He looked around. "Florenda, I could use a hug. Where is Babe?"

Florenda released Jock and ran out the door.

Sister Margaret sputtered, "She isn't … surely even a Negro would not presume to bring an animal …"

Moyer grinned. "Let's make room for him."

There was no mistaking the sounds of Babe's hooves. He tilted his head enough to clear his horns coming through the doorway and thrust his muzzle across the bedside rail. He rumbled in code.

Sarah, Florenda, and Henry burst out laughing.

Sarah explained to Dr. Moyer. "He told Jock that now he knows how it feels to be penned in."

Sister Margaret fanned her face. "I have never—"

"Never been privileged to see one miracle after another," said Dr. Moyer. "Sister Margaret, neither have I. I suggest that we leave all these, uh, individuals alone." He stopped in front of Henry. "I intend to get a lot better acquainted with you. The problem with your wrist?"

"Broken, sir. That is, I think so."

"Our colleagues call me Sam. We need to discuss your future. Oh, when you finish here, come to my office, and I'll make you a new cast. Won't do a better job than what you have; it just won't smell quite as earthy."

63

MacPherson surveyed the panorama before him. He drew breath deeply to savor the sweet scent of air blessed by *Kitchigami*.

The day was sunny—and warm where sheltered from a breeze off the lake. The shoreline of mighty Lake Superior was less than two blocks from the front of Saint Andrew's Hospital.

Jock MacPherson sat in a wheeled chair, facing toward the water. He swept his gaze around the circle that included him— Sarah, seated by his side; Henry; Florenda; and Ashawa, with Babe lying on folded knees.

"Council, family," Jock said, "we need to decide a few things. I had an unexpected visitor this morning while the four of you were still at the hotel. Paul Bunyan has just returned from the West. He offered me my old post in Minneapolis. He wants Ashawa to take Richards's place with next winter's camp in an area just west of Jericho. Babe? Want to tell them what he said about you?"

Babe signaled, "You tell. Quicker."

Jock smiled. "Babe fascinated Paul. When he discovered that he could communicate with him ... I have never seen the man as excited. He asked Babe to join him as he moves about from camp to camp. For all his success as head of his logging company, he still regards himself as basically a lumberjack."

"And proud of it," rumbled Babe.

Sarah's voice was choked. "But what about the family?"

Florenda said, "Girl, you know the answer to that. A flower doesn't hang on to its seeds. Where Ashawa goes, there I go too. And you. Did y'all plan to leave Jock? 'Course not. Babe, what do you want?"

He rose to his feet and faced the rest. In code, he rumbled, "You are my family. My salvation. But I am *Bos*. I am what my parents were and what they created. Transformation turned me into something caught between two realities. I heard the word 'chimera' one day, a creature made of two different beings. Even a monster."

"*No!*" a chorus of voices responded.

"Hush. You, my family, treat me like one of you—not as a *Bos* but as a person. Do you know how rare you are, willing to look inside me instead of just at the way I appear? You've seen the turmoil my being here has caused. It won't change in Duluth or Minneapolis. At Jericho, up in the woods, for the first time in my life, I had a purpose, a skill that not another creature could equal. It felt good. This Paul Bunyan and I clicked, on the same level as you, my family. Like Petr and Shag when they used a saw, we can be a team. I have learned what love means from all of you. That I won't forget, but I believe I belong now with Paul. That is my thought."

Tears flowed, and Sarah said, "I never knew that a steer could cry."

Reality settled in, and they looked at each other with new understandings—with love that blesses but does not cling. Sarah thought, *The family has achieved what families are destined to do.*

Amen!

64

Babe chews a cud, his mind working as vigorously at arranging his thoughts.

In a sense, any life is a series of hellos and good-byes; acknowledging that fact does not diminish their meaning. The day for my most personal good-byes is upon me. My family gathered for the last time on the lawn of the hospital.

Jock MacPherson is ready to leave the hospital, with its fuss-budget Sister Margaret—and good riddance there!

It comforts me that Jock and Sarah are safely past the emotional nonsense that occurred during the winter. And yes, I had a small part to play in making things better. I nod, pleased with the thought. The MacPhersons will catch the noon train bound for Saint Paul. No boxcars this time, although I have trouble envisioning what the alternative might look like.

Henry—dear Henry, special friend and fellow student

Henry—he will stay in Duluth, studying with tutors arranged for by Dr. Moyer. Lessons, I was told, designed to smooth off the rough edges to his knowledge base. The boy—no, the young man—will matriculate in Duluth Normal College come fall.

Now I, Babe the Blue Ox, stand with head raised and legs planted firmly, and my back is strong. A curious mist affects my vision when I look to each of these Two-Legs who has become such a part of my life.

One thing I finally understand. Kissy-kissy means special love, to be shared only with those precious few.

So …

I touch my nose against Ashawa's chin. Against Florenda's cheek. She throws her arms as far around my neck as she can reach, and I taste her tears on my muzzle. Salty.

I nuzzle Jock's neck; he circles my neck with his arms. Jock kissy-kisses me enthusiastically.

And Sarah—the look we share at nose-tip range tells me that love is immortal.

Henry's voice is barely audible when he lays his head against mine. "You haven't seen the last of me," he says.

I turn to look out over the lake. I snort to clear an odd nasal congestion before turning back.

We fall silent, caught in that awkward time when intimates must leave each other.

I shall cherish memories of this first chapter of my life. How Paul Bunyan and I relate to each other remains to be seen. Who knows?

Perhaps the next chapter will also be memorable.

AFTERWORD

December 1928

We *Bos* do not live as long as Two-Legs do. Thirty-eight years after Paul and I became a team, aches in my joints speak of all the punishment I have inflicted on them. Rest, with dreams or without, sounds better each cold morning. I have so much to remember …

My life as companion to Paul Bunyan has been recounted in the bunkhouses of hundreds of logging camps. Told and retold and, yes, perhaps exaggerated a bit. I understand that some of our exploits have even been written down in books for all to read. Paul and I were present when the last stands of primal white pine trees were harvested. How humbling to witness the end of an era.

In this, the twilight of my life, I find images from its beginnings to be the most indelible. Dear Florenda. She who followed her Ashawa from logging camp to remote camp, enforcing her standards, lovingly, on those rowdy jacks, "her boys." "No spitting tobacco juice on the mess room floors, and no head lice allowed."

There is Ashawa, a true man of the forests, who turned out to be a gentle leader of men. He and his beloved Florenda are both gone; he followed her less than a year after she moved on to whatever comes next.

Jock survived the loss of his leg, even designed an artificial limb that included a flexible knee. The man is as feisty as ever. I give him Babe back-rides whenever he returns from Minneapolis for a visit.

Sarah. What can I say about the woman who saved not only my life but did so much to ensure my dignity? Love must be experienced. I leave attempts to capture it in words to those braver than I.

And finally, Henry. I understand that he has earned acclaim in Two-Leg society. Professor of surgery at the University of Minnesota Medical School. His passion for planting trees is unabated. White pine and black walnut. He has not forgotten his old long-horned friend. Just last week he went with me on a dark cold night to a nearby lake, where at last I heard ice singing.

The days seem shorter, perhaps because I sleep so much. The light appears dimmer. I must finish my cud … must tell Paul how much I have … also … enjoyed … our time …

Printed in the United States
By Bookmasters